SCOURGE OF FATE
ROBBIE MacNIVEN

SCOURGE OF FATE

ROBBIE MacNIVEN

BLACK LIBRARY

A BLACK LIBRARY PUBLICATION

First published in 2019.
This edition published in Great Britain in 2019 by
Black Library,
Games Workshop Ltd.,
Willow Road,
Nottingham,
NG7 2WS, UK.

10 9 8 7 6 5 4 3 2 1

Produced by Games Workshop in Nottingham.
Cover illustration by Anna Lakisova.

See Black Library on the internet at

blacklibrary.com

Find out more about Games Workshop
and the worlds of Warhammer at

games-workshop.com

Printed and bound by CPI Group (UK) Ltd, Croydon, CR0 4YY

From the maelstrom of a sundered world, the
Eight Realms were born. The formless and the divine
exploded into life.

Strange, new worlds appeared in the firmament, each one
gilded with spirits, gods and men. Noblest of the gods was
Sigmar. For years beyond reckoning he illuminated the realms,
wreathed in light and majesty as he carved out his reign. His
strength was the power of thunder. His wisdom was infinite.
Mortal and immortal alike kneeled before his lofty throne.
Great empires rose and, for a while, treachery was banished.
Sigmar claimed the land and sky as his own and ruled over a
glorious age of myth.

But cruelty is tenacious. As had been foreseen, the great
alliance of gods and men tore itself apart. Myth and legend
crumbled into Chaos. Darkness flooded the realms. Torture,
slavery and fear replaced the glory that came before. Sigmar
turned his back on the mortal kingdoms, disgusted by their
fate. He fixed his gaze instead on the remains of the world he
had lost long ago, brooding over its charred core, searching
endlessly for a sign of hope. And then, in the dark heat of
his rage, he caught a glimpse of something magnificent. He
pictured a weapon born of the heavens. A beacon powerful
enough to pierce the endless night. An army hewn from
everything he had lost.

Sigmar set his artisans to work and for long ages they toiled,
striving to harness the power of the stars. As Sigmar's great
work neared completion, he turned back to the realms and saw
that the dominion of Chaos was almost complete. The hour
for vengeance had come. Finally, with lightning blazing across
his brow, he stepped forth to unleash his creations.

The Age of Sigmar had begun.

My name is Vanik.

Within the Eight Realms I am known by many titles. In Chamon, they call me the Warpclad, the Blacksteel and the Eighteenth Hammer of Chaos. In Ghyran, I am Bough-Sunder and Kindle-father. In the tribal cant-stories of the arid hills of Al'khut, I am the Dawn Hate, and to the worshippers concealed among the merchants of the highland ports of Entoth I am the foremost of the Coven of Iron. Somewhere in Ghur, amidst the fjords and ice-caves of the Splintered Coast, an aged chieftain calls me father.

These titles are all of equal unimportance. Only one matters to me now, the one that I have sacrificed everything for.

Varanguard.

My name is Vanik. When I was a newborn, clad only in my mother's blood, my father tried to dash my soft skull against the ice outside our lodge-hut. A daemon cut his head from his shoulders, and now his flensed bones sit among the countless trophies of the Great Warhound's throne room.

During my first winter, a pox-blessing was visited upon my lodge and the lodges of my entire village by a passing leper. The tallymen came for us seventy-seven days later. They taught me to count. I bear their marks still.

During my ninth winter, the skinwolves attacked my tribe. They took me but did not kill me, and I lived among them for two more winters and three summers, hunting as one of their pups.

On the last night of my eighteenth year I seized the eldest daughter of the chief of the Skorani in a feud-raid. The sixty-six Skorani bondsman scalps that were taken with her that night were a tribute to her beauty, a great blessing from the Golden Serpent. She bore me a son, my firstborn, and after his birth the Gods sent their heralds to me. My life ended that night.

I am Vanik. Many of the tales told about me are false. Many of those untold are true. All of your lies will not change that. Yes, I know of your scheming, and I know too of the fear that you harbour, fear at my arrival here amidst your host, fear at what my coming portends.

You are right to be afraid. I am Vanik, and you will bow to the will of the Three-Eyed King, daemonic wyrdspawn, or I will pluck the wings from your back, rip the horns from your skull and feed your essence to my steed.

In the name of Archaon, Exalted Grand Marshal of the Apocalypse, *submit*.

ACT I

THE EIGHTH QUEST

PART ONE

THE BARROW KING AND THE BLACK PILGRIM

In the Death-Realm of Shyish, the village of the Necris burned.

Its people burned with it, their slaughtered bodies flung onto the pyres kindled from their homesteads. Those who attempted to flee were chased down, killed and immolated. The Black Pilgrim's instructions had been clear – neither flesh nor bone was to escape the flames that night.

The pilgrim himself saw little of the grisly work. He had ridden on from the village, leading his razor-fanged mount up the narrow, snowy tracks that wound their way into the Barrow Hills. He carried on now on foot, the firelight of the burning village long ago swallowed up behind him, bitter darkness and eddying snow pressing in on every side.

Hold your course, mortal. The voice echoed through the pilgrim's head, colder than the biting wind.

He climbed higher. He was a towering figure, tall and

broad-shouldered, his natural bulk accentuated by his armour. The black plate was baroque, edged with burnished silver bands and inscribed with dark runes of protection. Over his shoulders was draped a pelt cape, the hard blue scales of a slain Dracoth, now thick with snow. His helmet bore a slit visor and a crest of red-dyed horsehair, flanked by two horns that curled outwards like those of a ram. At his left hip was a heavy sword, sheathed in a scabbard of cured aelf-hide, while two long daggers were crossed over his chainmail cingulum. A shield of thick warp-steel was strapped to his left vambrace, embossed with an iron crest – a sea wyrm coiling beneath an eight-pointed star.

Glory awaits you.

The voice in the figure's head was growing louder, its sickly tones quickening with excitement. It wished for nothing more than to be free, and the Black Pilgrim represented a chance for just that.

The man – if man he was – passed between the burial cairns of the ancient dead, the stone mounds almost lost beneath the thickening snow. He ignored them – he had not come this far for some brass trinket or rusting blade. His destination lay ahead, rising out of the swirling darkness, a pillar of cold stone set into the fallow earth at the heart of the hilltop.

The barrow of the Frost King, eternal lord of the Necris.

Step closer, my champion.

The Black Pilgrim halted at the barrow's entrance, which was framed by two cornerstones of snow-clad rock. For a moment, he might have been a statue, cast from black iron, set to guard the king's tomb for eternity.

The illusion was shattered as he reached out with his right hand, the spiked gauntlet passing just beyond the entranceway flanked by the two great stones. Immediately, a thick coating of hoar frost closed like a vice over the black metal, threatening to shatter it. The figure withdrew, flexing his fingers and breaking the ice with a crack.

He raised the gauntlet again, this time to the left-hand stone. A crunching blow shuddered away the snow that clung to it in a white cascade, revealing the markings carved into the rock.

The figure spent some seconds assessing them. Then, with abrupt force, he slammed the edge of his shield against the first of the etchings.

Did they truly believe their corpse-wards would keep him at bay?

The Black Pilgrim broke them with his shield, each in turn, until all were reduced to shattered stone strewn around the entrance to the barrow. Their power dissipated and he stepped into the darkness beyond, no icy death-spell closing about his heart.

He had come to retrieve a fellow servant of the True Gods, and he would not be dissuaded.

At first, he could see nothing in the barrow's depths. He murmured a prayer to the Silver Fin, asking for guidance. Slowly, the interior of the burial place resolved itself around him, though whether that was because his eyes had grown accustomed to the darkness or because great T'char had answered him, he knew not.

The tomb was large, a circular space of drystone walls against which were set a dozen plinths. They were carved with mortuary emblems – skulls, bones, hourglasses and all the weak esotericism of the servants of the so-called Great Necromancer. Upon them rested the remains of twelve warriors, all skeletal, clad in ancient battle armour and with long, two-handed blades clutched to their rusting breastplates.

They occupied the pilgrim's attention only briefly. His gaze was drawn to the far end of the chamber, to the stone sarcophagus that stood there, flanked by the twelve plinths. Its upright lid bore a crudely worked depiction of a skeletal figure standing in triumph, praised by the outstretched arms of living tribe folk prostrate beneath it.

Weak. So very weak.

Yesss, hissed the sickly voice of Nakali in the pilgrim's skull, slithering around like the Golden Serpent. He shrugged it off, approaching the sarcophagus and slamming his warpsteel shield against it without hesitation.

The blow reverberated through the barrow, and sent a split running from the lid's top to its bottom, breaking the effigy in half. He clenched his fangs and slammed home a second blow, then a third. The tomb continued to shake, and finally with a cracking sound the front of the sarcophagus crumbled and came crashing down before him.

He took a step back. A figure lay slumped within, another skeleton. This one was more finely armoured than its guards, and bore upon its helm a circlet of bronze. It was not the barrow king's attire that held the pilgrim's attention though, but the weapon it clutched.

The sword was large, its hilt gripped in two bony fists. The length was black steel, its double edge jagged and irregular. The pommel was crafted in the likeness of a golden serpent, its long fangs bared and its forked tongue darting out. The crosspiece was likewise fashioned into a two-headed snake, also cast in gold.

It was no rusting barrow-blade. It was an exquisite weapon, forged in the daemon furnaces of the Varanspire. It was what he had been hunting for, the debaser of the Lightning Temple and the great serpent-daemon of Slaanesh.

Nakali.

There was a glimmer of illumination. It was not the wholesome flicker of flames, but was cold and bitter, like grave-dirt caught in the back of the throat. The pilgrim realised that blue dead-lights had flickered into being in the sockets of the barrow king's skull.

The Frost King wakes, Nakali hissed. ***Quickly, champion!***

He reached out with his right hand to snatch the sword from the king's grasp, but before he could touch it the skeleton shuddered. There was a rattle as its bones re-formed and straightened, dragged tight as though by the sudden twitch of a marionette's strings. It stood fully upright, its armour scraping against the stone of its tomb. With a snap, its head turned to face the pilgrim, and the deadlights in its sockets flared with an unnatural, immortal awareness.

Fool! Nakali shrieked.

The Black Pilgrim drew his own sword, Serpent's Fang, the sensation of the heavy blade in his fist sending a familiar thrill through his body. It was always a blessing to kill, even when the enemy was already dead.

The Frost King stepped from its shattered resting place and hefted its own sword: Nakali, desperate to be free, desperate to be saved from the deathless grip of a warrior who could never be tempted by its whispers or tainted by its perverse aura. Though nothing but bone, the ancient undead champion carried the heavy blade without any difficulty, lent strength and vitality by the sorcerous tricks of its False God.

'Come to me, corpse,' the pilgrim demanded. 'That I may release you from your long bondage.'

He attacked. Serpent's Fang met Nakali's edge, the clash of Chaotic steel ringing through the barrow, and he knew at once that the king's weapon was superior. The realisation brought a smile to his thin lips. It was good to know he was not wasting his time.

He turned his right-handed stroke into an overhead blow, then a thrust, relying at first on his strength, then seeking to drive the reanimated corpse into the stone at its back. Neither tactic worked – the death magic binding the thing together was at least as strong as he was, and the master of the Necris had no human regard for self-preservation. It refused to take a backward step as he rained blows down upon it, its motions clumsy but enough to parry each strike. It was not trying to attack, he realised. After another flurry of blows, he understood why.

More light had filled the chamber. He heard the rattle and clatter of bones and the scrape of worn armour, and noticed that the twelve guards had risen from their plinths. At first their motions were jerky and uncoordinated, but as they moved to surround him he knew his time was up. Soon every barrow and cairn across the hillsides would have awoken.

'Tzatzo!'

The pilgrim roared the name, the sound shaking the burial place just as surely as the first impact of his shield against the sarcophagus. The undead were unperturbed – they had no eardrums to burst, no brains to addle. The word had not been uttered for them, though.

The Frost King attacked. Nakali clashed against Serpent's Fang once, twice, and then scored a jagged blow down the pilgrim's left pauldron. He realised the corpse was becoming stronger and faster as it fought, the magics animating it taking a firmer hold of its remains the longer it was awake.

He took its next blow against his shield. Nakali rebounded violently from the hexed warpsteel, and he seized the chance to thrust Serpent's Fang into the king's open guard. His sword punched through the rusting breastplate and split its ribcage. Half a dozen shattered bones came away as he dragged the steel free, but the undead champion showed no sign of injury – it attacked, forcing him to take a step back or risk having his guard opened. He snarled with frustration, fangs bared.

The barrow-guard were upon him as well, and he was forced to turn away to meet them. They were slower and weaker than their king, but they were a distraction he could not afford. He shattered the skull of one with an upward thrust of his shield and cut another from collarbone to pelvis with a tight, spinning blow. The broadsword of another clattered ineffectually from his back, snagging in his Dracoth-pelt cape, but he was forced to turn to the king before he could break the one who dared strike him.

The undead master of the Necris had used the distraction well. It struck with an overhead blow. Made with the likes of Nakali, it would have cut open even a favoured champion of the Four. The pilgrim barely managed to get Serpent's Fang up to meet it, and the clang of the two blades striking one another jarred up his arm. The blow was too much – with a clatter, the upper half of Serpent's Fang came away, sheared in two, its tip impaling the frost-covered soil at his feet. He just managed to take enough of a step back to avoid Nakali's descent.

The moment seemed to slow. Death was reaching for him, its icy fingers scraping along his skin and tightening around his heart and throat. He brought the shorn hilt of Serpent's Fang up with all his strength, angling for the Frost King's arm as it swung downwards, cutting towards the exposed bone just above its brass vambrace.

Even in death, Serpent's Fang served the pilgrim well. The blade's remains – a wicked stub – bit through the skeleton's limb, splintering the ancient bone. Its fist came away, and with it Nakali, the sword spinning through the air for longer than seemed possible.

As the Frost King's shorn limb disintegrated, the pilgrim reached out and, with a bellow, he grasped the sword's hilt.

A landscape of writhing flesh consumes him. There are drumbeats on the perfumed breeze, primal and brutal. The vision comes apart, rent open with blood and screaming. In its place stands a boulder, a great block of pulsating green stone. Its outer surface cracks and splits, and verminous creatures spill out, gnawing the verdant substance with maniacal energy. It is consumed whole, and the flesh returns, crawling, writhing with lust-maddened need. Ahead of him, the Black Pilgrim sees a tree, its bark and boughs formed from intertwining bodies and grasping, fleshy limbs. A serpent is coiled about its groaning form, its scales golden and glittering with a lustre that fixes his eyes in place. It hisses his name, slowly, as though savouring it for the first time.

Vanik.

It lunges at him, its long fangs bared, and he lashes out with one hand, the motion born of instinct. The serpent is gone. The sky above is a black thunderhead, flickering with lightning. A single bolt slams down with a deafening crash, striking him, shattering him, splitting him into a thousand thousand broken shards–

He returned to the present, to reality. Somehow, he was still whole. The roar died in his throat.

Vanik blinked and, in the darkness, realised that his assailants had been flung back against the barrow's walls. A shock wave of daemonic power had picked them up and hurled them away, the Frost King included, and now the barrow-guards lay shattered and broken around the edges of the tomb. The Frost King itself was slumped against its broken sarcophagus, head hanging to one side, a single flicker of deadlight still lingering in one eye socket.

Vanik looked down. Nakali was clenched in his gauntlet. The whole blade was vibrating, buzzing with the ecstasy of release.

Free me, the daemon's voice slithered in his skull, full of hideous desire. *I know your thoughts now, pilgrim. Release me, and all your desires will be realised.*

'Never,' he replied, out loud. There was a cracking, scraping sound, and he half turned before the daemon could reply.

A femur was scraping through the barrow's frozen dirt, as though tugged by an invisible string. Vanik realised that all of the shattered bones around him had begun twitching and rattling – they were coalescing, each one reknitted by whatever sorcery animated the tomb's guardians. A pathetic necromantic trick. Even as he realised what was happening, the Frost King twitched. Its other eye socket ignited with deathly illumination once more, and it reached out with its one remaining skeletal hand, gripping the side of the sarcophagus.

Free me, Nakali reiterated. *It is the only way we can escape this place.*

'No,' Vanik said again, even as the reanimated barrow-guards began to rise around him, bones crunching and clacking. He had heard a noise from outside the tomb. A familiar scrabbling of claws on icy dirt.

The entrance to the barrow burst inwards, old stone and grave-dirt cascading down around the creature that had forced its way inside. It was a massive beast, moving on all fours and clad in thick barding, as though it were a Freeguild warhorse.

But it was not a warhorse.

It was his steed, Tzatzo.

The creature shrieked and lunged with her elongated, quill-studded head, her twin sets of serrated fangs clamping over the skull and upper ribcage of one of the barrow-guards. It came apart with a snap of splintered bone, and the rest of it turned to dust in her jaws. Tzatzo shrieked again, furious at having found neither flesh nor blood on her prey.

Vanik sheathed Nakali, but the blade snagged and snarled against the aelf-hide scabbard, and it took what felt like an eternity for him to break his grip and remove his gauntlet from its hilt. Had he grasped it with the bare skin of his palm, he doubted he would have had the strength to ever release it again.

Nakali snarled, but Vanik ignored the daemon – his mind was his own again. He moved to Tzatzo's side and from there past the broken remains of the barrow entrance. The Chaos steed was screaming and snapping, her great fangs breaking apart the skeletal guardians while their blades slid from her flanks, unable to pierce either her armour or her reptilian hide.

'Come!' Vanik snapped at her. The Frost King had fully recovered itself and was approaching from across the tomb, the sword of one of its guards in its bony grip. Tzatzo snorted in disgust and turned, a violent hind-leg kick sending more bones scattering across the barrow. Finally, she cantered outside.

Snow was still descending, swirling thicker than ever. He grasped Tzatzo's mantle and put a foot in one stirrup, pulling himself up into the saddle. He could hear ethereal screeches in the air, and the drumming of hooves. In the distance, barely visible through the snow and darkness hemming them in, he made out mounted figures emerging from the other barrows and cairns surrounding them – spectral horsemen, come to avenge the insult he had dealt their master. His pride stung, he felt the mad desire to turn his steed and face the oncoming warriors. To his surprise, it was Nakali who dissuaded him.

Don't be a fool, the daemon snarled. Nakali clearly had no desire to run the risk of remaining an immortal prisoner of the Necris.

Vanik overcame his ennui and turned Tzatzo right, back down the winding track. There was little enough time as it was – delay any longer, and claiming the sword would count for nothing.

Below, in the heart of the valley of the Necris, the hunters had become the hunted. The screams of burning villagers had turned into the icy howls of the disembodied – the newly dead had risen.

Vanik came upon the scene as his retinue, the Eightguard, re-formed in the centre of the village's remains. The hovels surrounding them were ablaze, lighting up the snow-streaked darkness all around and providing the illumination that was driving the shadows back and keeping the small war party alive.

The dead were assailing them from all sides. Though the bodies of the villagers were charred embers, the necromantic energies that wreathed Shyish had already resurrected their spirits. The pallid, ethereal things were now shrieking down at the Chaos knights, kept in check only by ensorcelled blades and the flames that had consumed their corpses, which they seemed to fear.

Vanik rode in amongst the melee, Tzatzo blowing hard, her thick muscles bunched in rage. The spectral riders were close behind, unimpeded by the snow or the rocky earth of the high hills. Seeing their lord thundering into the light of the fire, the Eightguard opened their circle, admitting him into their midst. As they did so, a clutch of the wailing phantoms swooped from the darkness above, out of the ash and snow, their screams making the living warriors' ears ache.

Vanik tugged Tzatzo round hard, sawing on the steed's chains, and brought up his shield. The things that had once been the villagers were nightmarish, their ghostly forms echoing images of sloughing flesh, liquefied organs and hideously burnt faces. Ethereal flames clung to them as they dived down, talons flaring with witchfire that reached for the Chaos knights.

One crashed into the pilgrim's shield with the force of a duardin's greathammer. He grunted but held, trusting in the warpsteel to repel the undead sorcery. The apparition burst apart around the thick metal, leaving it blackened and scorched but failing to pass through. The howls of the other spirits redoubled as the Eightguard resisted them, their Chaos-blessed blades capable of harming the otherwise incorporeal nightmares. The True Gods would not abandon their servants so readily.

'Is it done, lord?'

Vanik twisted in his saddle. Shielded at the centre of the circle of riders was his retainer, Modred. The youth was wearing no greater protection than a black leather doublet and plain cap, and was sat astride a wild-eyed, nameless nag. Both rider and mount were dwarfed by the towering armoured warriors surrounding them.

'It is,' Vanik said curtly. 'The blade is mine. You have looted the village?'

'We have, lord,' Modred said, indicating the small chest strapped across the nag's rear. He cringed as another spirit screamed overhead, trailing witchfire.

'And a living prisoner?' Vanik demanded. 'You saved one from the fire?'

'Yes, lord,' answered one of his knights, his bannerman, Kulthuk. The Black Pilgrim realised that the body of one of the villagers had been slung over Kulthuk's saddle, unconscious.

'Then let us be gone,' he said, urging Tzatzo towards the track that led from the blazing village. 'Skoren Blackhand has already claimed his prize, and there is no more time for us to waste. There is no glory in this place. Only death.'

With phantoms shrieking at their heels, Vanik and the Eight-guard lashed their steeds towards the dawn.

PART TWO

CASTELLAN GRULGRIX'S TRIBUTE

The dolorous clanging of the plaguebells announced the retinue's return to the Festerkeep.

The staunchest bastion of the Eightfold Path in the realm of Shyish rose up out of twilight's gloom like an overripe pustule, glistening in the icy rain. Vanik and the Eightguard approached it from the south, descending from the Barrow Hills along winding mud tracks thickened by rain and meltwater.

It had been five days since they had left the burning hovels and unquiet spirits of the Necris behind. They had ridden hard, stopping rarely, and never at night. None but a madman would use Shyish's long hours of darkness to try to sleep. Eventually, as the high, barren hills had begun levelling out, Vanik had permitted a slower pace, mindful that his retinue's horses could not keep up with Tzatzo's hellbred stamina. The Chaos steed snarled and snapped at the accompanying animals, sullen as ever in their presence, but occasionally permitted Vanik to calm her with fresh meat sliced from the captured Necris peasant. They'd killed him a few hours after leaving the village, confident his unquiet spirit would not return to haunt them once his body had been cut apart and consumed.

Vanik felt his spirits lift as his gaze fell upon the Festerkeep. It was not a feeling he had anticipated, but the rotbringer dreadhold represented something precious – an escape from Shyish. Vanik had ventured into the Realm of Death threescore times since he had first started on the Path to Glory, and no other place, mortal or immortal, cursed or blessed, crushed his soul quite like it. There was always so little to be gained and so much to be lost during any quest into the Necromancer's kingdom. The Four cared little for the slaughter of dead men, and hewing walking corpses or warding away screaming spirits advanced neither their favour nor personal skill at arms. Worse, to fall in such a place was to risk having the soul's essence stolen away by the creatures that inhabited it. The Gods, both True and False, guarded a mortal's soul jealously, and Vanik's was already promised to others. There were few fates worse than being bent in eternal service to the withered night-things that infested the lands of the dead.

That danger was receding now, as Vanik and the Eightguard descended onto the plain that stretched around the isolated dreadhold of Castellan Grulgrix. The Festerkeep had been built on a rocky outcrop, a lone, jagged rise that stood apart from its many brothers and sisters in the bleak hills beyond the plains. From a distance, it was as miserable a spectacle as anything in Shyish. Rugged parapets and leaning towers rose up out of the swampy ground that surrounded it. As Vanik drew nearer, however, the fortress' many blessings became more apparent.

The Festerkeep had been constructed not long after the

Three-Eyed King had taken the Eightpoints, built to protect one of the greatest of the Allgates that led into Shyish. It had been founded by Grulgrix, a rotbringer lord high in the esteem of both Archaon and the Grandfather. Grulgrix's descendants had manned it ever since, using it as one of the main staging points for any Chaos incursion into the Necromancer's kingdom. It was the means by which Vanik had first passed into the Gods-forsaken realm, and it would be his means out of it.

As he rode, he felt his scabbard shudder. Nakali was furious. The daemon bound to the black sword hadn't spoken since Vanik had grasped it, but he could feel its anger and its resentment bleeding into his own mind. Only mutual benefit was keeping it from lashing out. It was biding its time. For now, they shared the same objective – escape from Shyish. Once they were both free, he had no doubt it would try to wrest control from him, as it had done when he had first gripped its hilt.

Nakali's voice had been like sweet honey, drooling slow and thick through his skull, but he knew it for what it was. Mortals too often mistook daemonkin for men and women like themselves, albeit with more diabolic minds. They were not. They were wolves, starving wolves that had the gift of speech. To contend with one once it had dropped its pretences was to contend with a ravenous animal, an untameable predator whose immortal cunning was matched only by its hunger.

It was a struggle Vanik had been preparing himself for since he had set out from the Eightpoints. He felt the sword shudder once more, as though sensing his thoughts. Then he realised it was reacting to the sound of the plaguebells tolling out across the marshes. The Festerkeep was close.

They rode over a groaning wooden bridge, Tzatzo's claws clacking on the thick, maggoty timbers. Beneath them, the marshland bubbled, the black surface of the toxic bog barely disturbed by the sheeting rain. Vanik had stood atop the Fester-keep's walls and seen the potency of the surrounding quagmire first-hand. The shambling undead could make no headway when they attacked through it, their bodies coming apart and dissolving amidst the ooze. It soaked up and swallowed the greatest of assaults, and with supplies readily brought through the Realmgate within the dreadhold in the event of a siege, even the undead's immortality did not offer them an advantage. The Festerkeep had never fallen.

The bog was not the only reason for that. As they passed into the shadow of the gatehouse, the stench of decay struck Vanik – a sickly-sweet scent that was at once repulsive and delightful to his senses. The walls of the fortress, rising up from the black rock on which they were sited, had been almost completely consumed by mould and decaying growths. Thick fronds of rotmoss and pulsing fungal blooms covered every inch of the crumbling stonework in a tangled mass, all woven together with slime-slick vines and furry clumps of mycological infestation. The whole dreadhold was a delightful extension of Grandfather Nurgle's garden, an outpost of fecund life standing proud and virulent in the Realm of Death. It was the forever-weeping sore on the aspirations and sovereignty of the Necromancer. Vanik rarely felt prouder of the Grandfather's work than when he gazed upon the pus-ridden defiance of the Festerkeep.

The gate yawned before them. It was a living maw, a great parasite of rotten daemonic flesh that had burrowed itself into the dreadhold's walls. Its gullet was a tunnel of yellow teeth and blackened, diseased meat, like gums that had been left to decay. Beyond it, the thin light of a dying Shyish day glimmered.

The knights passed through, thick strands of mucus and saliva splattering their black armour. Tzatzo's claws dug into the flesh underfoot, making the whole gateway shake. They passed through, riding into a wide, cobbled courtyard spread out before the jagged spike of rock that bore the dreadhold's central keep. That final fortification was more thickly blotched with growths than any other part of the fortress, and its mould-heavy flanks were draped with mildewed banners bearing the sigils of the Grandfather – the triple buboes, the fly, the horn-and-eye. The cobbles of the courtyard surrounding it were thick with rancid-looking mushrooms and other slimy growths, a fungal carpet that crawled with writhing, sightless insects. The air was fogged with green spore clouds and thick swirls of buzzing, fat-bellied flies, airborne despite the rain. The stench redoubled, so pungent and sickly now that even Vanik, who had long had dealings with the Grandfather's subjects, felt his stomach churn.

Grulgrix's guard had assembled, warned by the tolling of the great, rusting bells high up in the keep's towers. A procession of two dozen blightkings had formed up either side of the stone stairs descending from the keep's port, hulking warriors whose distended, diseased flesh had burst forth from plate armour and chainmail straining to contain their spilled guts and oozing buboes. They had drawn pitted axes and maces, but did not move to impede the new arrivals.

More rotbringers gathered as Vanik hauled on Tzatzo's chain, bringing the Chaos steed to a snorting, ill-tempered halt before the keep's steps. The fortress was permanently garrisoned, but the size of the courtyard indicated the dreadhold's status as a staging point for larger invasion forces. Vanik had never quite been able to discern how such a space could exist atop the jagged hilltop, whether it was a trick of the land or whether the Gods had blessed the Festerkeep in such a way as to extend its natural boundaries from within. If Castellan Grulgrix himself knew, it was unlikely he would share the information.

The master of the Festerkeep had emerged and was descending

the steps towards Vanik. He was as bloated and corpulent as his warriors, his belly swollen beyond the ability of his armour to contain it. His ruined left leg, gout-riddled and bulging, forced him to lean heavily on a gnarled stave as he came down. A mace hung at his side and a cloak of bristling mould-fur was draped over his shoulders. His helmet had been removed, exposing a face riddled and swollen with cancerous growths. He came to a stop a few paces from the bottom of the keep's stairs, remaining above Vanik, and took a deep breath of the foul air. For a few seconds, the only sound was the buzzing of flies and the rain seething down around them. Even the plaguebells had ceased their mournful peals.

'Castellan Grulgrix,' Vanik said. 'As promised, we have returned. I require passage to the Eightpoints.'

'Black Pilgrim,' Grulgrix replied, his voice rattling and phlegmy. 'I did not expect to see you again. And I can sense by the bloodlust that now fills the air of my keep that your quest was a success.'

'The daemonblade stolen by the Necris has been returned to the service of the True Gods,' Vanik said. 'You were wrong to doubt me, rotbringer.'

There was a scrape of rusting battleplate as the nearest blight-kings hefted their weapons, and the buzzing of the flies around them grew more intense. Grulgrix hawked and spat a thick globule of green filth onto the cobbles before Vanik.

'I doubt that very much, pilgrim. I have seen enough of your kind fail before. Tell me, what tribute do you bring back for me from the Barrow Hills?'

Vanik twisted in his saddle and gestured to Modred. The retainer hastened to dismount, hauling the chest off the rear of his nag. He looked pale-faced and ill. Vanik doubted he would survive the exposure to the Festerkeep's noisome atmosphere.

Modred carried the chest to the foot of the keep's steps and retreated, clearly desperate to remain as far away from the rot-bringers as possible. Grulgrix put his weight on his good leg and reached out with his maggot-chewed stave, knocking the chest's lid back. He leant forward, peering out from the mask of cancerous growths that covered his face, then let out an angry grunt.

'Trinkets. Worse than worthless. I will have more dead at my door soon because of your inept thievery.'

'Then return it to them,' Vanik said carelessly, signalling at Modred to remount. 'What concern is it to me?'

'You have more to offer than just this,' Grulgrix said, knocking the chest's lid back down with a thud. 'You have the blade at your hip.'

'You think I would come here, complete my quest and then simply surrender it to you?'

'Perhaps I'm of a mind to take it regardless of what you would do, pilgrim. You won't make it back to the Eightpoints, not unless I permit you to use my gate. Is the blade worth your life?'

'It is,' Vanik said. 'There are other Realmgates that can take me to the Eightpoints besides yours, castellan.'

'Even with night falling and the dead abroad in the hills? Yet you won't fight me or my blightkings to keep the sword and gain passage. Why is that? When has one of the Black Pilgrims ever hesitated to draw steel in his master's cause?'

The rotbringer descended the last few steps and moved to Vanik's side, the fungi underfoot ground to mush, his stave clicking. Tzatzo threw her head back and snarled, but Vanik kept a tight grip on her. He suspected Grulgrix would have been smiling, had his diseased face permitted it.

'I know why, pilgrim,' he went on, now within touching

distance of Vanik. 'It is because you are afraid to draw your daemonblade. Afraid to even grasp its hilt. You haven't tamed it yet, have you? You haven't bound Nakali?'

The sword shivered slightly in its aelf-hide scabbard. Grulgrix emitted another wet chuckle.

'It thirsts for your soul. Lay a hand on it and it will tear you apart.'

'I have already used it once. Nor do I need so noble a weapon to remind you of your place, rotbringer.'

Vanik allowed his gauntlet to rest on the pommel of his long knives. Grulgrix let out a grunt of anger.

'I should have you slaughtered and riddle your body with bloatworms for the insults you heap upon me, pilgrim. In my own keep, as well!'

'Karex Daemonflayer will offer you more than insult if she hears of how you have delayed me here.'

The words gave Grulgrix pause. Vanik watched the castellan's pale, rheumy eyes dart about in the swollen flesh of his face, before fixing on Vanik's own.

'You did not know that she is the one I serve?' Vanik went on, relishing the sudden doubt in the castellan's gaze. 'I can assure you, the Fifth Circle will return to this pitiful conglomeration of rotten stonework with fire and sword if you do not permit me to pass through the Realmgate. *Now.*'

Grulgrix said nothing. Vanik could sense the desire to shed blood all around – in Tzatzo, tense beneath him; in the Eightguard at his back; in the blightkings and the other assembled rotbringers, fingering the rotting wood and rusting steel of their heavy, brute weaponry. He knew that he and his retinue would be slaughtered if the castellan gave the word.

He also knew that the master of the Festerkeep would do no such thing.

'You may pass, Black Pilgrim,' Grulgrix said finally, turning back towards the keep. 'But do not think I will forget this day. And do not show your face at this dreadhold ever again. If you do, I will cut you down myself and feed you to my plague drones.'

'This fortress exists at the pleasure of the Three-Eyed King,' Vanik said. 'I'm sure I will return to remind you of that someday, Castellan Grulgrix.'

The Realmgate stirred as they approached, the barest ripple passing across its black sheen. It was sited on the far side of the courtyard, atop another, smaller outcrop of the jagged dark stone that predominated in Shyish. It took the form of an inky expanse, like a pool but unmoving and wholly unreflective. The perfection of its nothingness seemed to drag the eye to its heart. Vanik had known many favoured champions of the Gods to stand for days on end, simply staring into the void of its lustre. The fungal rot that infested the rest of the Festerkeep seemed unable or unwilling to grow near it, the rancid blooms ending in a perfect circle around it and leaving its deathly cold stones and surface untouched.

A wind caught them as they approached, hot and sulphurous, out of place amidst the foetid air of the keep. Tzatzo tossed her head, eager to be gone from death's realm. Vanik's own spirit was no less willing. He let her take the lead, and she launched herself up the broad steps leading to the pool's glassy surface. She plunged into its depths, unhesitating, and the black substance shifted around rider and mount, slow like tar, shuddering as though with some sort of sentience. It reached upwards, oozing thickly around the steed's barding and then Vanik's legs, its grip like ice. Tzatzo carried on regardless, and Vanik heard the sound of his retinue entering behind him. A moment more, and then Tzatzo was wholly submerged in the pitch-like substance. The pilgrim followed, fighting the instinctive urge to take a breath.

They were not beneath the black surface any more. It had taken them somewhere else. Reality bent and distorted, like a dream. A piercing chill gripped Vanik's body, and he heard screams – so many screams, the howls of a billion dead souls calling out to him, some in despair, others in anger. No living thing left the Necromancer's kingdom without feeling the hatred and misery of those left behind.

The experience may have lasted only a second, or it may have been a lifetime. It did not matter. Reality dissolved and re-formed in a heartbeat. He was through, still mounted, Tzatzo passing over stone of a different sort – the dry, hot rock of the Eightpoints. They were rising, the spine-covered steed dragging herself free of the black morass. The substance retreated, sliding and wriggling from their armour, returning to the strange pool, a mirror of the one on the other side of the gate. It warped and distorted again as more riders emerged, Vanik's retinue, sloughing off the Realmgate's deathly cold. Modred was trembling, eyes wide and white with terror.

Vanik paused to ensure all of the Eightguard were present, and nodded to Kulthuk. The bannerman unfurled his standard, once the wyrm-and-star crest, now a simple length of featureless black cloth, the mark of a pilgrim.

Ahead lay the Festerkeep's twin, built on the Eightpoints side of the Realmgate. It also owed allegiance to Grulgrix, and the virulence of the Grandfather's garden was as evident here as it was in the Realm of Death. Tzatzo's claws crushed and pulped blooms of furred fungi as she cantered for the living gateway, the retinue falling into formation behind. The foetid air, dank and sulphurous now that it was free from death's bitter chill, resounded with the tolling of the plaguebells announcing their arrival.

The gate yawned, discoloured slime and liquidised rotten flesh pattering down like hail as the Chaos knights cantered through. The Leper's Way – the stone-clad road leading into the Eightpoints – opened up ahead. Jagged peaks of rock surrounded the fortress, and the sky overhead was far removed from the low, black clouds of Shyish – here an ugly crimson light suffused everything, and the heavens were full of strange, ever-shifting constellations. Orbs and spheres weaved illogical patterns around one another, some distant, some so close they filled great portions of the sky. There were other shapes too, creatures, circling in the aetheric void far above. Looking at them for too long hurt the eyes.

Vanik dragged his gaze from the maddening heavens and pinned it to the road before him. It was full, packed with dirty, rag-clad people who let up a great wail as they saw the Festerkeep's gate-maw spit the knights out.

The retinue rode in among them. They were a seething, lousy horde – men, women, children and other things, all cursed with only the most minor of the Grandfather's blessings. They choked the Leper's Way and swarmed around the Eightpoints side of the Festerkeep, night and day, desperate to be visited by the greater and more glorious illnesses that hung over the rotbringers within. They would regularly mob those returning through the Realmgate, praying loudly that whatever contamination might have been picked up by visitors to Grulgrix's fastness would be spread to them. Often the only way into the Eightpoints was through them.

'Blades,' Vanik snarled, feeling his anger stir. He had not come here to negotiate his way through a legion of the Grandfather's disowned. He was running out of time, and Nakali's shudder confirmed it. Or perhaps the daemon sword merely wished to taste blood. He prayed that was the case.

The swords of his retinue rasped free in unison, and the dolorous begging of the Unafflicted turned to screaming and shrieking. He dropped back to the heart of the armoured phalanx as his knights dug in their spurs, plunging like a wicked spear tip into the unkempt, filthy masses. The thud of blades through bone and the sudden tang of blood in the hot air helped assuage his doubts.

Tzatzo bucked beneath him, enraged at not having been permitted to sink her fangs into any of the scattering mob. He tightened the chains binding her and ripped his barbed stirrups along her flanks, reminding her that all he needed right now was her speed, not her bloodlust. She snarled but lowered her head and lengthened her stride. He left Nakali in its scabbard, unwilling to draw it and risk another mental battle, let alone grant it the strength of a bloodletting. The daemon remained silent.

The retinue broke free of the Unafflicted, the armour of Vanik's knights splattered and dripping with their blood. After a while he wheeled them off the road and south-west – or as much an approximation of the direction as was possible in the shifting landscape of the Eightpoints – and took the lead once more, through the vast, jagged rocks that ringed the Festerkeep. They crested a shallow rise of barren dirt, the red-tinged heavens still nebulous above them, and saw an encampment spreading out ahead.

It was clustered around a small hill, its steep, rounded flanks betraying intelligent design. Its top was crowned by the ruins of a shrine, not a place sacred to the True Gods, but built to supplicate some weak idol of mortal veneration. Its priests were long dead, and the bones of its structure had been daubed with icons pleasing to the Four and the lesser deities that ruled under them.

Vanik's banners also flew from its ruins, lengths of unadorned black. Those who inhabited the tents pitched around the hill's base were his own, warriors and families all. Until recently, they had been his personal warband. Now their allegiance was to the Darkoath warqueen, Jevcha, though she was bound to him still.

Renki's white-pelted hounds caught their scent, and the barking echoed out across the surrounding plains. The noise alerted the rest of the warband, and the blare of tusker horns signalled their approach. Vanik allowed his retinue's herald, Aramor, to sound the half-carnyx in response. Families were emerging from the tents and covered wagons, mothers snatching children to stop them running out to greet the returning knights. There were warriors too: Jevcha's own Darkoath kinsmen, Kjarlmer's raiders and Lo Faug's sallow-skinned scalp-takers.

Silence fell as Vanik cantered up, a weight of fearful expectation reducing the noise of even Renki's dogs to uncertain whimpers. Then someone caught sight of Nakali's hilt, and a cheer rang out. It spread, and the crowd parted as the Black Pilgrim carried on through them, his retinue staying close to his flanks.

He urged Tzatzo on up the steep slope to the ruined shrine, the tribe's acclaim washing over him. It was meaningless – even with the quest completed and the sword in his possession, he would have failed if he did not reach the Varanspire with it before Skoren Blackhand.

Jevcha, alerted by the commotion in the camp below, was emerging from beneath the shrine's broken archway. She was a powerful woman, her toned body – much of it bared in the Darkoath way – criss-crossed with a hundred old scars. Her red hair was worn up beneath the curling horns of her half-helm, and she carried a heavy war axe easily in one fist. Her yellow eyes, watchful and cunning, were alive as they caught sight of Vanik.

'The daemon sword is yours, my lord?' she called over the shouts of the warband, following like eager pack hounds up the slope.

'Do not call me that, sister,' Vanik said, halting Tzatzo at the edge of the shrine. The mount stood quiet – Jevcha was one of the only mortals he had ever known the Chaos steed not to snap at.

'Black Pilgrim,' the warqueen said, correcting herself. 'Or Varanguard, now that the blade is yours?'

'The blade means nothing,' screeched a new voice. Vanik grimaced as another figure emerged from the shrine's ruins, lingering warily in Jevcha's shadow. It was an old woman, swathed and bent over in sackcloth, her bony fingers clutched around a gnarled staff hung with the small skulls of children. Her face was haggard with age, one eye milky and blinded by cataracts, the other a startlingly light shade of blue. Tzatzo snarled at her.

'The Blackhand is already at the Seat of the True Gods,' the crone, Mother Yogoth, crowed. 'Your many quests are all for naught, young Vanik!'

'Waterskins,' Vanik said to Jevcha, ignoring the decrepit witch. 'I do not know how long the wastes will take this time.'

'Skins!' the warqueen barked, gesturing at two of her Darkoath tribesmen. Vanik called back to the Eightguard, turned to keep the rest of the warband from mobbing him.

'You will ride with me for the Varanspire. Drink and eat while you can.'

'Your plans are all undone!' Yogoth cackled, daring to edge closer. 'Did you really think you could outrun the destiny chosen for you by the True Gods?'

Tzatzo snapped her double fangs, tugging at her chains, and the crone let out a shriek and scurried back behind Jevcha.

'Nakali has yet to taste blood by my hand, witch,' Vanik snapped, pointing at her over Jevcha's shoulder. 'I will feed it with yours when I return if you do not hold your tongue!'

Yogoth hissed but said nothing more, skulking out of reach of Tzatzo's wicked jaws. Jevcha approached and placed one hand on the steed's muzzle, quietening her once more.

'Even if the Blackhand has reached Varanspire ahead of you, all is not lost,' she said, looking up at Vanik. 'The Gods favour you, dear brother, regardless of what Mother Yogoth says.'

One of the Darkoath had returned, a waterskin in each fist. Vanik took one, unstoppered it, and quenched his thirst before responding.

'Perhaps. I would rather not test their graces.'

She nodded. 'Then go. I will keep the warband here for a few days longer. There is food enough from the Laushen caravan we took before you rode for the Festerkeep.'

'Do not wait for me, sister,' Vanik replied, his eyes already on the horizon. 'I will send word to you if I succeed. If not… may the Four watch and bless you.'

PART THREE

A PILGRIM'S ARRIVAL

They rode. There were no complaints from the Eightguard. There never were. The fifteen warriors – kinsmen all – had followed Vanik loyally since before he had set out on the Black Pilgrimage. Each trod their own Path to Glory, relishing every new quest and battle he brought them. A few were close to becoming champions in their own right. Whether they stayed with him or not was their own choice, but he suspected he would have their services for many struggles yet to come.

It was good to have such men at his side during days like these. The pilgrim's life was a lonely one, and even in times of greatest surety, in the midst of battle or while contemplating the ways of the Eightfold Path, Vanik knew doubts. At least for now his way could not be clearer. He had to reach Karex and the Fifth Marshal before Skoren Blackhand. That was all that mattered.

His destination waited over the next rise. They mounted the ridgeline and saw it sprawling before them – at last, the

Seat of the True Gods, the throne of the Three-Eyed King. The Varanspire.

He was sure that the sight of it would never fail to set his spirits soaring. It was the greatest fortress in creation and uncreation both, a fastness whose glory defied the imagination of those not blessed with immortality. It covered the horizon from end to end and rose up like a mountain range, a continent-spanning forest of vast towers and walls, bastions, bulwarks and gateways. It was a beacon in the red-tinged gloom that swathed the Eightpoints, lit by a million flaming braziers and crimson hell-light. Dark energies beamed from its highest towers, up into heavens torn and broken by the glorious power of Chaos. Shattered worlds and the moons of far-flung constellations hung in torment above the vast citadel, their spheres crumbling and broken into thousands of slowly circling fragments.

Despite their haste, the sight of the vast fortress gave him pause. His eyes were dragged by a will that was not his own towards the heart of the citadel, where the spires and turrets, barbicans and keeps rose highest and thickest, clustering like the spears of a thousand lifeguards around the heart of the fortress. There stood the Varanspire itself, a colossal tower dwarfing all those around it, a spike of blackest stone and metal so high its bladed parapets seemed as though they would scrape the remains of the celestial ruination far overhead. Crimson lightning arced and crackled around its pinnacle, and billowing flocks of shadowy things, wailing and half immaterial, circled its flanks endlessly. To look at it made Vanik's skull ache and his heart quicken.

'Lord?' Modred's voice broke the dark allure of the unmentionable fortress. Vanik snapped his eyes away with a grunt, and realised blood had broken forth from his nose. He cuffed it away with the back of his gauntlet and, without turning to the retainer, dug his spurs in.

The landscape around the Varanspire was barren and tortured. Blackened earth stretched away, littered with the desiccated bones of countless thousands of creatures – men, beasts and immortal beings whose material forms had failed them. The ground was riven by crevasses and fissures exposing the fiery heart within, thick streams of lava and bubbling, white-hot magma crawling ponderously across the open plains. The skyline to either side was dotted with strange outlines: monoliths, totems and lonely shrines to the Four and to the thousands of lesser deities that demanded veneration from those who inhabited the wastes.

Every time Vanik's eyes returned to the Varanspire itself, there seemed to have been an almost imperceptible shift in its distant structure. Towers no longer stood where they once had and great gateways had become unbreakable cliff walls. Only the central spire remained constant, a lance piercing the dark heart of the immense fortress. He had long ago learned not to ponder its impossibilities, nor worry about the fact that, like a mirage, the Varanspire seemed to grow no closer as one approached. A warrior could travel for years towards it and never reach it. Only those with the necessary blessings and willpower could ever hope to arrive at its soaring walls. Doing so was a rite in and of itself. These were the Chaos Wastes, and here the greatest of champions and the mightiest of armies were as nothing, laid bare before the eyes of the Gods.

He did not know how long they rode for, and nor did he stop to wonder. Those that did were always sure to become lost. Eventually, he saw signs of life amidst the expanse of dry bone and magma around him. Off to his right a convoy of lumbering wagons dragged by brute, shaggy tuskers trailed away along the horizon, doubtless carrying all manner of trophies and captives, or the fodder consumed by the fortress and the vast armies that eternally surrounded it.

Those armies became visible not long after. At first, they were nothing but a smudge in the distance, a line of black smoke set before the backdrop of the Varanspire's soaring glory. Soon they resolved though, and distinct warhosts became apparent. Hide tents and dark pavilions stood clustered in their thousands beneath warpsteel icons and great banners that bore the runes of the Four and the heraldry of chieftains, warlords, knights and champions. A few Vanik recognised. Many he did not. The camps were bustling, men, women, children and less easily discernible things roaming freely and intermingling. Many were warriors, many more were those who followed them – retainers, lifeguards, families, captives. These were the armies of the True Gods, and for a thousand different reasons and purposes they had come to stand in the long shadow of the greatest fastness.

So many overripe souls, desperate to be plucked, hissed Nakali. It was the first time the daemon had spoken since Shyish. Vanik had felt its hunger building, the presence of so much living flesh around it for the first time in so long almost more than it could bear. He ignored it. Its whispered urges meant nothing to him.

Vanik and his retinue rode in among the encampments without slowing their pace, taking a well-beaten path between two warbands whose sigils the Black Pilgrim did not recognise. The boundaries of the countless different factions and sub-factions were staked out with totems, banners and rune sticks, or impaled cadavers. The peoples either side of him appeared to have come from very different corners of the Mortal Realms – those to the left were broad and dark-skinned, and wore jagged gold-plated armour. Their tents were draped in the speckled or striped pelts of strange predators and surrounded by carved wooden icons bearing the All-Seeing Eye of great Tzeentch. Those to the right were squatter, clad in white furs not dissimilar to the pelts of Renki's warhounds. Their flesh, where exposed, had been smeared with blue woad, and they had used it to grease and spike their hair. Their shelters were crude brushwood lean-tos, and they had chalked out warding sigils and Dark Tongue litanies on the cracked black earth around them. Dozens of them, old and young, stopped to stare at the Chaos knights as they thundered past.

Let me feed, Nakali urged, shivering in its scabbard. *They would rejoice at such a blessed end to their pathetic lives!*

Vanik ignored both the sword and those it hungered after, his eyes on the camps they rode through. The peoples of Chaos were without end. They flowed into and out of the wastes continuously, some at will, others under the bondage or leadership of some warlord or daemonkin. Sometimes the most favoured champions of the Four would amass vast armies from their numbers and lead them on grand campaigns through the Mortal Realms. Always, however, there were more, seeking the Gods' favour and trying to eke out an existence in this harshest of places.

They passed around the edge of a sutler enclave, where merchants and traders from across the dominions of Chaos were peddling their wares to the encampments – hides and pelts, fresh meat, gritbread and lard, herbs and root-plants, coarse ales, and garments of leather and linen, fur and silk. There were trinkets in abundance, tokens and icons of wood and stone, brass, iron, clay and bone, and less identifiable substances, etched in a thousand different shapes and sizes and dedicated to any of the multifarious ways of the Eightfold Path.

Captives were auctioned too, some for slavery, some for sacrifice, others for worse fates still. Their wailing was drowned by the insistent demands of the crowds.

Beyond the sutler wagons and the spiked slave pens, a mobile ironworks churned smoke and steam from dozens of copper chimneys, a pall of ash falling softly on those unlucky enough to be encamped alongside its clanking route. It was a blockhouse of black metal, lit within by a furnace-glow, its great tracks clattering as they dragged it along. A dozen duardin of the Legion of Azgorh surrounded the mobile structure, guarding its slow passage, and as Vanik rode nearer they hefted axes and flare-muzzled harquebuses. The thunder-strikes of hammers and the hiss of quenched metal rose above the animalistic snarling of the moving, smoke-belching structure. Vanik signalled for the Eightguard to keep to the left of the track, and raised his hand in the three-fingered salute of the Everchosen as he passed.

None of the daemon-worshipping duardin returned the gesture. He could sense their greedy eyes, assessing the heavy armour of his knights, lingering on his own Azgorh-forged battleplate as he passed. He did not slow.

There was no time for confrontation.

They continued. The path took them around one of the shrines dotting the wastes, this one little more than the great skull of some multi-eyed beast, set alongside a stone slab upon which a captive had been bound. His ears were being carved off. The slab and the skull were surrounded by a baying mob of tribespeople, naked but for the blood daub swirling across their filthy bodies, their hoarse voices calling upon Khagaroth, Korneth or another of the Warhound's lesser guises. A little further on, tents formed from rainbow-coloured feathers or long sheets of gleaming fish scales had been pitched in ordered rows beneath blue, yellow and purple pennants bearing the device of the eye-and-fin. The clash of steel rang through the air, and he saw warriors armoured in brilliant silver plate and scale mail sparring on an expanse of open dirt. These he recognised – the Silver Knights, paladins of Tzeentch, come to the Varanspire to pay another tribute-cycle to the throne of the Three-Eyed King.

Ahead, a train of wagons was filling the track, laden down with thick bushels of grain. He signalled Aramor to sound the half-carnyx and the teamsters hurried to shift the lumbering transports to one side. They snatched caps from their heads and averted their eyes as the knights thundered past, then scrambled to tug blankets across their cargo as a brief squall of blood pattered down, churning the dirt to a reddish paste and sending crimson lines streaking across the retinue's armour and barding.

Finally, they broke free from the hordes. Despite Vanik's haste, he was thankful. It could take weeks to traverse the musters and encampments, let alone reach them from across the wastes. Something was speeding his arrival, and he resolved to make the proper offerings of thanks at the first opportunity.

Before him, the Varanspire now soared, as eternal and immutable as it was ever-shifting. Between the retinue and its cliff-like walls, a great lake of lava boiled and bubbled, a motte fit to encompass a continent. Arching bridges crossed the infernal expanse, vast highways of daemon-forged metal, their sides hung with the blackened corpses of hundreds of thousands of apostates, their scarred and worn roadways rarely clear of sacrificial blood. Here the true glory of the Gods began to manifest itself in sights and sounds that were unequalled in one reality or the next.

He did not pause to drink in the spectacle, but urged Tzatzo forward, through the shimmering heat and sulphurous smoke. The bridge directly ahead – wide enough for Vanik's whole warband to have marched across side by side – was teeming with souls. They were tribes, warbands and covens come from all across the Mortal Realms, seeking to offer tributes of arms and armour, food, slaves and sacrifices, hoping for a daemon-blessing or boon from the Varanspire's darkling sorcerers, or perhaps even the gaze of one of the great marshals that ruled the vast fortress' eight circles. They were pilgrims all, but none were like Vanik. Aramor loosed the half-carnyx once more, and those ahead – kings and slaves alike – scrambled to make way. These were not the Unafflicted. They recognised the black banner, fluttering from Kulthuk's fist in the hot air. They knew that he would not spare any delay.

Hooves and claws striking sparks from the bridge's surface, they rode into the shadow of the gatehouse. Its vastness made Vanik's skull ache, a chasm that seemed as though it could swallow a city, all dark stone, black bedrock and blood-rusted iron. The portcullis, raised, was a thousand shards of warpsteel poised overhead, and searing fire gouted and belched from portholes above and to either side. The gates of the Varanspire's great curtain wall almost never closed, for the tide of supplicants was endless. Rarely did any pause to consider how few were leaving in the opposite direction.

He felt eyes on him as he passed through the gateway, not the fearful or jealous glances of the pilgrim masses, but the cold inspection of rivals and fellow warriors. He did not return them. He knew that the Varanguard were watching him – knights of the Eighth Circle, the infamous Unnamed and Unknown, their nature understood only by Archaon. They clustered around the flanks of the gate and on the spiked parapets high above, baleful and silent, assessing the mortals, beasts and wyrdspawn entering the great fortress unflinchingly. Sometimes they rode in amongst the masses, taking individuals or groups for unknown purposes, at other times slaying with sudden, cold precision, their reasoning always unfathomable. He felt their eyes fixed on his black banner. None moved to intercept him. Their baleful presence sent a surge of determination through his thoughts, and he dug his spurs a little deeper. If they did not view him as worthy of their attention, they would soon realise their mistake.

Beyond the gate, all was bedlam. A grand ward gave way to upward-sloping streets and thoroughfares, all twisting and turning, and all packed with more supplicant hordes. The fortifications either side were towering pillars of steel and stone, embossed with bestial images and runic sigils of allegiance. Braziers blazed above watch posts, barrack blocks, vestries and armouries, and vast banners of silk, cloth and the hides of countless creatures flapped in the infernally hot air. Here the pilgrims were split and divided by the Varanspire's castellans: beast-headed brutes and bellowing overseers, acting under the silent gaze of more cohorts of Varanguard. The air shivered and pulsed like a living thing, torn by the screamed praises and terrified shrieks of the hundreds of thousands pressing around Vanik, heavy with the primal stink of blood and sweat, and the cloying, underlying reek that permeated every Chaos-blessed stone of the great fortress.

Unlike most of those around them, Vanik already knew which path to take. He rode the cobbled street branching right along the rear of the cliff-like curtain wall, then turned left, uphill, passing by the great brass statue of Engra, a champion-spirit of the World-That-Was. Tzatzo snapped and hissed at those who didn't get out of the way fast enough. The Eight-guard stayed close behind their master, hands on the hilts of their swords. Despite the eternal truce that lay over the sacred ground of the Varanspire, bloodshed was a constant. Daemons, beastmen, spawn, men driven mad by the truths of the Gods – it was rare that something didn't try to impede those who sought to travel deeper into this greatest of strongholds.

There were eight concentric circles of defence within the Varanspire, one of the few absolutes that could be applied to the sprawling fortress. Each was ruled by an order of the Knights of Ruin, the Varanguard, paladins of the Gods and foremost servants of the Three-Eyed King. Vanik's destination was the Inevitable Citadel, a chief fortress within the Fifth Circle. It was there that Fifth Marshal Neveroth had his fastness, and it was to him that Vanik had to pledge Nakali. Doing so would bring him a step closer to the goal he had been striving towards for as long as he could clearly remember – entry into the ranks of the Varanguard. He was but one of a host of Black Pilgrims seeking the same honour. He feared that he was too late already, that others had sworn his pledge before him. The Fifth Circle would only be inducting a single pilgrim into its ranks – all others faced nothing but spawndom and damnation. He could only ride, and trust in the Eightfold Path to carry him straight and true.

The streets became less crowded as they climbed higher. For all the desperate masses teeming in through the great gateways, the Varanspire was not a city, and was not inhabited like one. It was a fortress, a seat of war, the greatest martial stronghold of the thousandfold armies that would one day conquer eternity itself. They passed through an Azgorhi foundry district, leering bearded effigies wrought from strange metals glaring down at them from the walls of brutalist stone and iron factories. Clusters of dozens of chimneys great and small belched forth all manner of alchemical smog, some of it thick with ash and black smoke, others exuding gouts of glittering, multihued mist – the raw stuff of magic drawn from the daemon-forges.

They went on through the seventh and sixth gates, each – impossibly – larger than the last, each teeming with cavorting throngs of beasts, mortals and, occasionally, the baleful presence of a daemon-servant glorying in the manic adulation of the creatures around it.

Eventually, past a slaughter yard where stooped, one-eyed creatures butchered all manner of flesh-beasts for the banquet tables of the Varanspire's lords, they found the Inevitable Citadel rising before them. It stood hard against the great wall of the Fifth Circle, like a broken shard of black metal jutting forth from its sheer flanks, a looming tower-keep studded with spikes and chains hung with the rotting remains of those who had failed the True Gods. A smaller curtain wall surrounded it, its parapets draped with the banners of the Fifth Circle.

'The Gods have guided us true,' Kulthuk called as their steeds clattered towards the curtain wall's main gateway. 'Surely reaching the citadel so swiftly is a good omen?'

'The Gods do as they please,' Vanik replied, unwilling to tempt their good humour with hope. 'We shall see what they have in store.'

A horn blared as they pulled on their reins before the gateway, and Vanik caught movement on the spiked parapets of the gatehouse above. A face appeared overhead, bestial and furred, with two great gold-tipped horns curling from its brow.

'Who dares come to the fastness of Lord Neveroth?' it demanded. Vanik recognised Shorgul, the beastman gatekeeper of the Inevitable Citadel. He motioned Kulthuk forward with his black banner.

'It is Vanik, Black Pilgrim of the Fifth!' the bannerman called. Shorgul made a grunting noise and disappeared from the battlements. A moment later there was a thud and a clank of chains, and the portcullis began to rise. Vanik urged Tzatzo on under the wicked spikes before they had locked in place.

The retinue came to a halt once more in the courtyard before the keep, hooves and claws drawing sparks from the cobbles. Shorgul had descended, the hulking, armour-clad beastman peering with its goat-like split pupils at the new arrivals. It was rare for such an animal to rise to so high a station within the Varanspire, but Shorgul had been master of the citadel's gate-house for as long as Vanik had known of the eight circles. The thing picked at the grey fur of its throat and let out a braying noise Vanik realised was laughter.

'I did not think to see you again, young Vanik,' the thing grunted in its garbled half-tongue. 'You must hurry.'

'Modred, take Tzatzo to the stables,' Vanik said, without reply-ing to the beastman's jibes. 'The rest of you, find lodgings within the citadel. I will send for you as soon as I have need.'

He barely heard the affirmations of his retinue – his eyes were on an assembly of black-armoured figures that had gath-ered on the steps of the keep directly ahead. Modred scrambled to take Tzatzo's reins, flinching back from the beast's jaws, as Vanik dismounted with a clatter of battleplate. Shorgul's bray-ing laughter still ringing in his ears, he approached the knights massed around the keep's inner gate.

They parted before him, their expressions unknowable behind the bestial effigies that adorned their visors. All except one. She was waiting beyond the rest, at the bottom of the keep's steps. Her expression – accentuated by her ritual scars and shaven scalp, and by the nubs of the two horns growing from her tem-ples – was one of rawest anger.

'My lady Karex,' Vanik began. He got no further. A backhand blow from Karex's gauntlet crashed against his face, snapping it to one side and causing him to stumble. He shook his head, blinking the stars away, trying to unclench his fist from around Nakali's hilt and ignore its murderous urging.

'You are too late,' snarled Karex, Varanguard and Knight Templar of the Fifth Circle. 'Blackhand is already here.'

'He has presented his blade to Lord Neveroth?' Vanik managed to say, finally unclenching his gauntlet from around Nakali.

'Perhaps not. The Gods may have blessed you in that regard. Last I saw, the fool was still wandering the citadel's corridors. They have confounded him.'

'Then there is still hope,' Vanik said.

'Pray so,' Karex replied, standing aside for him to pass up the keep's steps. 'For if you have failed, and Neveroth chooses to spare you, I shall not. Go.'

The corridors and halls of the Inevitable Citadel were a nightmare to traverse. It was something no sane mortal could hope to accomplish, for the place was ever-shifting. Vanik could recognise individual corridors and walkways, but they never led to the same location. Doors and archways could change position in the time it took to blink. Some said it shifted based on the whims of its master, Lord Neveroth, others that it had been placed under a curse by a Gaunt Summoner of Tzeentch, others still that it was the Gods themselves who refashioned the stronghold depending on who had their favour and who had earned their ire. The truth, Vanik knew, was that there was no truth, and no point in trying to guess the whims of the fortress. It shifted because it desired to, and in such a place as the Varanspire, no desire, no matter how impossible, was denied.

He passed down stone hallways lined with strange statues fashioned from all manner of materials – clay, wood, metal, crystal, flesh. Beyond, he discovered a corridor composed entirely of a glassy substance that cast crazed, endless reflections as he hurried along it. He knew better than to look at the images, or the beast-headed idols that filled the niches in the passageway's walls.

A sharp left turn took him up a spiral turret, the steps of which abruptly – impossibly – turned one way and then the other as he climbed. He tried to ignore the sickening unease in his stomach, the instinctive revulsion that even a mortal long accustomed to the ways of the Gods felt in the presence of such madness. He had to hurry.

He emerged from the turret, limbs aching from the climb. The glass corridor stretched out before him once again. His myriad reflections were laughing at him, silently.

'Gods, guide my path,' he growled, setting out once more for the archway at the far end of the prismic passage. Past it he found himself on the edge of an amphitheatre. The tiered stone steps were lined with figures in red robes, their features hidden by their raised cowls. The ceiling mirrored the floor perfectly, stone steps arrayed in concentric circles around a central dome. In both the pit below and the dome overhead, something formless and fleshy writhed, tentacles and eye-stalks questing towards one another as the creature sought some form of congress. The robed onlookers were screaming.

Vanik skirted the amphitheatre. On he went, moving through the passageways and chambers of the Inevitable Citadel, praying as he went that the Gods showed him favour and guided him through the great keep's illusions. He travelled through a fleshy tract, like the intestinal passage of some great beast, thick with stinking, decaying matter and greasy globules of fat, then passed on abruptly into an armoury forge. There, muscle-bound creatures with featureless black masks welded to their faces beat and hammered at all manner of blades and armoured plates, their sweat-streaked labour lit only by the flames of their furnaces.

He met other beings as he went, usually stooped servant-things in the black robes of the Varanguard's retinues, hurrying through the citadel on some errand or other. Occasionally he passed the knights themselves, sometimes alone, other times in twos or threes, conversing as they traversed the maddening architecture of the fortress. He knew better than to meet their gaze in a place such as this – his status as a Black Pilgrim made him in many ways less worthy than even the knights' retainers. At least they served, and by extension bore the protection of the Knights of Ruin. Vanik was only permitted within the citadel because of the mentorship of Karex Daemonflayer. Without her, he would have been seized, slain or worse.

He passed along an outer corridor studded with arrow slits. The Varanspire itself was visible beyond, a bristling cluster of keeps and towers rising towards the central pinnacle, mind-aching in its scale. Vanik didn't pause to stare at the impossible panorama. He had to carry on, no matter how long the citadel's madness sought to confound him. To fail now was unthinkable.

You're too late, Nakali cackled in his head. *The one you call the Blackhand is already knelt before your master.*

'Be silent,' Vanik snapped out loud.

He rounded a corner in a bending, maze-like passage of bone archways that seemed to repeat over and over, and finally saw the great doors of Neveroth's court ahead, emblazoned with an iron design representing the Fifth Marshal's daemonic skull heraldry. He ran, silently praying to the True Gods that the entrance was not another trick.

The doors swung inwards before he touched them, scraping ominously across the stone floor beyond. Vanik slowed as he crossed the threshold, fierce exultation surging through him as he realised it truly was Neveroth's throne room that he had found. The feeling didn't last long.

Neveroth's court was assembled, the inner warrior cabal of the Fifth Circle, dozens of figures gathered by the light of burning braziers beneath the ever-shifting black fluxwood beams of the chamber's arched ceiling. They were Varanguard mostly, some fully armoured, others in leather jerkins or daemonhide doublets, disdain on their features as they turned to witness Vanik's arrival. He recognised some from the tales he had been told as a child, growing up in the ice lodges of the Splintered Coast. There was Ogold the Flenser, the three-armed champion of the Thousand Eyes, and there Lord Galorix, the great warhammer that had famously smashed the Lightning Gate asunder slung across his broad back. Closest to Vanik was Sandruil Halfborn, half a dozen sightless retainer-things clustered against the bristling golden scales that constituted that thrice-blessed warrior's outer skin.

The Black Pilgrim took them in with just a glance, his eyes dragged past the assembly to the far end of the chamber. There he saw a great throne, set beneath a shimmering black-and-silver banner, marked by the blazon of the Three-Eyed King himself. The throne was forged from twisted golden metal that Vanik recognised as sigmarite, the cursed material crafted by the False God Sigmar to armour his petty warriors. Hundreds had to have been broken from their protective plate to create the throne, their golden greaves, breastplates and helms stripped from the Stormcast Eternals' bodies and hammered by Azgorhi smelters into a seat for one of the most powerful lords of the Varanspire. It gleamed in the torchlight, a testimony to the triumphs of the True Gods.

Upon it, Neveroth sat waiting. The Master of the Fifth was

clad head to foot in bone armour, the thick warpsteel plates fashioned and polished in the likeness of femurs, sternum and ribs. His helm was a fanged daemon skull, ram horns not unlike those on Vanik's own helmet curling from his brow. Something cold and dark kindled behind his visor, and flared as the Black Pilgrim entered.

Vanik's hopes plummeted. Another figure was already before the throne, knelt in supplication. He wore black armour similar to Vanik's, edged with silver, a rust-red cape clasped about his shoulders. His head was bared, revealing a topknot and a lean, hungry face that rapidly became a mask of hatred as he caught sight of Vanik.

Skoren Blackhand had reached the court of Neveroth before him.

'You are too late, Vanik,' Skoren hissed, still kneeling before Neveroth's golden throne. 'The sword is mine, as is a place with the Knights of Ruin.'

The despair that had settled upon Vanik when he had seen Skoren vanished, replaced by a surge of determination and anger. It was not over. It couldn't be.

He strode towards Neveroth. None in the assembled court moved to stop him, until Skoren himself rose and barred his path. The warrior's hand was on the hilt of his weapon, a long, curved blade that Vanik recognised as the daemon sword Skoren was tasked with recovering. Vargen, the Prince of the Apocalypse.

'Take another step and I will cut you down,' Skoren snarled, face contorted with anger.

'You may try,' Vanik replied, before addressing Neveroth directly. 'Lord, has the Blackhand yet sworn his oath to you?'

'You dare address my lord?' Skoren shouted, pushing himself in Vanik's face.

'Is he your lord?' Vanik demanded, meeting his rival's ice-blue eyes. 'Or has he yet to accept your oath?'

It was taking Vanik all of his control not to lash out at Skoren. In that moment, he would have given anything, anything at all, to grasp Nakali's cursed hilt and plunge its blade into his rival's guts. The daemon in the sword was whispering in his skull.

Let me feed on him, pilgrim. I will rend him for you. Flesh, blood and soul.

He could see the same struggle in the other Black Pilgrim's eyes, Skoren riven with the desire to obey his new, bloodthirsty Khornate blade and cut Vanik's head from his shoulders.

The realisation that Skoren wanted to kill him just as much was what gave Vanik the strength to resist. If Skoren didn't succumb to his bloody urges before the Master of the Fifth Circle, then neither would he. He was better than that. Stronger.

'You are late, Vanik.'

The words, breathed like an icy Shyish corpse-wind, immediately quelled the rage in Vanik's soul. Neveroth had spoken. Though the bone-clad giant on his throne of conquest hadn't moved since Vanik had entered, the chill in his declaration sent an involuntary shiver up the pilgrim's spine. He said nothing in reply. Skoren too had gone deadly still and silent, though a cruel smile had taken to his thin lips.

'You are late,' Neveroth repeated, each word scraping with frosty malice from the jagged grin of his daemon helm. 'But what you say is true. Skoren Blackhand has not yet completed his oaths to the circle. Your interruption has saved your life, for a time.'

Skoren's smile burned away in a flash, and he spun to face the throne of tortured sigmarite. Vanik was convinced he was about to howl his outrage at the Fifth Marshal, and he prayed that he was fool enough to do so. The rest of the court had frozen in a mixture of anticipation and shock, and hands had dropped to sword hilts and axe hafts.

Eventually, common sense succeeded in overpowering Skoren's fury. The pilgrim shuddered visibly with the strain of keeping his peace, his full plate armour clattering. He said nothing though, and after a pause Neveroth continued.

'The knightly code is clear on matters such as these. The True Gods have chosen you for your rivalry, and their will might be made clearer to us through deeds of hatred and bitterness.'

Neveroth paused, as though to give time for a response, but Vanik said nothing, and Skoren managed to maintain his silence.

'Only one of you can bear the sigil of the Three-Eyed King and become a Scourge of Fate,' the Master of the Fifth went on. 'To determine who, you will engage one another here in my halls, in an unsanguinary duel. The first to disarm the other without shedding blood will be judged the victor, and will swear his oath to the Varanguard before me. The loser will be thrown to the spawn.'

Silence settled once more in the wake of Neveroth's pronouncement. Vanik didn't let it stretch. He spoke.

'As my lord wishes. Say the word, and I will draw Nakali in your honour.'

Skoren snarled audibly, glancing back at the other pilgrim. Vanik knew he had outplayed him – Skoren couldn't now complain without setting himself against Neveroth's direct command and risking his wrath.

'I will give you one hour to prepare yourselves,' Neveroth declared. 'If you are not here by the appointed time, for whatever reason, your soul will be forfeit. You will be reduced to spawndom, and when the power of the Eightstar has finally ripped your changed flesh apart, your essence will be tormented for eternity by the higher powers.'

The Blackhand will seek to goad you as soon as you are both beyond this hall's doors, Nakali's voice whispered in the wake of Neveroth's declaration. *Go now, pilgrim, and do not give him the opportunity.*

Vanik bowed low towards Neveroth. Then, without another glance at Skoren, he turned on his heel and strode from the hall.

PART FOUR

THE UNSANGUINARY DUEL

'Why the Gods have spared you I will never know,' Karex hissed, her lean-boned face twisted with disgust. 'I can only pray I live long enough to find out.'

Vanik was learning to endure her chiding without response. It washed over him now, where once it would have needled. Jevcha claimed it was all part of the pilgrim's test – the Knights of Ruin were a far cry from the bloodthirsty and arrogant warlords that began many a Black Pilgrimage. The Varanguard served selflessly, seeking no boons or favours from the Gods, not even the immortality so many servants of the Eightfold Path yearned for. Service was in itself a reward, and dedication to the circle, the Varanspire and the Gods was a blessing. Most of all, to serve the Three-Eyed King was a glory beyond compare. Archaon was all. Without him, the eternal struggles that gripped the Mortal Realms were meaningless.

'Pay attention,' Karex snapped. 'Or must I strike you again, boy?'

It had been many decades since any being, mortal or immortal, had called Vanik a boy. The word brought a smile to his lips, unbidden. Karex's eyes narrowed further.

'You are bold, Vanik,' his mentor said. 'Bold and foolish. I should never have sworn to guide you down the pilgrim's path.'

The two of them – Black Pilgrim and Knight of the Varanguard – were standing in the sparring chamber used by Karex's *konroi*. The stone walls bore the six warpsteel shields of Karex and her fellow knights, emblazoned with their crests and heraldry, while metal stands were laden with their equipment. There was a rack for their lances, and serried ranks of swords, axes, maces and hammers lined the walls, their wicked edges gleaming in the red-hued light that pulsed, raw and bloody, through the arrow slits in the chamber's far side.

'You saw the favour of the Gods in me,' Vanik reminded Karex. 'Only Skoren and I have returned with a tamed blade. That must count for something?'

Modred entered and started to remove Vanik's armour as he and Karex spoke, fixing it to one of the stands that held the Varanguard's spare battleplate. An unsanguinary duel forbade protection of any type, and Vanik would go into the fight without his rune-etched steel. The warriors would be stripped down to their leggings, torsos bared, every effort made to ensure the spilling of blood. To draw even the slenderest cut from an opponent was to immediately forfeit.

Vanik could guess what would follow for whichever pilgrim lost – at best, an agonising death being ripped apart or slowly digested in the spawn pits, and at worst an eternal soul-rending at the clawed hands of one of the Varanspire's daemonic torturers.

The Path to Glory permitted no failure.

'Is the blade truly tamed?' Karex demanded. She reached

out, as though to grasp Nakali's haft, still strapped to Vanik's waist. Though her gauntlet stopped short, the daemon sword quivered in its scabbard, and Vanik felt the Slaaneshi creature's sickly lust surge through his mind.

'As soon as you draw it, it will claim you,' Karex said. 'Have you learned none of the lessons I taught you?'

'I have already used it. I have overcome it.'

'What? You drew it for a few moments in Shyish's miserable depths to use against some soulless, flesh-rotten corpse?' Karex said. 'That is even worse, you idiot. It will have tasted you now. It will know your soul. Your desires, lusts, ambitions – every weakness your thoughts can conceive of.'

'I know my own mind better than any daemonkin,' Vanik said, holding both hands out for Modred to unbuckle his gauntlets. 'I will tame it.'

'Still so arrogant,' Karex said. 'You think you can fight two foes at once. You think a daemon will let you shackle it while Skoren is coming at you with Vargen?'

'Has he tamed his own blade?' Vanik demanded.

'We had best pray to the Four that he has not. It is our only hope.'

'Vargen is a daemon of the World-That-Was,' Vanik went on, moving his bared arms wide now for Modred to unbuckle his breastplate. 'It will be desperate for blood. I can end this duel early.'

'Without having to draw Nakali?' Karex demanded. 'Besides, winning an unsanguinary duel is of little value if you find your head cleaved from your shoulders.'

'I will not fail you,' Vanik repeated, forcing his voice to remain level. 'When a new errant joins the ranks of the Varanguard tonight, he will be in your konroi, not Zubaz's.'

Karex's expression darkened at the mention of her rival within the Fifth Circle, but she said nothing. Vanik stepped away from Modred as the retainer finished removing the final pieces of his armour, the scrawny youth straining beneath the heavy black plates. He had unbuckled Nakali and his long knives to allow Modred to undo his lower armour, but now he strapped them around his waist once more.

'I have not seen Blackhand fight before, but if he has learned anything from Zubaz it will be patience. Unless his blade provokes him, he will seek to emulate his master and draw you into the attack, then counter with speed and force. That is where you may get the better of him.'

'I will draw his counter-strike onto me and force him to shed blood,' Vanik said, nodding his understanding.

'Yes, but be wary,' Karex elaborated. The scorn in her voice had vanished, replaced by the calm, measured advice of a sparring tutor. For all her acerbic comments, it was at moments like these that it became clear why Karex sought an apprentice. Knights within the Varanguard accrued support among future ranks of warriors by mentoring them into their circle. Vanik represented an investment, one which Karex surely hoped would pay off in the form of an able future ally. When the Daemonflayer's tongue was most cutting, Vanik reminded himself that she would not have chosen him had she not seen some form of potential.

'A daemon sword thirsts like no other,' the older knight went on. 'Allow it so much as a taste of you and it will rip the soul from your flesh. That is doubly true for a blood-creature like Vargen.'

'But exploiting that is our best opportunity,' Vanik concluded. He checked Nakali's scabbard, and offered a brief bow to Karex.

'My thanks for your counsel,' he said. 'As ever.'

Karex muttered something, but clasped a gauntlet to his shoulder, the spiked metal digging into his pale, bare flesh.

'Come then, boy. The court awaits us.'

* * *

Neveroth's throne room had been cleared ahead of the impending duel. The courtiers and knights of the Fifth Circle had removed themselves to the chamber's edges and corners, and the low hubbub of conversation rose as Vanik entered. The torchlight picked out the hardened muscles of his arms and torso, and the tough, cracked flesh of his left shoulder that spread down to his right forearm – a boon of the Gods, though which he had not yet been able to decide.

Karex paced behind him. Allies and rivals alike, all present were aware of the threat the duel posed to the Daemonflayer's standing – lose and her apprentice would be slain, and her own position within the Fifth Circle would suffer. Win, and the number of knights loyal to Karex would increase, not only because of Vanik's initiation, but also the inevitable drift in support that occurred whenever a champion of the True Gods rose to prominence.

Karex's rival stood to reap the same dangers and rewards. Skoren and his hulking mentor knight, Zubaz, were already present when Vanik and Karex entered. The former was stripped, like his rival, down to his lower garments, his lean, sinewy musculature criss-crossed with the ritual scar-marks of the tribes of the Bone Mountains. Zubaz was fully armoured in his baroque silver-and-black battleplate, still adorned in his silver cape and great helm. His emotions were unreadable behind the inlaid warpsteel, but Skoren's were plain enough to read – he sneered as Vanik strode through the hall towards him, folding his arms across his chest.

'I had thought you would have fled by now,' he said, voice rising above the murmuring of the spectators. 'You could have lived, Vanik, if you'd only taken your pathetic spiked steed and ridden for the wastes.'

Vanik didn't respond. He wasn't looking at Skoren, but at

Neveroth. The Fifth Marshal was still seated on his throne of broken sigmarite armour, though now he had drawn his greatsword and was clutching it in one bone-clad fist, the tip resting on the stone floor. The huge weapon gleamed, the jade eyes inlaid into its heavy skull pommel gleaming with dark sentience.

'My lord,' Vanik said, halting before the throne and kneeling. Karex did likewise, a pace behind and to the left of her apprentice.

'You return to death or glory, Vanik,' Neveroth said, voice as cold as ever. 'Rise, and prepare yourself.'

Vanik did so, stepping away from the foot of the throne towards the hall's centre. Skoren mirrored him, while Karex and Zubaz took post on either side of Neveroth. The conversations around the chamber died, leaving behind a silence that was broken by the cold sound of armoured footsteps ringing off the stone floor. One of the Varanguard, a tall, raven-haired warrior with piercing green eyes, had left the assembled onlookers and now strode between the two combatants. From his breastplate, fashioned after the likeness of the Eightstar clutched in the talons of a soaring wyrm, Vanik took him to be Lanstred, the most favoured of Neveroth's personal konroi and purportedly the greatest swordsman in the Fifth Circle. His daemonblade, Vor'ga'traxis, was the weapon that had cut the head from the aelf prince Athandril at the Battle of the Six Peaks. Vanik forced himself not to stare at the Varanguard as he offered a short bow to Neveroth before turning on his heel to address the rest of the hall.

'Lords and daemonkin, brother and sister knights of the Fifth Circle, bear witness now before the mark of the Three-Eyed King. See the final trail of Vanik and Skoren, Black Pilgrims both, Servants of the Path. Here today the True Gods will decide which of them is worthy to serve.'

Skoren was glaring at Vanik with undisguised hatred, icy eyes glinting in the torchlight. Zubaz remained looming and inscrutable behind him – Vanik had rarely heard of a member of the Varanguard not removing his helmet in the presence of Neveroth's court, yet Zubaz still wore his. Karex's expression was set, but the grim line of her mouth betrayed her unease. Vanik resisted the urge to snarl. She was a fool to doubt him, and he would prove that to her now, before the eyes of the Fifth Circle's chosen.

'You know the rules of the unsanguinary duel?' Lanstred asked, the words jolting Vanik. He glanced at the tall knight and nodded, once. Skoren merely bared his teeth.

'If a warrior loses his grip on his sword or is by any other means disarmed, he is defeated,' Lanstred said. 'If a warrior draws even a single drop of his opponent's blood, he is defeated. The duel continues until one of those conditions is met. Black Pilgrims, are you ready?'

'By the True Gods, I am,' Skoren barked.

Vanik just nodded again.

Neveroth raised one skeletal gauntlet from the side of his throne, and let it drop. Vanik placed his bare hand on Naka-li's haft.

Immediately, his breath choked in his throat. His other hand went up and grasped something, something that had latched itself around his neck and was rapidly crushing his windpipe. He found himself gripping the smooth golden coils of a serpent, a great, sinuous creature that was winding itself around his shoulders, throttling him with slow, irresistible force. He gritted his fangs and snarled an oath. It was Nakali.

Something jarred up his arm, and a vicious clang resounded in his ears. He blinked. He realised that, far from clutching a serpent's coils, his fist was gripping the hilt of his daemon sword. He'd drawn it without realising, and now one of Skoren's blows was shuddering along the length of the warped black blade as it parried another downward strike. The serpent at his throat had vanished, the illusion shattered, but Nakali's voice still slithered about in his head.

Submit to me.

'Silence!' Vanik shouted as he took a backward step, seeking to put some distance between himself and Skoren. The rival pilgrim had taken the precious seconds Vanik had spent mentally wrestling with his daemon sword's illusions to throw himself at him. Vanik turned another blow, then another, feeling his sword's consciousness dragging at his arm, helping to guide his parries. As much as it wished to wrestle control from him, Nakali also clearly didn't want its new master slain by another Black Pilgrim.

I see what is in your heart, Vanik, the daemon whispered, its seductive tones riven with frustration and anger. *You will serve the Varanspire, but first you must serve me. No knight is anointed by the Three-Eyed King without first earning his blade.*

'The sword serves the knight,' Vanik growled. 'Not the other way round.'

He felt another vision intruding on his consciousness, Nakali using the physical link between the flesh of his fist and its hilt to try to overwhelm the mental barriers he had prepared for the duel. He saw, as though in a distorted vision of the present, Neveroth upon his throne. He knelt at the Varanguard marshal's feet, fully clad in his battle armour, head bowed as he swore himself to the circle and completed the blood-oath on Nakali's bared blade.

Let me guide you, Nakali begged. *And this will be yours. If not, I will let you die, here and now.*

The vision dissolved into the point of Skoren's blade. It slid just past Vanik's throat, its curving, toothed edge whispering by the pilgrim's pale flesh. Vanik dodged to the right, away from the stroke before Skoren could turn it into his neck.

He isn't trying to disarm you, Nakali hissed. *He's trying to kill you.*

Vanik had come to the same realisation, despite what Karex had told him. It had been all he could do to keep both the daemon and the pilgrim at bay simultaneously, but while his mind had wrestled with Nakali, a part of him had realised that something was very wrong with Skoren. Karex had predicted a slow, measured style of combat that would wear away at Vanik's usually more aggressive stance. According to Karex that was how Zubaz fought. Yet Skoren was attacking in a near frenzy, apparently desperate to kill Vanik in spite of the fact that doing so would forfeit his own life and soul.

The rest of the court continued to watch in silence as Vanik parried a stab towards his stomach and then another slash at his throat, a blow that would have beheaded him with ease had it passed through his guard. He'd been forced halfway back to Neveroth's throne, and Skoren was showing no sign of either tiring or relenting. Vanik felt his own anger flare.

It's his daemonblade, he willed.

If so, Vargen cares only for your death, Nakali replied, voice riven with scorn.

Vanik didn't have time to respond. With near-flawless footwork, Skoren had danced around a desperate counter-thrust and lunged up from a low hold, almost carving open Vanik's stomach. He backed off once again, the razor-toothed sword in Skoren's grip visibly shuddering as it came close to his skin.

By upping the stakes, Skoren seemed intent on ensuring neither of them survived. While Vanik was more than happy to go blade to blade with him in mortal combat, he couldn't see any way of disarming him without dealing him at least a minor wound. And a single drop of blood was a drop too many.

Skoren's blade dragged along Nakali, striking sparks and making the daemon hiss. Vanik had no choice. He had to attack.

He turned his parry into a crude but forceful sideways cut, putting his weight behind it. Skoren blocked the strike with ease, but its suddenness forced him to take a step back for the first time. Vanik didn't hesitate. Fangs bared, he pushed himself into Skoren's guard while their blades were still locked, and slammed the scaly flesh of his left shoulder into his rival's chest.

Even doing that was dangerous, but Vanik couldn't deny the surge of exultation as he felt the thumping impact, and saw Skoren stumble back again. His rival was shorter and leaner than him, and Vanik intended to use that to his advantage. He swung once more with Nakali, before Skoren could recover, forcing him into a desperate series of parries that barely withstood the force of Vanik's blows.

For the briefest second, as Vanik blinked, he saw Yogoth hanging dead from the boughs of a Chaos-warped tree. A smile curled his lips. Nakali was still trying to distract him with his own desires.

Cease, he snarled mentally. *You parried Skoren's first blow before I knew it was falling. You know you are surrounded by warriors who will bind you tighter than I ever could if I fall. You are in the hall of your enemies. So help me.*

The daemon in his sword hissed at him, but did not deny he spoke the truth. If Vanik was killed, it was likely a member of the Varanguard present would claim his sword, if not Zubaz himself, and Nakali would be no closer to the freedom it craved.

The reverse edge of his blade, the daemon said. Skoren had backed up far enough to recover from Vanik's sudden change of pace, and now the two warriors circled one another slowly. Skoren was panting, his face a rictus of blood-fuelled hatred. Whatever Nakali's lies, Vanik was convinced the sword had possessed him. Nothing else could explain his sudden frenzy.

His blade, you imbecile, Nakali snapped again. Vanik's gaze was drawn to the reverse side of Skoren's weapon. While the leading edge was serrated like the maw of a Khornate daemon-hound, the other was flat and weighted. It gave the sabre-like weapon a cutting edge that, combined with a champion's strength and a bound daemon's fury, could cleave an armoured warrior from skull to groin in a single blow, but it also meant that any sword that caught that flat edge wouldn't snag on the teeth that perforated the other side.

Vanik realised what to do. As Skoren charged him once again, a howl building in the warrior's throat, he swung Nakali overhead to his left side, dropping into a low crouch and half twisting his body as he did so. Ordinarily, such a change of stance would have been difficult to achieve so swiftly, but fighting bare-skinned offered a degree of freedom he intended to use. The sudden change on the angle of Vanik's sword, coming from his left, forced Skoren to change his own right-handed back-cut to avoid leaving his guard open while Vanik dropped beneath his own swing. Vargen came back clumsily, and Nakali met it on its flat edge. There was a shriek – part the collision of Chaos-forged metal, part the intertwined hatred of two bound daemons – and more sparks flew as Nakali's razored black blade scraped brutally down Vargen's flat edge. Vanik put his strength into the blow, forcing his sword against Skoren's, grinding it down until it slammed against the other weapon's cross-guard.

Skoren realised the danger too late. Vanik slammed himself in close and twisted his body, rising as he did so, muscles bunched and straining as he locked Nakali against the cross-guard and brought his blade up and around, twisting Vargen out of Skoren's grip. Skoren snarled with fury and tried to fight back, tried to twist his own body away and bring Vargen down and across Vanik's back as he turned on him, but Vanik was bigger and stronger, and well inside Skoren's guard.

Vargen left Skoren's fingers. The daemon sword slid past Vanik's back even as Nakali came back round after the disarming twist, slashing past Skoren's bare forearm. Vanik felt the sword tug, and let out a bark of anger mixed with denial as he tried to force the weapon back, but he was off balance after the twist. Nakali would not be denied. The razor edge of the black weapon nicked across Skoren's arm, and Vanik saw, as though in a moment of perfect, frozen clarity, a slender stream of blood well up from the pilgrim's cut and slither across Nakali's edge as the daemon sword passed by.

The gut-wrenching moment came unstuck and both warriors slammed past one another with a bellow, finding their balance again and spinning to face one another. Vargen slammed into the cobbled flagstones with a clatter, the daemon snarling audibly at finding the blood-pulsing flesh-grip of its wielder broken. Nakali was still in Vanik's fist. Skoren blinked as though awaking from a dream. He seemed surprised to realise that his sword was no longer in his hand. His expression became one of anger as his gaze turned to Vanik and then, slowly, he held his forearm up. A trickle of blood ran down to his elbow to drip to the floor, and a dark smile split the pilgrim's lean, cruel features.

Vanik looked down at Nakali. The single drop of blood had run to the blade's tip, but rather than fall, it melted into the sword's glassy black metal, absorbed by the daemon's thirst. He heard Nakali let out a small groan, and felt the sword vibrate.

'You betrayed me,' he hissed out loud to the daemon.

Skoren laughed, the noise echoing away to the fluxwood beams overhead. The rest of the court remained silent.

Vanik made to take a step towards Skoren, his rage flaring. As he did so, however, a pain in his back made him flinch. He came up short and, with his free hand, reached around, slowly, as though in a daze, to touch his back. His fingers came away bloody.

As he had tried to saw his blade back across Vanik, Skoren had managed the slightest nick across the small of the rival pilgrim's back. It had drawn blood the very same moment Nakali had slid its razor tongue across Skoren's arm.

Both pilgrims stared at the blood on Vanik's fingers for long seconds. Then the silence shattered. An uproar gripped the court, as its members gesticulated and descended into angry debate. Karex surged down from beside Neveroth's throne, pointing furiously at Skoren and then Vargen, still lying on the flagstones.

'He disarmed him!' she was shouting. 'They both drew blood, but Vanik disarmed him!'

Zubaz hadn't spoken or moved to his own apprentice's defence, his silence mirroring the statue-like stillness of Neveroth. As the rest of the chamber argued, the Fifth Marshal sat upon his throne of shattered sigmarite, his skull helm bowed slightly. Vanik shook, his body and mind torn between the uncertainty over the duel's outcome, and the burning, immediate need to stride over to Skoren and cut him limb from limb. The other pilgrim seemed to share his feelings – he bent quickly and snatched up Vargen, quivering as the daemon latched on to him once more.

Karex reached Vanik's side. She hadn't drawn her own sword, but her gauntlet was on its hilt. She leaned in close to Vanik, the unyielding spikes of her armour nicking his bare torso.

'Say and do nothing. I will handle this.'

Vanik managed to nod. The wound in his back, though tiny, ached – the sure mark of a daemon's bite.

I will punish you for this, he willed to Nakali. The daemon didn't answer, though he felt the sword in his hand shudder again, as though suppressing its own amusement.

Neveroth raised a gauntlet, and the tumult in the chamber died instantly. The Fifth Marshal spoke.

'The Gods test us this day. The duel is inconclusive, and I will consult my mages and those members of the Eightstar present here. Until a judgement is reached, the two pilgrims are permitted to bear arms, but they will remain confined. Clear the chamber.'

'Do not resist,' Karex hissed forcefully as the voices of those crowding the hall rose once more. 'And sheathe that thrice-cursed blade.'

Vanik hesitated, but with Karex's gaze burning into him he sheathed Nakali. To his surprise, the daemon didn't try to resist.

Two Varanguard closed around him, giants in black-and-silver plate mail. They grasped his arms and dragged him around, towards the door. Every instinct cried out at him to resist, but he forced himself to remain still in their vice-grip. Now was not the time for defiance.

Before he was marched out through the doors, he caught sight of Skoren. The pilgrim was protesting furiously as two more Varanguard gripped him and began to haul him away. Zubaz had finally moved, and seemed to be in conversation with Neveroth. Karex was striding towards the sigmarite throne, her every step hinting at barely suppressed rage.

That was the final sight he got, before the great skull-doors of Neveroth's court slammed shut behind him.

PART FIVE

THE FLY AND THE FISH

There was a daemon in the cell they threw Vanik into. It was a pathetic thing, bound in flesh, but Vanik still considered banishing it with Nakali before restraining himself. It was down here for a reason, and he doubted his current predicament would be alleviated by slaying its hostflesh and freeing it to return to the Realm of Chaos.

The cell the Varanguard thrust him into was little more than a small square cut from the rock upon which the Inevitable Citadel had been sited, its jagged stone walls, floor and ceiling daubed in blood and chalk inscriptions forming layer upon layer of hexagrammic wards and runic sigils in a thousand variations of the Dark Tongue. The only illumination came from burning green torchlight. Vanik sat in its corner, away from the amorphous thing he shared the cell with, putting his mind elsewhere. Even without the monotony of being confined to a cell half filled with warped daemonflesh, time in the Inevitable Citadel did not pass as it did in the Mortal Realms.

Vanik did not know how long he remained confined for. He did not even know if he slept. The only certainty was that at some point the scrape of a lock and the squeal of hinges made him shift. The cell door creaked open, revealing a silhouette of armoured might. Karex.

Vanik stood, grunting at the ache that had worked its way into his limbs on the cold, uneven stone floor. The daemonhost at the far end of the cell had begun to drag itself forward at the sound of the cell opening, but recoiled with a gibbering screech when it saw Karex. The Daemonflayer didn't even so much as glance at it. Her eyes were on Vanik.

'Come.'

He checked the straps of his sword and knives, and stepped out of the cell. The screams of the daemonhost still within were abruptly muted as the door slammed shut behind him. Karex turned a heavy key in the lock, and handed it to a hunched, shaking creature in a soiled black cloak, its features hidden by a cowl. A sinuous tentacle uncurled from the folds of its stained garments and clasped the key.

Karex turned her back on the gaoler and motioned for Vanik to follow. She led him through the citadel's dungeons, past iron grates holding back shrieking, many-limbed things and door-bulwarks inscribed with runes that blazed with sorcerous energy. She spoke as she walked, following the twisting, rocky corridors of the citadel's bowels seemingly by instinct.

'Always when I think you have reached the end of the Path, you are blessed with another chance,' she said, not looking at Vanik. He hurried to keep up.

'Lord Neveroth has passed judgement?'

'No. Matters have grown... even more complicated. Last night the court of the Fifth Circle played host to a visitor. It travelled from the pinnacle of the Varanspire itself.'

'One of the Grand Marshal's inner council?' Vanik asked, trying to make sense of the news.

'Indeed. Neveroth received it in a private audience. Beyond that, I know nothing. Other than the fact that he has granted me leave – in his mercy – to free you for now, and demands that we attend the Tournament of the Fly and the Fish tomorrow.'

'The Fly and the Fish?' Vanik said. 'A joust?'

'Yes. I will explain when we are there. In the meantime, you are to be given back your armour, and provided more salubrious meal and lodgings. By the Eightstar, it stinks down here, daemonic filth!'

The last, shouted words dragged further screams from the things bound in the dungeons either side of them. Karex grimaced, her temper clearly even shorter than usual.

'Will Skoren be at the tourney?' he asked as they mounted the stairs leading up to the citadel's middle levels.

'He will, and so will Zubaz. For the love of the Gods, speak to neither. You know well enough that Skoren will seek to provoke you.'

'Neveroth's decision was unjust. I disarmed him before I cut him.'

'You will keep that opinion to yourself as well.'

Karex carried on through the keep, leading Vanik through its maddening corridors and halls without a second thought. Vanik found Modred waiting for them outside the sparring chamber where he had first removed his armour before the duel.

'You will lodge with my konroi,' Karex said as they entered, and Vanik's retainer set about clothing and armouring his master once more. 'Their presence may dissuade Zubaz from making an attempt on your life.' She paused. 'No, I do not think he would, but...' She trailed off, face contorting in anger once more. She was frustrated – for once with more than just Vanik – but she clearly did not wish to say more either.

'We will speak further tomorrow,' she said, turning to leave while Modred was still strapping on Vanik's warpsteel. 'You know the way from here?'

'I do,' Vanik lied, sensing Karex was in no mood to linger with him further. She left.

For a while, Vanik was silent as Modred continued to armour him. Eventually he spoke to the retainer.

'What of Tzatzo? She is stabled?'

'Yes, sire,' the retainer replied. 'With the steeds of the Eight-guard. She seemed… *distressed* to be so, but I was able to secure some live slaveflesh for the next few days.'

'Good,' Vanik replied. After another pause, he went on. 'You were not ill-treated in my absence?'

'No, sire,' Modred said, grimacing slightly as he put his weight behind buckling one of Vanik's pauldrons. 'Your sigil kept me safe.'

He glanced down at the simple black token pinned to the breast of his doublet, the mark of a Black Pilgrim's retainer. Vanik grunted.

'You've been with the Eightguard?'

'Yes, sire.'

'Where do they reside?'

'They have lodgings near the gatehouse, sire. They are await-ing word from you.'

Vanik lapsed into silence once more. It was Modred who broke it next, speaking as he continued to work.

'You are not to be a prisoner then, sire?'

Such inquisitiveness would have been treated harshly by many warlords Vanik had known. For his own part, he did nothing to discourage Modred's occasional questions. They helped him to order his own thoughts.

'In a sense, no,' he said, raising his arm at Modred's prompting and checking the pauldron was properly secured. 'By the will of the Gods, something has stayed Neveroth's hand. I am to submit to him once more tomorrow, during the Tournament of the Fly and the Fish.'

'The joust?' Modred said.

Vanik frowned. 'You know of it?'

'The Eightguard were speaking of it, sire. It is the talk of the retinues and the citadel garrison.'

'Tell me of it,' Vanik commanded.

'It's the knightly orders, isn't it?' Modred said, warming to his tale. 'Not the Varanguard, sire, but from among the supplicants. The Order of the Fly and the Silver Knights are both here seeking the boons of the Gods and the favour of the Three-Eyed King. They are testing their blessings against one another in a tourney in every one of the eight circles, on their way to the pinnacle of the Varanspire.'

'And they come to the Fifth tomorrow,' Vanik surmised. 'Lord Neveroth is hosting them.'

'It shall be a grand day I'm sure, sire,' Modred said, buckling the last of the straps and hefting Vanik's ram-horned helm.

'And you shall be blessed enough to witness it,' Vanik said, taking the helm. 'Neveroth will pass his final judgement on me there.'

'Then may the Eightstar bless you, sire,' Modred said earnestly. Vanik said nothing, looking down at his helm, tracing the Dark Tongue runes engraved in it. The visor glared back at him, gleaming and black, the raw light filtering in through the chamber's arrow slits picking out its sharp edges and brute angles.

'I will become Varanguard,' he said, slowly. 'I will become a Knight of Ruin. A Scourge of Fate.'

Modred said nothing – he knew when to hold his tongue. Eventually Vanik hooked the helm to his belt.

'Come,' he said. 'And tell me what else the warriors of this keep have been saying about tomorrow.'

It began with a hundred and twenty deaths. Vanik was not sure of the number's significance, but he had no doubt there was some occult reasoning behind it. Everything in the Varanspire was bound to ritual and superstition, and the imagined whispers of thirsting daemonkin. Something, somewhere, had demanded a hundred and twenty deaths, and Lord Neveroth was in a mood to oblige it.

Whatever it was, it was not a servant of Khorne. The one hundred and twenty prisoners were all warriors. They had been dragged from the Inevitable Citadel's depths and stripped of their belongings, and were now on their knees in the coarse black sand of the jousting lists. From his seat in the stands Vanik could discern prisoners from across the Mortal Realms – humans, aelves, duardin, even green-skinned orruks straining at their bonds. They all died the same way. Tarron, Executioner of the Fifth, a member of Neveroth's inner circle and a figure feared even amongst the Varanguard, went among them one by one. He was a tall, gaunt figure, clad in close-fitting silver plate, his features shrouded beneath a blue hood trimmed with silver weave. From his back sprouted two atrophied wings, replete with raggedy black carrion feathers, a strange and foreboding mark of the Gods. His usual method of killing – a long, curved glaive – had been forsaken in favour of a simple flat-headed hammer.

Tarron crushed the skulls of each warrior in turn. He never took more than a single blow, and the relentless, brute efficiency of each killing stroke as it fell, over and over, brought a chill even to Vanik. How many who had failed the Three-Eyed King had received a similar end, beheaded by the Executioner's silver glaive?

Most of the Varanguard seemed to share his thoughts. The hundreds arrayed in the tiered seating overlooking the lists remained silent as the killing went on and on, a contrast to the wild cheering of the crowds that mobbed the spiked railing on the far side of the arena. Word of the Fly and the Fish's tournament through the circles had travelled far through the Varanspire, and many supplicants had already witnessed the two knightly orders face one another in the Eighth, Seventh and Sixth as they made their way to the fortress-city's heart. Those who had survived to reach the Fifth were more eager than ever to see their respective champions emerge, and they revelled in every crunch of Tarron's hammer as he prepared the stage.

'The fools would not be cheering if they were beneath Tarron's blade,' Karex grumbled beside Vanik. 'Neveroth is bold to greet the visiting knightly orders with such warmth.'

'He honours them with so many deaths?' Vanik asked as Tarron staved in an aelf's skull with a loud crack, stalking to the next in line like a gaunt, gleaming carrion bird.

'Not just the number,' Karex clarified. 'But the nature too. The Executioner is staving in the skulls of warriors. He is denying them as tribute to Khorne and his throne of beheaded skulls, and in doing so he honours T'char and the Grandfather.'

'Surely such an act is not worth angering the servants of Khorne?' Vanik asked, watching the brain matter of a duardin splatter out over one of the wooden lists. He had noticed that some of the more prominent Varanguard he'd heard tell of in the keep seemed to be absent, and Karex herself – often sympathetic to the martial causes of the Blood God – was obviously ill at ease being forced to attend the tourney.

'It is all part of the cycle,' she said, though she glared as she spoke. 'The freedom of the Varanspire must be maintained, but here on the threshold of the realm of the Gods, that isn't easy. Today, the Varanguard remind the Lord of Skulls of our independence, that we serve Archaon above all others, and hold this fastness in his name first and foremost. Tomorrow, it will be the turn of another of the great powers to be reminded.'

Vanik nodded, his gaze travelling across the tiered seats of the Varanguard and their retinue. To his left the main stand rose up, black fluxwood daubed with runes and hung with the banners of Neveroth's inner court. Neveroth's sigmarite throne had been hauled to the highest seating by dozens of manacled slaves, and the Fifth Marshal was now taking his seat along with his closest champions, advisors and sorcerers. The supplicants across the lists from the stand were straining for a glimpse of the giant, bone-armoured warrior, and a flurry of beats from the cyclopean drummers seated at the foot of the stands whipped up their excitement.

'There it is,' Karex said, following Vanik's gaze. 'Look there, next to Neveroth. That is the one from the spire he took counsel with, the one who had you brought here.'

Vanik leant forward slightly, peering towards where the Fifth Marshal's throne had been installed. He saw Neveroth himself, clad in his grim bone plate. Upon the armrest of the throne, cast from the gauntlets of broken sigmarite plate, was a messenger-thing, a stunted, crablike creature swaddled in black robes. Two champions of the Varanguard, Kol Oneblade and Marston the Hollow, stood behind and to the side of the Fifth Marshal's throne, but closer to it, leaning over to converse with Neveroth, was a small, hunched figure. Vanik got an impression of grubby brown robes and a dishevelled hat, drawn down low over a wizened face and long grey beard. In one bony hand the old man clutched a simple walking stave, while the other was cupped close to Neveroth's helm. Vanik frowned.

'He is from the spire?' he asked. The contrast between the slight, decrepit-looking mortal and the armour-clad giants that surrounded him could not have been greater. He looked nothing like one of Archaon's chosen.

Karex huffed audibly, a sure sign that a sharp rebuke was coming.

'Are you blind as well as stupid, pilgrim? How often must I tell you? Nothing in the Varanspire is as you first assume. Look again, and concentrate this time. Its appearance is only for the benefit of those supplicants across the lists from us. It is hiding itself.'

Vanik looked at the stand once more, his frown deepening. He fixed his gaze on the figure Karex seemed so apprehensive of, looking more closely, trying to pick out every detail possible at such a distance. And as he did so the thing beside Neveroth seemed to shimmer. Like a heat haze, the air between Vanik and the old man rippled. He blinked and, for the briefest second, saw its true form.

The thing beside Neveroth was inhumanly gaunt, clad in strange silver armour and blue robes that hugged its spider-like form. Its arms were multijointed, the flesh of the hands clutching its staff and cupped near Neveroth's helm corpse-blue. Multihued feathers were draped around its hunched shoulders and hung from its arms and staff, which bore at its tip the coiling fish-and-eye rune of Tzeentch, riven with energy that seemed to warp and bend the very air around it. Most distressing of all, however, was its head. It bore no facial features other than a sharp-toothed maw, its smooth skin an icy shade of blue. Even more startling were the long, flat horns that rose from its temple. They were webbed with flesh, flesh that bore ninety-nine blinking black eyes. Vanik did not know how he was certain of the exact number. All he knew was that ninety-nine eyeballs, all gleaming and black as pitch, were set into the thing's horns, and roved about as it whispered its secrets into Neveroth's ear.

Vanik recognised it from the stories that abounded through the Chaos Wastes and beyond. It was a Gaunt Summoner, favoured of T'char and advisor to the Three-Eyed King, one of nine councillors who did the bidding of Chaos throughout the Mortal Realms.

The vision collapsed in on itself as abruptly as it had appeared. Vanik found himself looking at the unkempt, unassuming old man once more. Only now it was no longer bent over, in counsel with Neveroth. Now it was standing straight, and looking directly at Vanik. He leaned back hastily on his bench, feeling the otherworldly attention of the Gaunt Summoner's eyes burning into his soul.

'Do not fear it,' Karex ordered, though a rare hint of uncertainty had entered her voice. 'They hold no sovereignty over us. They are fellow servants of Archaon, at least as long as they remain bound by him.'

'But they are powerful?' Vanik asked.

'The Summoners hold great influence in the Infernal Court,' Karex admitted. 'In his wisdom, our great king makes use of their prophecies and foresight, and utilises them for tasks of greatest import. They do not fail him.'

'They are daemons?' Vanik asked.

'None but the Gods themselves know for certain, but if they are not then no other creature could parley so closely with daemonkin as they do. The name of that one, so far as we are permitted to utter it, is Kar'gek'kell.'

The blare of daemonhorns interrupted before Vanik could

respond. The cheering of the supplicants redoubled, and Vanik saw movement amidst the tents at either end of the lists. The knightly challengers were emerging.

From the right side came the chosen champion of the Most Suppurating and Blightsome Order of the Fly. His name was Sir Vulgarix, of Festerfane's Rancid Glade, and he was a deathly figure, his plate armour rusting and pockmarked, his shield composed of heavy boards of rotten wood bolted over one another by corroded strips of metal. He rode atop a famine-ravaged horse draped in a mildewed, blotchy caparison, the steed looking as though it shouldn't have been able to stand, let alone carry the knight's weight. A decaying strip of cloth, its heraldry lost amidst blotches of mould, hung heavy from the tip of the knight's raised lance.

His opponent came from the opposite direction. Truz the Changeworthy was a champion of the Silver Knights, his armour burnished to a mirror hue. His helm bore a thick plume of flowing blue and yellow feathers, and his shield was emblazoned with a coiled silver fish, set against a field of yellow and blue, quartered. His mount was hunched over and reptilian, covered in multicoloured feathers that rippled as it loped forward. Truz's lance bore at its tip a length of silver fish scales that snapped in the breeze. His whole form seemed to shimmer, not unlike Kar'gek'kell's, as though distorted by a heat haze. The power of the Changer of Ways was clearly strong within him.

The supplicants' cheering reached fever pitch as the two knightly figures came together at a trot before Neveroth and the main stand. They turned to face the sigmarite throne, and dipped their banners in salute. Neveroth rose, and the rest of the main stand followed suit. Silence followed before the Fifth Marshal spoke.

'Knights of Chaos, fellow servants of the True Gods and our

master, the Three-Eyed King. I bid thee welcome to the Fifth Circle of the Varanspire. May your chosen Gods favour you in this tournament, and may you honour them with your deeds. Glory to Archaon, and the Eightstar!'

Sir Vulgarix and Sir Truz saluted the stand once more, the horns and drums struck up a crescendo, and the crowds went into rapture.

'Sir Vulgarix will be victorious,' Karex said, watching as the two knights parted and returned to their separate ends of the lists.

'What makes you think that?' Vanik asked.

'I've seen them both fight before, Vulgarix at the Maidenport and Truz at the Nine Hands. Vulgarix might look crippled, but he bears all of the Grandfather's resilience.'

Vanik pondered Karex's words as they watched the knights go through their final preparations. Vulgarix was testing the weight of a rust-eaten axe, passed up to him by one of his obese rotbringer retainers. Truz was receiving a blessing from a blue-robed priest of T'char, the knight's head bowed before a stave bearing the All-Seeing Eye.

'Has Truz not been visited by the Changer's blessings since the Nine Hands?' Vanik wondered aloud. 'He may be more formidable than you recall.'

'Perhaps,' Karex allowed. 'Most of the Fifth here today have him as their favourite. The Silver Knights certainly need a victory – the Order has already defeated them in two of the last three circles. Their chances of being permitted an audience in the spire are slipping away.'

Vanik nodded in agreement, his eyes straying back to Neveroth's throne. The Silver Knights' chances were not the only ones slipping away. Understanding that he too would soon be judged made it difficult for Vanik to concentrate on the spectacle below. Where was Skoren? Why had he been summoned here? His stomach churned as he wondered what judgement Neveroth was to enact upon them.

Below, both knights raised their lances, signalling their preparedness. The drums abruptly ceased their thundering tattoo, and the crowd once more fell silent, this time out of expectation rather than reverence. For a few seconds, all was still as the two knights surveyed one another from across the lists.

Then the moment passed. Sir Vulgarix and Sir Truz dug in their spurs, and charged. The Nurgle knight's steed accelerated with a burst of speed that should have been impossible in such a disease-ravaged creature, while Sir Truz's Tzeentchian mount darted forward with a predatory gait, its feathers rippling. Hooves and claws pounding the blood-and-brain-slashed dirt, the two knights closed on one another in just a few heartbeats, their lances sweeping majestically downwards.

They struck. Wood snapped and shattered and metal thumped into meat, the sound of the collision a hideous, wet crunch overtaken almost immediately by the frenzied howls of the crowd.

Sir Truz's yellow-and-blue lance had found its mark. Though it had splintered into a hundred shards, it had also ploughed squarely into Vulgarix's shield, splitting it in half and physically slamming the putrid knight from his saddle.

Sir Vulgarix, however, had also found his mark. Even as his rival's lance broke his shield and arm and unhorsed him, his own lance had ploughed into the reptilian guts of the Tzeentch knight's steed. The thing let out a trilling screech and went down, its forward momentum driving the great length of steel and wood deeper into its body, puncturing whatever infernal organs it possessed.

Like Vulgarix, Truz was thrown from his saddle. He crashed

into one of the lists and smashed the wooden boards, splitting the runes emblazoned there.

Both knights sprawled in the dirt, while Truz's steed's claws scrabbled in its death throes. Vulgarix was the first to recover, rising unsteadily, his broken arm clutched to his rusted breastplate. He drew his axe from his belt and started to stumble towards Truz, the roaring of the crowd rising with every step.

The Tzeentch knight finally began to rise as well, using the broken remnants of the lists to drag himself up. He seemed to sense Vulgarix's approach at the last instant, and dragged a gleaming silver blade from its scabbard just in time to meet the downward stroke of Vulgarix's axe.

Silver steel bit into maggot-gnawed wood as the blade checked the axe's haft. Truz recovered from the clash first, sweeping his sword around and off Vulgarix's right pauldron. The crowd gasped at the audible clang, and the Nurgle knight stumbled.

Truz kept attacking, raining a trio of blows on Vulgarix in quick succession. The champion of the Order of the Fly was hampered by his broken arm – Truz used the wound, attacking from the left repeatedly. It seemed Vulgarix had no response, though his heavy armour absorbed blow after blow. An axe was no defensive weapon either, especially not single-handed.

'He must yield or perish,' Vanik said incredulously.

'They are one and the same here,' Karex replied, her expression grim.

Vanik glanced across at the main stand. Neveroth was impassive as ever on his throne, but Kar'gek'kell bore an unnaturally wide rictus grin on the flesh of its disguise.

A crunch and a loud gasp drew Vanik's gaze back to the melee. A wide swing by Truz had slammed open Vulgarix's faltering guard and, lightning-fast, the Silver Knight had whipped his sword back in and punched it into his rival's torso. The blade had buried itself in Vulgarix's stomach.

Both knights froze, Truz's hand still on the hilt of his sword, and the crowd went silent once more. Then, with a leaden slowness that spoke of the inevitability of decay, Vulgarix raised his axe and ploughed it into Truz's skull. The rusting blade split his plumed helmet and crunched through the Silver Knight's head with a sickly crack. The blue and yellow feathers turned red. Truz swayed, sword still buried in Vulgarix's guts, then fell back with a clatter.

The crowd went wild. Vulgarix reached down and grasped Truz's sword, slowly dragging it free from his body. Dark blood and milky-white pus spurted from the wound as he tossed the blade aside, then placed one foot on Truz's silver breastplate and ripped his axe from the Silver Knight's skull. The champion of the Order of the Fly took a few faltering steps forward and raised the weapon in salute, first to the supplicants and then to the main stand, Truz's blood pattering down on him. The smile had gone from Kar'gek'kell's false face. The cheering redoubled.

It masked the sound of Truz's vengeance.

The Silver Knight twitched. A leg spasmed, then an arm. Then, like a macabre puppet, the Silver Knight rolled onto his front and curled up, brain matter still spilling from his split skull.

Vulgarix turned as the crowd's adulation turned to shock, and he realised something was wrong. Truz's back arched hideously, and there was a wet crunching sound, followed by the squeal of buckling metal. Something burst from the knight's back amidst a shower of blood and uncoiled itself. Through the viscera Vanik could make out blinking eye stalks and writhing tentacles.

Change ripped Sir Truz's old form apart. His right arm burst, the flesh reknitting into a gross bony growth. The right followed suit, blue and yellow feathers unfurling like strange flowers, matted with gore. Fresh bulk was added from some Eight-blessed source, rending apart the knight's once flawless silver plate armour. His skull split further, the brain matter changing to a multicoloured torrent. A beak, the snapping maw of a cephalopod, emerged from the wreckage.

Sir Truz let out a shrill shriek and heaved his new bulk up on quivering backjointed limbs, the flesh translucent and newborn.

Sir Vulgarix charged. His axe hewed the raw meat of Truz's spawn body, more of the oily fluid spilling from the wounds and making the creature vent another avian-like cry. It was useless. The spawn towered over Sir Vulgarix, its distorted body apparently untroubled by the hacking strokes of the rusted axe.

It lunged. Vulgarix, still wounded, was too slow to get out of the way. The spawn's gaping beak-maw snapped down over the knight's head, the flesh at the sides of its mouth ripping as it distended unnaturally. It forced Vulgarix's shoulders into its gullet then heaved back on its legs, raising his lower half into the air and forcing the rest of him down with a hideous peristaltic motion. In a few seconds, all that remained visible of the once proud knight of the Order of the Fly were his kicking heels, and then they too vanished as the spawn's jaws snapped shut with a loud clack.

Some of the supplicant crowd had broken past the arena's railings, driven insane by what they had witnessed. Armed stewards were cutting them down, and groups of men-at-arms from the citadel's garrison were rushing to reinforce them.

The uproar was hardly less apparent among the Varanguard. Most of the knights had surged to their feet, and now dozens of warriors and their retinues were engaged in furious debate. Vanik looked up at Neveroth, who remained unmoved. Kar'gek'kell, however, had thrown off its disguise. Purple energy arced from its staff and from the tips of its eye-horns. The sight made Vanik shiver despite himself. To be in the presence of a creature so God-blessed was never easy. It was part enrapturing, part sickening, wholly terrifying.

Truz reared, and howled in triumph. Vanik looked at Karex. She grimaced and shook her head.

'Neveroth will wish to speak with us now,' she said. 'Again, say nothing. Leave that to me.'

Vanik didn't respond. The monster that was Truz had ceased its cry, and now doubled over. For a moment, no one noticed the spawn's sudden change in stance, too busy with the carnage breaking out around the arena.

The thing started to shudder visibly, and Vanik half expected fresh growths to burst from its foul body. It howled again, and this time its unnatural voice was riven with pain.

'By the Eightstar,' Karex murmured, leaning forward as she stared at the spawn. Vanik had rarely seen her shocked by anything before.

Truz the Changeworthy was transforming again. The front of its feather-lined stomach began to morph and bulge, before splitting open. More brilliantly coloured ichor burst out, splattering the dirt where it congealed into more fleshy, lumpen growths. Vanik's lip curled as he watched, expecting more tentacles to uncurl from the wound.

Instead, something more solid emerged. At first it was so coated in ichor and viscera that Vanik couldn't make out what it was. Then he realised. It was an axe head.

He realised why Karex was so shocked. The axe was followed by a haft, and then a hand. With agonising slowness, like some vile parody of childbirth, Sir Vulgarix emerged back into the Varanspire.

He fought his way free, inch by inch, Truz's torn flesh sucking and dragging on him. He was almost unrecognisable, drenched in the spawn's innards, and even from a distance Vanik could see that the creature's slime had eaten away his flesh and armour. Still, however, Sir Vulgarix fought for life, fought from the vitality that the Grandfather blessed his offspring with. His flesh reknitted and reworked itself, unbending before the Changer's wrath.

Finally, the ravaged knight tore himself free, stumbling out through the writhing filth that had spilled from Truz. The spawn let out one last scream – disturbingly human this time – before slumping forward, its bulk shaking. Vulgarix hacked his way out through its innards, and not even the morphing power of Tzeentch could recover Truz's mangled body this time.

The knight of the Blightsome Order of the Fly faced the main stand and, drenched in Chaotic effluvium, raised his old axe once more.

Even before he had done so, all sense of order about proceedings had broken down. The fighting between the supplicants had degenerated into a full-scale battle on the other side of the arena's railings, as mortals driven to the brink of physical and mental endurance by their journeys through the wastes and the Varanspire broke down entirely. Even among the Varanguard, relationships were strained. Oaths and curses flew, and Vanik's eyes widened as he saw one knight he recognised, Talith Redmane, strike another across the jaw with the back of his gauntlet. Retinues and other members of the Varanguard near to them pitched in, and the seating a dozen rows below Vanik descended into carnage.

He dropped his hand to Nakali's hilt.

Show these unworthy dogs their place, Nakali hissed, the daemon's desperate urges bleeding through into his own thoughts. *Kill them all!*

Vanik ignored the daemon's slithering imperatives and looked to Karex.

Below them, half a dozen mounted Varanguard had ridden out to encircle Vulgarix, mainly to protect him from the shrieking rush of Tzeentch worshippers that had come spilling from the Silver Knights' tents. Other members of both knightly orders were assembling, mounting steeds and receiving arms and armour from their retinues. Karex, however, was not looking at any of it. She was looking at the messenger creature, the small, hunched, crab-thing wrapped in black robes that was scuttling towards them from Neveroth's dais.

She extended one arm, allowing it to crawl up onto her shoulder and murmur its words in her ear. When it was done, she brushed it off and it scurried away.

'It is time,' she said to Vanik.

'Amidst all this?' he asked. Below, the Varanguard around Vulgarix had drawn their swords, and another contingent were riding out to keep the Tzeentch and Nurgle factions separate.

'Yes,' Karex said. 'Stay close, and remember what I told you.'

They moved along the lower stands, Vanik grasping Nakali. The sword was still begging just to be drawn, but he resisted. Ahead Neveroth's main stand rose up, his silk-and-hide banners rippling. A Varanguard admitted them to a side entrance. They climbed the wooden staircase beyond and emerged into Neveroth's presence. Marston the Hollow moved to intercept them, but the Fifth Marshal waved him away. Karex and Vanik went down on one knee in the space before the sigmarite throne.

'Rise,' Neveroth commanded. He sounded bored, a sharp

contrast with the carnage unfolding below. 'You favoured the Fly in this bout, didn't you, Daemonflayer?'

'Yes, lord,' Karex said as she stood.

'Perhaps I should seek your assistance in matters of prophecy, Varanguard,' Kar'gek'kell said. The Gaunt Summoner was still standing beside Neveroth's throne, its true form unveiled. Vanik found that, though he tried, he could not look at the creature while standing so close to it. His eyes shied away, his head throbbed and his flesh crawled, as though merely being in the Chaos-blessed thing's presence ran the risk of changing and warping him like Truz. Even Nakali had gone silent.

His own weakness sent a spike of anger through his thoughts. A warrior of the Varanguard answered only to Archaon. He would bow to no other, and when he had cast off the mantle of Black Pilgrim, he would spit upon God-slaves like the Gaunt Summoner.

Kar'gek'kell laughed, almost as though it had read his thoughts. Then it spoke.

'Vanik, son of Uthor, lodge-warrior of the Vhargs, child of the Splintered Coast.'

Vanik had expected the pallid, scheming creature to have a sibilant or papery voice, but the smooth-skulled sorcerer spoke in a deep tone, the words spilling rich and thick from between wickedly pointed teeth. Vanik felt his unease redouble as it recounted his origins effortlessly.

'You stink of fear,' the Gaunt Summoner went on. 'In that regard, you flatter me. Too many of your kind hold so little regard for the Summoners.'

'He is not of our kind,' Neveroth interjected, a hint of displeasure in his cold voice. 'You know he has taken neither the oaths nor the sigil-brand, Kar'gek'kell.'

'But he still may,' the Tzeentch sorcerer responded, and an

ugly smile split its pale skull, made more unnatural by the smooth, featureless skin where its nose and eyes should have been. The black eyes clustered across its left horn blinked in unison.

'You are wondering why you have been summoned here, Vanik,' it went on. 'Let me show you, just as I did Blackhand.'

It reached out one unnaturally long, slender finger, towards Vanik's brow. His first instinct was to recoil, but he found himself held in place by some invisible force, every muscle bound up with sorcerous potency. He grunted, body quivering, heart pounding in his chest as the Gaunt Summoner placed a digit against his forehead.

Abruptly, he was elsewhere. The Varanspire was gone, replaced by a grassy expanse, framed by distant mountain peaks. His consciousness hurtled across the plains at speed, a comet, bound up in flame and fury. Ahead he saw a city materialise, set into the cliff-face bedrock of one of the great mountain peaks. He recognised duardin architecture in the foundations of its great protective walls, built upon by human masons. He was going to strike it.

He sped over the farmland that now sprawled beyond the mountain city's walls, and down, inevitably down, past the stony peaks and bluffs. He roared as he fell, charged with destructive power, his heart and mind surging. He struck in a blaze of light, and there was nothing.

The nothing resolved. He stood upon a battlefield, amidst blood and mud and steel. Rain slashed down, a deluge riven with thunder. Ahead of him, a warrior raged, rampant with the intoxicating fury of combat. He was clad in the plate armour of the Free Cities, with a royal circlet upon his helm, and a great warhammer grasped in both fists. His heavy auburn beard was matted with sweat and blood, and he bled from a wound in his right shoulder. Before him, the servants of the True Gods fell, broken by his hammer or thrust aside by his armies of men and duardin as Sigmar's thunder rumbled overhead. He saw the icons of the Eightstar and the Four trampled in the press, and screamed his frustration.

Before he could lash out, the vision changed. The battlefield was whipped away, and in its place were the soaring towers and walls of the Varanspire. They were not as he remembered them, though, even in the warped realm of the Chaos Wastes. Now the bastions and barbicans were aflame, and the parapets shattered. A million beings warred across the broken landscape, and the cast motte of fire and lava that had once surrounded the unassailable fortress was now quenched, choked with countless bodies. As Vanik watched on in horror, the Varanspire itself began to topple, its foundations laid low, its glorious, agonising peak splintered by a bolt of lightning.

Its brilliance engulfed Vanik. He screwed his eyes shut against its light, flinching. When he opened them again, it had receded. He was back, back standing before Neveroth and Kar'gek'kell. The Tzeentch sorcerer had removed its finger from his brow.

'Tell them what you saw,' it commanded.

'A champion of the Free Cities,' Vanik said, blinking as his eyes adjusted. 'Slaying the servants of the True Gods. There were many duardin, and humans too. After it, I saw... I saw this fortress conquered. I saw the Varanspire toppled and the triumph of the lightning.'

'The warrior you saw was Castellan Albermarl of the Free City of Helmgard,' said Kar'gek'kell. 'He holds it for the Lightning God. The fall of the Varanspire is what might come to pass if he is not stopped.'

'How?' Vanik demanded. 'He is but one mortal warrior.'

'For now,' the Gaunt Summoner replied. 'Within his court

is a Lord Ordinator of the Stormcast Eternals. I believe his presence implies that Albermarl will soon be raised up to the ranks of the damnable Stormcasts by the Lightning God. Just as our prophecy foretells, I suspect that Sigmar's lackey also says as much.'

'And what has that got to do with me?' Vanik demanded. He sensed Karex stiffen, but he was tired of Neveroth's silence and the Summoner's veiled words.

If his tone stung Kar'gek'kell, the otherworldly creature gave no indication of it.

'I have seen you before, Vanik,' it said. 'In nine hundred and ninety-nine dreams, since the end of time. I see you now, and tomorrow, and yesterday, and in all iterations I see you ride forth against the lightning at Helmgard.'

'You wish me to sack this mortal city?'

'No. Far simpler than that, Black Pilgrim. I wish you to slay Castellan Albermarl, and end any chance he has of ascending to the ranks of the Stormcasts.'

Vanik looked from Neveroth to Karex. Neither moved or spoke.

'Why me?' Vanik began to ask. Kar'gek'kell was suddenly right before him, the air around it twisting and shuddering visibly, as though even a place as blessed as the Varanspire could not hope to contain the magical essence of such a creature. Its strange smell – spices, rotten milk, scorched metal – engulfed the pilgrim, and his words turned to ash in his throat as its black eyes leered down at him.

You do not defy the True Gods, it hissed, and now its words reverberated around inside Vanik's very skull – not the slow, honeyed ooze of Nakali's suggestions, but scraping about like a bared blade, making him twitch with pain.

You should rejoice that a creature as pathetic as yourself has been singled out for such a task.

Vanik stumbled back. He tasted blood on his lips, and realised his nose was bleeding. His vision swam, his only constant those black eyes, bulging and blinking down at him. He felt a grip on his shoulder, and realised Karex was steadying him.

'He will strike warpsteel to stone and pass through the Third Eye to Chamon, to the Ironroot Mountains, where Helmgard lies,' he heard Neveroth saying to Karex, the voice sounding distant. 'There he will slay the mortal known as Albermarl. He will bring evidence of his victory back here, to my court. Then, and only then, will he be admitted to the Knights of Ruin.'

'And what of the Blackhand?' Karex asked.

'He has been granted the same objective. Whoever slays Albermarl and returns will be judged the final victor.'

Karex had to lead Vanik away then, back down the main stand's stairs and out onto the lower terracing. There he doubled over and was sick, the acrid taste of bile stinging his throat and making him choke and gasp. His vision returned, and he managed to stand straight.

'Well, we're both still alive, so I suppose I should give thanks to the Gods for their smallest of blessings,' Karex said.

'We should,' Vanik said tersely, struggling to keep his anger in check. He had parleyed with daemons and bested warlords blessed by each of the Four, but never before had he encountered anything like Kar'gek'kell. The memory of the thing's invasive presence in his mind sent a shudder up his spine.

'Mortal flesh rebels around a creature so favoured,' Karex admitted grudgingly. 'If it so desired, it could have torn you apart with a word, or refashioned you into something even more hideous. Though probably no less stupid.'

'Why?' Vanik demanded. 'Why has it chosen me?'

'You should know by now not to ask those questions,' Karex said. 'The Gods do as they please. Though that being said...'

She trailed off, looking down at the lists. It seemed the knights of Tzeentch and Nurgle had thought better of engaging in a pitched battle before the greatest warriors of the Varanspire's Fifth Circle – they were separating, though the supplicants continued to slaughter one another in an orgy of madness-riven violence.

'It is more than just prophecy,' Vanik said slowly. 'There are politics at play here, aren't there?'

Karex grimaced, as though acknowledging an unwelcome truth, then turned back to Vanik.

'You recall how Skoren struck at you during the unsanguinary duel? How he seemed to seek your death, even though it would mean his own?'

'Yes. A madness seemed to take him. I believe he failed to resist his daemon sword.'

'Perhaps,' Karex allowed. 'But there is something wrong, not only with Skoren. With Zubaz as well. I have not seen him anywhere at the tourney today, though I am certain Neveroth would have summoned him, as he did us.'

'Perhaps he fears the sorcerer,' Vanik said, unable to bring himself to pronounce the Gaunt Summoner's warped name.

'But why?' Karex pressed. 'Zubaz is a high-ranking champion of the Fifth. Kar'gek'kell would not strike at him publicly. And what reason would it have to do so anyway?'

'Why is Skoren being given the opportunity to complete this quest before me?' Vanik added. 'Neveroth should have him slain here and now.'

'Zubaz's influence is too strong to allow something so simple,' Karex said. 'But he has always had a thirst for power above and beyond that of his fellow-knights. He will stop at nothing to ensure Skoren is successful.'

'Perhaps he is seeking allies elsewhere, beyond the circle,'

Vanik wondered aloud. 'Skoren would be the perfect emissary, to be used while he completes his pilgrimage.'

'Maybe,' Karex said. 'Regardless, I do not trust him, or his motives.'

'You think the Summoner's prophecy is true? Could the Varanspire really be under threat?'

'Kar'gek'kell would not have left the spire and come here merely to foment a rivalry between myself and Zubaz. Something has unsettled it. Albermarl is a threat to the rising glory of Chaos. He must be removed. You have been chosen for that honour.'

'I ride for Chamon then,' Vanik said. 'I will leave immediately.'

'How will you do it?' Karex asked.

'How else?' Vanik responded. 'I will raze his city and cut his head from his shoulders.'

'You have yet to set eyes on Helmgard, at least in person,' Karex said. 'I was still a young champion when the forces of the Gods assailed it, before Ulgleth was Seventh Marshal. For a year we besieged it, but it did not fall.'

'Therein lies the mistake,' Vanik said. 'There will be no siege. We will storm it in a single night.'

'If you try, you will die,' Karex said. 'You are still too arrogant for the Varanguard. All you need do is slay Albermarl.'

'The more difficulty the Gods place before us, the greater the glory there is in overcoming it.'

'We are the Fifth Circle of the Varanguard,' Karex replied tersely. 'Do you have any idea what that means?'

The question was rhetorical, but he answered all the same.

'We are the Three-Eyed King's huntmasters. We are the Scourge of Fate.'

'Precisely. More so than any other circle, it is our task to *hunt down* and *slay* the greatest enemies of the Eightfold Path.

That, as much as any vision, is why Kar'gek'kell has come to our Black Pilgrims. That is why you have been tasked with a quest to kill this mortal fool. Do it, then you can indulge in your lust for glory.'

'We shall see,' Vanik replied. 'I still have favour with a number of warbands, in the wastes and beyond. I will summon them before I ride for Chamon. Helmgard will burn.'

'I do not doubt that Skoren will do the same.'

'Then all the more reason for me to depart now.'

'Go,' Karex said, waving him away. 'I cannot stomach your foolishness any longer. I will have your steed and your retinue sent for at the main gate.'

He bowed and turned away, before Karex's voice made him pause.

'And Vanik? May the Eightstar guide you.'

'And you, master.'

PART SIX

SIR CARADOC'S OFFER

Tzatzo, Modred and the Eightguard were waiting for him at the Inevitable Citadel's main gate. Tzatzo shrieked when he came into sight and broke free of Modred's grasp, trotting over to him. He managed to avoid the steed's maw, and grunted as he took her weight. Eventually, he managed to get a hold of the chains and calm the steed.

She was happy to see him. He knew well enough to use that while he could – in a few hours she'd be back to her snarling, vicious self.

The Eightguard closed up around him as he mounted, Modred joining him at his side.

'It is good to see you again, sire,' Kulthuk said, inclining his head towards Vanik.

'Praise the Eightfold, my path is not yet complete,' he responded. 'A new quest lies before us, and the Warhound willing it will be a bloody one. Lord Neveroth has given us a final task.'

'The Blackhand yet lives?' the bannerman asked.

'He does. We are both to seek a mortal champion, Castellan Albermarl, of Chamon. The first to slay him and return will be elevated to the Knights of Ruin. To that end we ride now for Jevcha and the main encampment.'

He glanced back briefly at the citadel, at its towering, spiked walls and corpse-hung parapets. How long he had yearned to make the place his new fastness, to become one of the knights who guarded its keep and rode out to do the bidding of the Three-Eyed King. There could be no greater honour for a warrior, no greater glory, and any who claimed otherwise was a fool.

Shorgul, the beast-headed gatekeeper, was still patrolling the battlements, and when he caught Vanik's gaze he called out in his rough tongue.

'Eightstar's blessings, pilgrim.'

Vanik raised a fist in salute, to both the beastman and the fortress of the Fifth, towering over him.

Then he turned Tzatzo and rode.

The mind-aching architecture of the Varanspire had changed during the time they had spent in the Inevitable Citadel. Vanik led his retinue along the Colonnade of the Vanquished, a wide boulevard bearing on either side great mountains of trophies taken from countless foes across the Mortal Realms – rusting arms, armour and banners of all shapes and sizes. At the far end, though, rather than the great gateway leading to the circle, he found the triumphal arch of the Varanguard champion Il'keth, a looming structure of iron and daemonflesh that whispered the names of every creature killed by the great knight.

The retinue passed through the triumphal arch's great maw, and on down a road paved with crushed and powdered bone. A sulphurous smog had fallen over the Seventh Circle as they headed into it, blanketing everything in a stinking, yellow-tinged miasma that seemed to grasp and claw at whatever passed through. The stench of the foundry stacks had redoubled, and always there was the deep, sickly-sweet scent that seemed to accompany daemonkin. It was an unnatural, cloying thing, at first pleasant to the senses, yet soon stomach-turning for all but the most favoured of worshippers.

Vanik murmured a prayer-blessing to the Blood God as they carried on down a narrow street lined with shrines and statues to the champions of the World-That-Was. Blood-supplicants stumbled and staggered out of the retinue's way, their howls filling the dank air. The wretched creatures were stripped bare and slashing themselves with ritual blades provided by the shrine's bullheaded keepers, until they were drenched head to foot in their own blood. They were permitted to wander the street, begging for the blessings of the Warhound, until weakness and exhaustion made them collapse. As soon as one did, other gore-drenched supplicants would swarm them, brutally hacking off the head to add to the offering piles stacked up outside each shrine. The gaps between the brazen cobbles were thick with blood and strings of viscera, and Vanik ordered the Eightguard once more to cut down any too slow to get out of their way.

As they rode, he realised that a part of what he saw disgusted him. There was nothing so vile as weakness, and in the blood-crazed things around him he saw little but that – weakness and helplessness.

To choose just one branch of the Eightfold Path, one God amidst the Great Pantheon, was to open yourself to that weakness. It meant that a warrior could no longer choose his own path, that he was dictated to by something that viewed him only as a plaything. It ensured that there was nothing to be bargained with, nothing to be withheld. Earlier, when Vanik had first left the lodges of his village, he had not understood such subtleties, but he had been fortunate – the first champion he had served under, Golgeth Eightpoint, had taught him the value of serving the Four in turn, how each could grant different boons, and presented different dangers.

Then he had met Karex Daemonflayer. She had completed his training. Now he knew the champions of a single discipline for what they were – cowards and fools, their lives forfeit now and forever in the service of a single God. A warrior did not scrape and debase himself before anything, not even the True Gods. He stood, and took what he wished, and demanded what he wanted. The Four rewarded strength, and despised weakness. Vanik despised it too.

His thoughts were broken by the clatter of armour. A figure had ridden out from the shadows. It was unmistakably a knight of the Varanguard – his plate armour was brutal yet simple, adorned only by the gilding so often adopted by the Knights of Ruin. His half-helmet bore tall crests, fashioned like the Blood God's stylised skull rune. His steed was bigger than Tzatzo, a muscular, bare-fleshed brute with the snarling head of a great furless canine, clad in more spiked barding. At the knight's hip was a war axe, sawtoothed similarly to Skoren's stolen blade.

The knight dragged brutally on the chains of its heavy mount, bringing it to a stop in Vanik's path and forcing the Black Pilgrim to halt likewise. As he did so more riders emerged, all similarly mounted on great hound-beasts and clad in the heavy arms and armour of the Varanguard.

For a few seconds, silence settled across the street. The supplicants forced aside by Vanik scattered, while he remained facing the foremost rider impeding him. The Eightguard were also paused behind him, but Vanik could feel their sudden battle-ready tension.

It was the Varanguard who spoke first.

'By the bones of the unworthy, do my eyes deceive me? A Black Pilgrim bearing the favour of the Fifth passing through the Seventh Circle. Where are you bound for, boy?'

The warrior's half-helm did not hide his mouth, and Vanik saw that his lips and chin were crusted with dried blood, and his teeth sharpened to wicked points.

'I go beyond the Varanspire,' he answered tersely, feeling his heart accelerate and his body flush with anger. He forced his voice to remain level. He was not some simple warlord any more, prone to striking down a rival at the merest imposition. This was no place for a challenge.

'Why do you bar my path, Knight of Ruin?' he asked.

'This circle of the city belongs to the Bane Sons,' the rider responded. 'Here, I do as I please.' His voice was a semi-feral snarl, the sounds coming thick and ill-formed, as though he struggled to produce human words through the throat of a beast.

'I am a pilgrim, of the Scourge,' Vanik said. 'And I am serving the direct will of Lord Neveroth. Let me pass.'

'The bone-clad collector of sigmarite,' the knight sneered, his bloody lips peeling back from his wicked teeth. 'You are Vanik, the pilgrim of Karex Daemonflayer.'

'I am,' Vanik confirmed.

'I am Sir Caradoc, and these are the brother-knights of my konroi.'

Too late, Vanik heard the clatter of more battleplate, and realised that there were four more of the knights behind the Eightguard, cutting off their route back towards the last circle's gateway. They hemmed the pilgrim's retinue in, the Eightguard's steeds stamping sparks from the gory cobbles and snorting in distress. Tzatzo snarled at Caradoc's mount, and the dog-headed thing snapped back.

'If you wish for bloodshed here, you will have it,' Vanik said, letting Caradoc see him slowly place his hand on his daemon sword's hilt. 'But it will not serve the Varanguard, or our king.'

'*Our* king,' Caradoc echoed. 'You have not yet taken your vows, pilgrim. Do not use the Exalted Grand Marshal's title for your own vanity.'

'Nevertheless, what I say is true,' Vanik responded. 'Why are you impeding me?'

'A part of me wishes to cut your head from your shoulders, boy,' Caradoc growled, edging his mount closer. 'Maybe one day the True Gods will so bless me, but for now I play the role of simple messenger. My lord Arken, Seventh Marshal, brings you an offer. He has heard of your recent quests, and your rivalry with the pilgrim Blackhand. In his wisdom, he offers you this – kneel before him, and swear fealty to the Seventh Circle, and you will receive the sigil of Archaon.'

Vanik's surprise made him hesitate, but when he spoke again he kept the uncertainty from his voice. He had long ago learned that the only way to treat with the Varanguard was by refusing to show any weakness.

'Your lord would have me abandon the Fifth Circle for his own?'

'He would,' Sir Caradoc replied. 'And it is not an offer he will make again.'

'He would turn me into a traitor? A knight without honour?'

'He would save your life,' Caradoc said. 'You do realise the Blackhand has passed through this circle already? He is ahead of you. And in slaying Albermarl, he slays you too.'

'Did he turn you down as well?' Vanik countered.

'He did not receive our offer.'

'Why not?'

'It is not my place to question my lord Arken's will. Nor is it yours. You may accept, or you may decline.'

'He seeks to turn me against the Fifth Circle, but sends a bloodstained warrior to lead the negotiations?'

'Do not try to test me, boy,' Caradoc snarled. 'My brother-knights and I were butchering mortals and daemons alike for the glory of the Varanspire long before whatever pathetic spawn-creature you call a mother gave birth to you. Insult me again and I will carve you and your pitiful retinue to pieces, regardless of my lord's will.'

'My point stands,' Vanik replied, forcing himself to smile at the Varanguard champion. 'Why would I wish to serve your lord over Neveroth?'

'He has many uses for many tools, boy. Neveroth is a wasteful master. He will not care for your deeds or glories, only that you serve his every whim. You are less a Knight of Ruin than a slave.'

'And the master of the Bane Sons is somehow different?'

'Lord Arken properly rewards those knights who prove themselves to him. The Bane Sons are a warrior brotherhood. We honour the Three-Eyed King and the Eightfold Path through victory. You will find none of the scheming and false plotting that infects the likes of the Fifth.'

'I doubt that,' Vanik replied. 'And even if it were true, if you are such a band of brothers why would you welcome me into your midst, if I were to break my bonds with the Fifth and sunder my own honour?'

'Serve Lord Arken and the Seventh, and all are welcome.'

'Your words ring false, Sir Caradoc,' Vanik said. 'I know not why you have impeded me here with this offer, but it reeks of the falsehood and manipulation you claim to despise. I will have no part in whatever plan is being hatched by you or your masters.'

'You are misguided,' Caradoc said. 'So you are well suited to being a Scourge of Fate.'

'Better that than a knight without his own honour. I will slay the mortal castellan, and I will slay the Blackhand if need be. When next you see me, I will be a knight of the Fifth.'

'Tread carefully then, pilgrim,' Sir Caradoc growled. 'Until we meet again.'

'As the Eightstar wills it,' Vanik replied. Caradoc seemed to regard him for a little longer. Then, with a grunt, he dragged his mount to one side, the other Varanguard behind him doing likewise, opening the road for them once again.

Vanik rode on.

They passed again through the wastes. It took a day and a night to return to Jevcha's encampment, at least insomuch as the duelling, broken constellations and dark lights above the Varanspire could be defined by night and day.

The Darkoath queen had kept her promise to Vanik. The camp remained encircling the old shrine-ruin, the cooking fires of its inhabitants pluming lazily away into the red-lit evening sky. The hounds announced their return once more. Vanik ordered his war chiefs to assemble immediately, ignoring the weariness in his bones. It had been a long, hard ride compared to the journey to the spire, longer and harder than seemingly even he had realised.

'It was over a week,' Jevcha told him as he dismounted and passed Tzatzo's reins to her. 'Some of the others wanted to leave.'

'They thought me slain,' Vanik replied, a statement rather than a question. Jevcha shrugged.

'None would dare say that in front of me.'

'But their thoughts are clear enough to see,' Vanik responded. 'Who?'

'Gulgrak, Moll, Svarbald.'

'The usual then,' Vanik said.

'They are just battle-hungry,' Jevcha said. 'The wastes are no place to keep an army, not permanently.'

'Then they will rejoice,' Vanik said, stalking inside the ruins of the old hilltop temple. 'Because I am about to lead them to the slaughter.'

The chiefs assembled, five besides Jevcha, the leaders of the seven disparate warrior-bands that made up Vanik's core war party. They stood amidst the weed-clogged stones of the broken shrine, muttering among themselves until Vanik strode from the remains of the vestry.

They took the knee without hesitating. He bade them rise, his gaze lingering on Gulgrak, Moll and Svarbald. They had the good sense not to meet his eye.

'I am returned,' he said eventually. 'And I come bearing good news. Your days of idleness are over.'

'Your pilgrimage is at an end, sire?' Svarbald, the big former pirate, asked.

'No,' Vanik replied. 'It is not. By the decree of the Varanspire's Fifth Marshal, Lord Neveroth, I am to bring him the head of a mortal lackey named Albermarl, before Skoren Blackhand does the same. Only once that quest is completed will I have been deemed worthy enough to complete the Black Pilgrimage.'

There were murmurs amongst the assembled chiefs. They were simple fighters for the most part, pelt-clad champions from the harshest corners of the Mortal Realms. Their type made up the fodder of countless Chaos legions. None bar Jevcha had the charisma or foresight to lead anything more than a few hundred warriors at most. Still, when their own parties were brought together – Splintered Coast raiders, Faug's Red Steppe horsemen, Dravga's corsairs or the Eightguard – they formed a warband of almost five hundred favour-hungry, battle-hardened warriors. Vanik had fought alongside them for years. Regardless of their current restlessness, he knew they would not fail him.

'Albermarl is master of one of the so-called Free Cities in Chamon, Helmgard. We will go there, burn it, and I will cut him to pieces and take his skull as a trophy for the Varanspire.'

The murmuring rose, the approval now obvious throughout the assembly. Only Jevcha's expression betrayed apprehension.

'I know of Helmgard. The Darkoath chieftain Morvis was amongst a great host that besieged it. They could not storm it, despite trying for many months. It is duardin-built.'

'You are right,' Vanik said. 'Five hundred of us, no matter how blessed, will not be able to storm it. But I will not be journeying to Chamon with only this war party. The time has come to send out the call. The Gods demand obedience, and will reward those who show it.'

'We are to muster a legion?' Svarbald asked, his voice hopeful.

'Yes. Time presses, but I wish to bring as many warbands to our banner as I can before we march on Helmgard. This is no raid into the Eight Realms. We seek battle, and will slaughter all before us. That alone should rally the chosen to our standards.'

'Olhandris and his kindred will come, if my riders can find them before we depart,' Faug said. 'He has been seeking atonement before the Gods ever since his loss at Silverrun. He will surely see this as a message from the Eightfold.'

'Scoll Skagson as well,' Gulgrak added, the Nurgle-worshipping champion scratching at the weeping sores that constantly left his bare skin red-raw. 'He will not refuse me again, not after the blessings the Grandfather inflicted on his tribe the last time.'

'And the Hidesails,' Dravga interjected. 'I am still their captain, whether they like it or not. They will reave once more in your name, lord.'

'This is a good beginning,' Vanik said, nodding. 'Svarbald, what of the Triborn?'

The chieftain shook his head. 'Vorlock fell in battle with the Sons of Baelloc last spring-tide. I have no sway with their new master.'

'I might be able to bring the Fifteenth Anointed to our side,' Moll said, his tone cautious. 'But I have not heard word of them or Lord Barrin for three seasons. They may have taken their campaign against the aelf scum deeper into Hysh. I doubt they would reach us in time if so.'

'Send a rider anyway,' Vanik ordered. 'Your fastest horses and your most trusted message bearers, all of you. If there are debts to call in, call them in. If there are threats to make, make them. The Gods will be watching us when we reach Chamon, of that I can assure you.'

The assembly dispersed. Vanik motioned for Jevcha to remain behind.

'You still have doubts, sister,' he said, sensing her unhappiness.

She shrugged. 'Even if we waited for months, and even if every warband you summon were to come, we would not take Helmgard. And we cannot wait for months. Skoren will find a way to reach Albermarl before then.'

'I know,' Vanik said. 'Karex was of the same belief. We will not wait for months. But nor will I take only five hundred blades into Chamon. To do what I intend, we will need at least a show of strength.'

'This is not a quest I have ever heard being demanded of a Black Pilgrim before,' Jevcha went on. 'Let alone two.'

'I have been chosen,' Vanik replied. 'You will lead the warband again until my return.'

'Leaving already?' Jevcha demanded, her tone coloured with anger. Vanik knew how much she disliked leading in his absence, how she preferred only the company of the Darkoath tribespeople who had adopted her, and not the disparate factions of warriors Vanik had brought together. Her discomfort did not concern him.

'I am going to find Ulek,' he said. 'With him, his warriors and his prowess, we will be able to attract more Bloodbound to our host.'

'But Ulek is dead,' Jevcha said.

'He was *taken*,' Vanik corrected. 'Taken a season ago by S'aai and his God-Seekers.'

Ulek was an exalted deathbringer of the Blood God, a battle-hardened slaughterer whose name commanded great respect among the Bloodbound brotherhoods. Ulek and Vanik had found common cause before, and the Black Pilgrim hoped to do so again.

'If S'aai has him then he is surely dead, and all his warriors with him,' Jevcha said.

'We don't know that, and we won't until we ask S'aai directly.'

Jevcha scowled. 'This is madness. Even if S'aai had permitted Ulek to live this long and retained enough of his body and soul to be of any use, how will you convince S'aai to release him? The Castellum of the Virtues is not a place even most of my Darkoath would consider attacking, and the forest that surrounds it is even worse.'

'I will take your tracker, Yori.'

'Are you listening to anything I'm saying?' Jevcha demanded, her voice rising. 'If you're lucky, S'aai will kill you. If not, you'll end up like Ulek. Assuming he even still lives!'

Vanik said nothing at first, letting Jevcha's frustration drain before him. When he spoke again, his tone was slow and measured.

'You have started to underestimate me, Jevcha. At times you

sound like the Daemonflayer. She does not know me, so she is permitted her mistakes. You, however, do.'

The tone would have cowed any other warrior in the warband. Jevcha only scowled harder, her yellow eyes aflame.

'You have changed since you took up the pilgrim's black, Vanik. Every risk you take is bolder than the last.'

'Such is the nature of the Path,' he responded, looking past her. 'I know you do not wish to remain here any longer. I know the war parties have grown restless. But do not worry about S'aai, or Ulek. I have already considered how to retrieve the deathbringer. I will return here with him, and have word sent out to every Khorne warband between here and the Brass River saying that he fights beneath my black banner. Then, we march on Chamon.'

'S'aai's dreadhold is a darkling place, even for those who seek the Lost God,' Jevcha said, her voice resigned now. 'To go there will be to place your life and soul into the hands of S'aai.'

'What other choice do I have?' Vanik demanded, his patience expended. 'Without Ulek or the warriors he can summon we do not have a host enough to storm it, and even if we did I could not risk losing so many warriors before we journey to Chamon.'

Jevcha nodded.

'Go with the Eightstar's blessing then, brother,' she said quietly.

'If Gulgrak, Moll or Svarbald speak ill of me, you, or question the Path, kill them,' Vanik added.

'With pleasure,' Jevcha said, a note of fire re-entering her voice. She had been leading warrior bands for years. Vanik knew that her hesitation was not uncertainty. It was a desire not to exceed his commands. He had no doubt that she could have bound the war party to her own will in a matter of days. It was not, however, her will that drove them, but Vanik's. Reminding restless champions of that while he was absent was one of the most difficult tasks to ask of any warrior of Chaos.

'You have honoured me with your service,' Vanik said, the caustic edge gone from his voice. 'For more years than I deserve. When I join the ranks of the Fifth and am anointed with the sigil of the Three-Eyed King, I will not forget you.'

'You chose your Path,' Jevcha said, shrugging off his words. 'I chose mine. The Gods will do as they please.'

'We will do the ice lodges proud, my sister. The first knight to be raised up from the Splintered Coast.'

She looked at him, and smiled.

'I do not doubt it. I will see you again, when you return.'

ACT II

THE PATH TO GLORY

PART SEVEN

THE COURT OF
THE SEVEN VIRTUES

Vanik assembled his retinue that night, to depart in the morning. The Eightguard ate and took on fresh steeds from among Faug's herd – such changes were necessary when Vanik's quests and trials bore him across the wastes of the Eightpoints. Only Tzatzo seemed never to tire, her and Modred's indefatigable little black nag.

To the Eightguard, Vanik added Yori, Jevcha's wizened old Darkoath pathfinder. Though grey-haired and white-eyed, the aged warrior had led the warband safe through cloying marshland and maddening mirror-mazes for years, seemingly relying on the preternatural senses the True Gods had blessed him with. He rode with a dozen of Faug's steppe horsemen, brought to act as outriders, scouts and messengers for the small party.

They rode as a trio of new, red suns bled ruddy light into the surrounding plains. Renki's dogs howled mournfully into the dawn, until the sound was lost to Vanik beneath the drumming of hooves.

It was difficult to tell how long they travelled for. Days and nights came and went irregularly. Vanik had counted eleven before they reached their destination, but Modred said nine and Kulthuk fourteen. Yori told the truth – he didn't know. They encamped when exhaustion took them, ate when they hungered, and prayed to all the Gods to speed their journey. At one point, they had to detour from the path suggested by Yori to avoid a travelling warband, for Vanik didn't recognise their distant banners and icons. During one night, when a deep chill descended on the plains and sword blades, axe heads and armour plates became rimmed with hoar frost, a pack of the feral hound-beasts that roamed the steppes caught their scent. All night they circled the small encampment, their howls and unearthly shrieks confounding any attempt at sleep. The retinue kept close to the fire, their weapons drawn. When dawn finally came, however, there were no signs of the feral creatures that had stalked the frigid darkness beyond the firelight.

On what Vanik thought was the sixth day they came upon an old shrine, a stone slab atop a low, flat-topped hill. Vanik inspected the runes carved into its craggy flanks. Though he couldn't discern the Gods or daemons it was specifically dedicated to, it certainly bore the blessings of the Dark Tongue. He drew blood from the back of his own forearm, and had every man and woman in the expedition do the same, smearing a portion of their lifeblood on the weathered old stones while Kulthuk led a short blood-rite dedication.

It seemed to work – the days were longer and the nights less disturbed. Eventually, after setting out during the hours of darkness, they saw the first signs of their destination amidst the light of the day, a dark green sprawl over the next barren rise.

The Castellum of the Virtues lay at the heart of a heavy, dark-leafed woodland, its expanse an unsettling contrast to the dead earth of the wastes that surrounded it. Vanik and his retinue entered it as the dawn spread across the wastes, a golden light that winked through the thick canopy.

The Black Pilgrim was on his guard. Jevcha had already warned him of the cursed glade she claimed protected the Slaaneshi fortress, but for the first few hours there was no indication of anything untoward. The woodland was thick and lush, the canopy heavy, permitting only the barest hint of the new day's light into the undergrowth. The path they followed was little more than an uncertain passage between the leafy boughs, and Vanik was forced to lean low in Tzatzo's saddle to avoid the branches and creepers that clustered the trail.

For its own part, Vanik's steed seemed in no mood to entertain the quiet woodland. She snarled and huffed, and the occasional crack or rustle of what Vanik hoped were mere woodland creatures made her twist and snap her fangs. She hadn't fed properly since they'd left the main encampment. She was restless.

On they ventured, led by Yori. Vanik only began noticing the changes slowly. He was sure one of the branches overhead was questing towards him, then realised that it was not a length of timber but a slow, sinuous, fleshy growth, seemingly reaching blindly for those passing by. Tzatzo tried to rear with a screech and rip it off, and it was only with difficulty that he kept her down and on the path.

Further on they found a golden tree. Its leaves were filigreed and its trunk seemed to have been forged and cast in purest duardin metalwork. It gleamed magnificently in a spear of light that shone down through a break in the canopy above, like an altar to the God of perfection. The sight of it made Vanik scowl.

'Don't touch it,' he ordered back up the line as they passed, refusing to look at the strange tree as he drew closer. It was a distraction, and he kept his eyes on the surrounding forest, looking for any hint of an ambush or creatures watching them. He was certain he caught movement, but every time he tried to focus on it he found nothing but quiet, undisturbed brush.

Past the golden tree a strange mist began to creep along the path, shrouding the undergrowth in a foggy, purple-tinged miasma. It grew thicker the further they travelled, and the canopy became denser, crushing the light and plunging them into a cloying realm of slowly shifting shadows. Strange cries began to haunt the air, unearthly, ululating. Whether they came from man, beast or something worse, Vanik could not tell. Ahead of him, he realised that Yori had started to falter. His unease grew, and he brushed a gauntlet against Nakali's haft. The daemon chuckled darkly, but said nothing.

Soon the mist had grown so dense that it took a long time for anyone in the retinue to realise the forest had changed as well. Yori discovered it first. He let out a disgusted oath and stumbled back from the edge of the path ahead. Vanik, who had dropped back to make sure the Red Steppe riders were keeping to the track, twisted in his saddle to see what had caused the commotion, a hand going once more to Nakali's hilt. He realised the daemon sword was vibrating softly.

'Flesh,' Yori barked back down the line, pointing into the fog. 'It's the trees! They're all flesh!'

Vanik turned back, looking more closely at the boughs around him, shrouded in the gloom. He realised Yori was correct. This was no longer a forest of wood, bark and leaves. The trees were trunks of flesh and bone now, their boughs limbs and writhing tentacles, their leaves fingers and ears. Eyeballs clustered like blinking fruit, and fissures in the outer bark revealed oozing blood-sap and throbbing, pulsating organs.

The mist was a soporific musk, a sickening perfume that was making Vanik feel light-headed. He forced himself to concentrate, to try to focus through the gently shifting fog. He realised that there was a certain beauty to the flesh-forest surrounding them, a sort of perfection in each grasping tentacle-root and groaning maw-hollow.

Are not my master's gifts beyond compare? Nakali whispered. *Is not his realm beautiful?*

Vanik didn't answer. He couldn't. His thoughts were elsewhere, sluggish and heavy. A part of his mind told him that it had been a mistake to come here. He shrugged the doubts off. Deeper, they had to go deeper.

The Lost God's corruption only grew the further they wandered. Tzatzo's claws began to dig and squelch in the forest path, and Vanik realised even the mulch underfoot had turned to pale, pastel flesh, puckered and bristling with slender, silver hairs. The steed's claws were gouging the skin, drawing more amber, sap-like blood and making the tree-growths either side shudder and groan as though in pain.

Why had he come here? The question became more abstract with every step they took deeper into the fleshwood. Thoughts of Ulek and the fearsome warriors his reputation could add to Vanik's banner slipped away. He decided he wanted to find the source of that wonderful scent tinging the fog. That was more important, wasn't it?

The trail was disappearing. The flesh was closing in around them, warm, soft and yielding, caressing his black armour. Tzatzo, her head low and labouring, came to a slow stop. Ahead, Yori appeared totally enraptured as he stumbled on into the forest's embrace. Vanik tried to call his name, but words felt like too much effort. He let out a groan instead, shaking his head slowly.

The sound was mirrored by a cry from behind. He managed to half turn in the saddle, so clumsy that he almost fell, and look back down the remains of the trail. Immediately behind him the Eightguard had maintained a degree of cohesion, but their slumped postures and bowed heads indicated they were as far gone as Vanik. The Red Steppe horsemen, though, were completely lost. Only a handful were still with the party, and as Vanik watched, another turned his horse off into the skin-thickets with jaw slack and eyes vacant. He vanished. The one whose cry had drawn Vanik's attention had been dragged from his mount by one of the branch-tendrils, which now coiled around his lower body like a great serpent and was hauling him away into the forest's perverse, corrupt depths.

The sight pulled something from the unsullied depths of Vanik's consciousness. A deep-set feeling of anger flared through the pilgrim's thoughts, igniting the fog clouding his mind, burning it away. He snarled, grasped Nakali's hilt and, ignoring the daemon's shrieked protestations, ripped the weapon free.

'Draw your blades!' he roared. 'In the name of Archaon, defend yourselves!'

The sudden defiance drew a response from the forest. The low murmurs of the mutated woodland rose, until the flesh and bone was screaming, making Vanik's ears ache and his skin crawl. The hands and tentacles that had been caressing him now struck and grasped, trying to heave him from the saddle.

He struck back, lashing out with Nakali.

Do not make me strike the flesh! the daemon wailed as it cleaved the boughs of its fellow servants, black ichor-sap splattering Vanik's armour. He ignored the Slaaneshi sword's pleas. Tzatzo had also recovered, and dug her double jaws into everything within reach, snarling.

The Eightguard closed around Vanik, forcing their own steeds back under control, the fug dissipating as their swords and axes hewed the flesh forest seeking to subsume them. Modred had attempted to wander off, vacant-eyed and drooling, but Aramor had managed to snatch the bridle of his nag and force him to the centre of the tight-packed formation.

As he cleaved at the nightmare undergrowth, Vanik became more aware of other things moving through the fog and writhing woodland around them. They darted to his left and right, too rapid to follow properly.

'We can cut a way out of here,' Kulthuk barked, pointing with his ichor-drenched mace back the way they had come. All sense of direction was rapidly disappearing as the forest continued to drag itself around them. If they didn't move, in a few seconds they would be smothered wholly by the sheer weight of the encroaching thickets.

'Go,' Vanik shouted over the forest's pleasure-addled screeching. Before any of the mounted band could turn, however, a sudden hush fell over the woodland. The warped trees ceased their thrashing and writhing and began peeling back, tentacle-roots slithering away from the panting, dripping Chaos knights.

'Hold formation,' Vanik growled, his battle-lust drowning out Nakali's continued rage as he kept the daemon sword raised, waiting for the next thing to rush them from the fog.

The forest completed its retreat, its screams reduced now to low, weary moaning. The pathway had opened up again ahead of them, though behind it remained barred by a bristling mass of limbs and trunks. This time, however, the forest track was no longer unoccupied. Two creatures approached, one mounted atop the other. The lower beast resembled a great serpent, purple-skinned and shimmering in the gloom beneath the flesh-boughs. Its skull was elongated, its eyes reflective and black as jet, while a thick, sinuous tongue darted from its maw, tasting the air.

The being on its back was clearly some sort of herald or champion of the Lost God. It wore a close-fitting breastplate, lacquered purple, and an enclosed helmet finished with a tall, bright pink crest. Its limbs were bare and unarmoured, unnaturally long, the flesh white as porcelain. A glaive was in its left hand, resting along the back of the serpentine creature as it coiled to a stop before Vanik's band.

'You are trespassing,' said a voice. Like the rider, it was androgynous, and Vanik couldn't tell if it issued from the knight, the serpent, the fleshy forest, or was reverberating inside his own head. Perhaps it was all of them.

'This is the sovereign fleshland of my lord S'aai the Virtuous, Prince Regent of the Longed-for. You have no right to be here.'

'I am a Black Pilgrim,' Vanik snarled, urging Tzatzo a few paces towards the serpent creature. 'And this… forest, is a part of the Eightpoints. Your lord has no right to impede me or attack my retinue.'

'The forest attacked them,' the thing said. 'They were unworthy to tread within the Prince of Pleasure's rapturous groves. It is only through his aching desire that you have been allowed to live. Now, if you wish that to remain the case, you will follow me and explain your blasphemous presence to my lord in person.'

'And if I would find my own way to your pathetic dreadhold?' Vanik demanded. He had hardly spoken the words before the forest around him twitched and writhed once more. The figures he had caught glimpses of before materialised all around the retinue – lithe, slender daemonettes, their pastel flesh and wicked claw-talons glistening in the murky light. He refused to look at them, knowing the dangers their daemonic allure held for even an experienced servant of the Eightfold Path. They were lust and seduction made flesh.

'Follow me, or give your soul the luxury of the forest's eternal caress,' the serpent-thing said. 'It is your choice.'

Vanik grimaced, forcing himself to focus through the mind-numbing, sickly-sweet stench of the forest and its inhabitants. They had almost entrapped him once. They would not do so again. Keeping a tight grip on Tzatzo's chains, he allowed the Chaos steed to follow the serpent as it turned back on itself.

'Stay close,' Vanik growled at the Eightguard. 'And fight your temptations. These things will seek to lure you from the path. Prove you are stronger. Prove you are worthy to be the retinue of a Knight of Ruin.'

'You have made a wise choice,' the Slaaneshi herald called back as Vanik began to follow it. 'But you must hurry. My lord can only deny the forest's desires for so long.'

The Castellum of the Virtues lay at the beating heart of the fleshwood. The final sickening boughs parted ahead of Vanik, and he saw the dreadhold of S'aai the Virtuous rise up before him, set against the brilliant firmament of the heavens. It was not what Vanik had been expecting, not some wicked citadel of razor parapets and flayed skins. Instead he found himself gazing upon a baronial fortress-home, a noble's dwelling that had been garrisoned and fortified. Walls of stone and heavy timber rose up to long roofs of slate tiles, patterned with the runes of the Lost God. Small windows and arrow slits perforated the mansion's flanks, while the corners were squared off by more tile-roofed towers, from which fluttered S'aai's lewd heraldry.

The forest clustered close around the grand manse's walls, root tendrils burrowing into its foundations, while latticeworks of throbbing veins webbed the flanks of the structure like perverse ivy. Like the mutated woodland that surrounded it, the manse seemed alive, presiding over the path that led to its great front doors with a malevolence that chilled even Vanik. For a second, as he passed into its shadow, his mind lingered on what perverted madness likely lay within. The thoughts were almost enough to make him quail. Of all the entities that constituted the pantheon of Chaos, the Lost God was the last he'd wished to fall into the clutches of. The pains inflicted by Slaanesh were beyond any mortal reckoning, and its pleasures were no less draining. To be left an agonised, broken husk would be a blessing.

One certainty comforted him. It was far too late to turn back now.

The heavy wooden doors of the manse lay directly ahead, framed by the trunks and overhanging boughs of the two largest flesh trees Vanik had yet seen. The groaning mass of quivering muscle and skin loomed over the retinue as they came to a halt outside the doors. Vanik had sheathed Nakali, but he could still feel the daemon sword vibrating against his hip. The thing that had guided them along the path carried on to one of the two overhanging trees and began to coil itself around its bulk, the hideous peristaltic motion of its serpentine body making Vanik's skin crawl. The herald on its back remained where it was as the Slaaneshi steed bound itself to its nest.

'Enter,' it commanded Vanik, pointing its glaive towards the mansion's doors.

'Jarll, Forvin, guard the horses,' Vanik said grimly, kicking his feet from Tzatzo's stirrups. 'Whatever you do, ignore anything that comes from the forest and tries to tempt you.'

He dismounted and leaned in close to Tzatzo, murmuring to the Chaotic creature. 'The allures of this place have no power over you. Let none of the others wander.'

The beast gave forth an affirming snarl. The remainder of the retinue had dismounted alongside the Black Pilgrim, hefting swords and shields as they gathered around their master. Vanik mounted the short steps to the manse's doors. They were studded with metal bolts, and up close he realised that each piece of black iron was warped into the shape of a tortured face. The timber of the door creaked as he approached. He paused before laying a gauntlet on it, catching sounds coming from the other side. Crying, laughter, the strumming cadence of string and wind instruments. He grimaced, and pushed.

The doors swung inwards, and the full madness of S'aai's fiefdom was laid bare.

A part of Vanik had expected the structure's insides to be like the forest outside – clad in skin, the rooms each the various organs of some titanic, daemonic entity. Instead, he found himself looking on a spacious entrance hall, a wood panelled atrium hung with tapestries and pieces of artwork. A baronial staircase opened up at the far end of the chamber, lined with busts and more paintings. The light of Hysh filtered in through high stained-glass windows, their refraction casting a kaleidoscope of colours across the hall.

At a glance, the space would have looked familiar to many noble families in the Mortal Realms, the fastness of some human baron or landed gentleman. What filled the hallway, however, was far beyond the most warped nightmares of any mortal noble.

S'aai's mansion appeared to be playing host to a grand celebration. The hall was packed with bodies lost in apoplexies of pleasure. Most appeared to be human, and judging by the remains of the silken gowns and shirts worn by the attendees, they had once been clad in wealth and finery. Now most of their clothing was in tatters, their flesh slick with sweat. They were dancing, wildly and senselessly, to the discordant melody of a band of vacant-eyed musicians playing at the foot of the staircase.

Vanik couldn't hide an expression of disgust as he took in the scene, and the stink of sweat and perfume washed over him. It seemed as though the revellers had been active for hours, perhaps days – he noticed that there were bodies on the wooden floorboards of the hallway, trampled and pulverised, either sacrifices killed at the beginning or members of the celebration who had fallen or collapsed from exhaustion and been crushed to death. The others still danced, oblivious to the insanity they were caught up in.

The urge to draw Nakali and end the debauched display with slaughter almost overcame Vanik. He remained on the edge of the main doors, seeking a route through the bedlam to the far staircase. After a while, it was created for him.

A figure slipped from the hedonistic press, buxom and lithe. Its skin was a pale purple hue, bare but for a few straps of leather and silk. Its features were like those of a woman, slender and beautiful, except instead of hair, its scalp was topped by a crest of horns and tendrils that coiled like a nest of vipers. Its left arm looked human, but the right ended in a long, crablike claw below the elbow. Despite being so unnatural, the deformities seemed only to complement and enhance its raw allure.

Vanik had steeled his soul for such moments. He knew he was looking upon a daemonette, one of Slaanesh's favoured servants. He knew such creatures drew their abilities from the seduction and trickery of weak mortal minds. Yet even after many decades fighting across the wastes and beyond – and many pacts alongside, and battles against, the servants of the Lost God – he found himself unable to tear his eyes away from the strange creature. It offered him a small, wicked smile, revealing rows of needle-like fangs. He felt his heartbeat quicken.

'Welcome, traveller,' the daemonette said, its voice a soothing lilt edged with lustful mockery. 'My name is Caelia. You must be weary. You are safe here. Come, take refreshments, and join our dance.'

'No,' Vanik managed to say, though he barely enunciated the word. 'Your master...' He trailed off. The daemonette giggled, a cruel, barbed sound that drew a longing shudder down Vanik's spine. It wore its nakedness with sickening pride, and he found himself staring into the depths of its eyes, jet-black and lustrous like the serpent creature outside.

'You have come to see my prince regent,' the daemon woman said, cocking its head slightly to one side, like a curious bird. 'You must be a bold and mighty warrior, to have passed through his forest without bearing his grace.'

'Take me to S'aai,' Vanik said between gritted teeth. He finally managed to look past the creature, then immediately wished he hadn't when he once more took in the full corruption of the hallway's maddening party.

Caelia giggled again. 'Come with me then, oh mighty champion.'

It turned and began to move in among the press, its posture brazen and sure in the knowledge that Vanik's gaze still followed it. After a moment, his thoughts re-engaged enough to push himself in pursuit. The Eightguard followed.

Not a single eye was turned as Vanik and his retinue crossed the threshold and entered the perverse manse. The revellers, though lost in their own madness, responded to the daemonette's presence with gibbering seizure-like convulsions or shrieks of awe, none of them noticing the knights who followed in its wake. They parted around Caelia, clearing a route towards the staircase. Occasionally the daemonette would reach out with its human hand and caress one of the revellers, though it rarely deigned to do more than glance at them. Whomever its touch fell upon would seize up and stumble, and be immediately dragged deeper into the mass of heaving bodies, to be crushed or torn apart amidst raptures of ecstasy.

Is the revelry not glorious? Nakali whispered, its tone mischievous. *Why not join in the dance, just for a moment?*

Vanik forced himself not to respond. With the daemonette's gaze no longer upon him, he was able to shake off the worst of the place's allure. The urge to lash out at the slick, writhing throng pressing against him from all sides redoubled, and he brutally shoved anything that came close, striking aside the hands that sought to grasp at him and pull him into the dance.

They reached the bottom of the staircase. The musicians there were the only ones in the hall still fully clad. Their eyes were glazed, their hands moving with a mindlessness that was almost as chilling as the mania of those dancing to their rhythms. As he passed them, Vanik realised that their fingers were ragged, and blood was dripping down the strings and boards of their instruments. He didn't pause to consider how long they had been trapped, playing their piece over and over in a fugue state.

'This way, champion,' Caelia called back over her shoulder as she climbed the stairs, winking at Vanik. He followed without meeting her gaze, checking to ensure Modred and the Eightguard had made it through the swirling chaos of the hallway.

They passed up the staircase. It turned back on itself, approaching a carved wooden archway covered by a purple veil. Caelia pulled it languidly aside, glancing back at Vanik again with a smile. He glared at her, gripping Nakali firmly. A sickly aroma wafted from beyond the veil, sweet at first but rapidly growing repellent. The sounds of debauchery coming from the hallway below had faded, though the music still rose up faintly.

'If anything lays a hand on you, kill it,' Vanik said to the

Eightguard as he approached the arch, deliberately loud enough for whatever lay beyond to hear him.

They passed through. Vanik found himself in a smaller chamber, wood-panelled like the rest of the manse, its fuller extent concealed by more drapes. He could see the suggestion of figures moving beyond the nearer veils, and heavy breathing and the scrape of claws across wood told him they were not alone. The room was full.

Caelia approached the veil directly ahead. There was already a figure standing beside it, apparently waiting on Vanik's arrival. Somehow, the herald that had greeted them in the forest had arrived in the chamber before them. It was without its serpent spawn now, but still armed and armoured, its tall, slender body and crested helm looming over Vanik.

'You have come into the presence of my lord S'aai, the prince regent,' the herald said. 'Kneel, and recite the Seven Virtues before his splendour.'

Vanik's retort was cut short by a voice from beyond the veil.

'There will be no need for that, Shor'qual. Admit them.'

The herald reached up and tugged the veil aside. More of the room was revealed, another space of finely crafted panels and thick purple rugs clouded by stale perfume and the vapours of half a dozen opiates. The far wall was a grand cast-iron fireplace fashioned like a screaming mouth, its embers providing a sultry glow to the room. A chaise longue was set before it, draped in cushions and silk. Candle holders, wrought like the grasping tendrils of the forest outside, held dripping wax nubs that provided further illumination.

A figure reclined on the chaise longue, while a number of daemonettes were draped around him, coiled like pets at his feet or standing over him. His lower half was clad in heavily embroidered purple and silver cloth, while his torso was bared.

The candlelight picked at slender, toned muscles and a face that was unmistakably inhuman. The aquiline features were those of an aelf, though the pitch-black eyes left few doubts as to his allegiances. Long white hair lay draped around his shoulders, and a slight smile tugged at his full lips as he looked Vanik up and down.

'I must admit, Shor'qual has piqued my interest,' the aelf said. 'Do you know of the Seven Virtues, my visitor?'

Caelia brushed past him and joined her kindred clustered around S'aai, pausing to kiss one before taking one of the long, strangely carved pipes several were smoking.

'You are S'aai, servant of the Lost God?' Vanik demanded, refusing to allow the fumes choking the room to distract him.

'The first Virtue is pride,' the aelf said, as though he hadn't heard him. His voice was cultured – he spoke clearly and carefully, but with an edge of disdain that plucked at Vanik's instinctive anger. 'Without it, why would we choose to tread the Path in the first place? The second is envy. If we did not envy the Gods, why would we try so hard to emulate them?'

'I have not come here to debate the tenets of your lost master,' Vanik snapped. The daemonettes around the aelf hissed, the beauty of their features contorting momentarily into hideous snarls, but the aelf seemed untroubled. He continued.

'The third is gluttony. With success we reward ourselves, and if a reward is good, there should be no limit to how far we indulge. The fourth is–'

'Lust,' Vanik said. 'For if the Gods themselves lust, why shouldn't we? The fifth is anger, the sixth, greed and the seventh, sloth. I know the base teachings of Slaanesh, aelf.'

The figure on the chaise longue laughed, though its daemon mistresses continued to glare at Vanik.

'It is always heartening to meet a fellow philosopher. I have built my fastness here upon the foundations of those seven fine and honourable merits. I am glad they are not wasted on you.'

'I told you, I have not come here to debate the tenets of your faith.'

The aelf nodded. 'Fear not, that much is readily apparent. I am indeed S'aai, master of all you have seen, see and will see. And you are Vanik, an aspirant of the great and glorious Varanguard.'

'I am,' Vanik responded, ignoring the mockery in S'aai's voice. 'And you owe me a dozen good horsemen and one tracker. I came here bearing the pilgrim's Black and in all good faith, and you have attacked my retinue and now seized us under arms.'

Vanik had bargained with warlords and daemons before. He expected the usual from such a being in a position of strength – a scornful sneer, dark laughter, threats, even anger. Instead, S'aai frowned slightly.

'Your riders discovered the pleasures of my fair woodland. They sought out Slaanesh's embrace, and they found it.'

'You insult me,' Vanik said to S'aai.

'I have done worse than that,' S'aai said, only now beginning to let dark humour colour his voice. 'If you wish to leave my castellum with your soul intact, let alone your body, you will choose your next words carefully.'

'I bear the Black,' Vanik said. 'I am under the protection of Karex Daemonflayer and the Fifth Circle. To strike me or my retinue is to strike a servant of the Three-Eyed King. It is you who should choose your words carefully, Lord S'aai.'

'Not in my own dreadhold,' S'aai responded, his eyes narrowing. 'You trespassed in my forest. This fiefdom has been granted to me by the Exalted Grand Marshal himself. You are nothing to him.'

'But you are?' Vanik said. 'If we were trespassing, as you

claim, why not simply kill us? Why bring me before you, here? Just to insult me? Or are you wiser than you first appear, Lord S'aai? Are you in fact perfectly aware that killing or torturing me would bring the wrath of at least one konroi of the Varanguard down upon this mansion?'

'Your assumptions are impertinent,' S'aai responded. 'So I'm sure you would fit well with the Knights of Ruin, were your fate not already sealed. I know why you are here.'

'Then I need not explain myself.'

'Your ally, Ulek, yet lives,' S'aai continued. 'It pleases me to let you know this. Pain is nothing without hope.'

'You will release him to me,' Vanik said. 'Him and any of his warband who are yet living.'

'Why?' S'aai demanded.

'Because in exchange, I will give you this.'

Vanik drew Nakali. The daemonblade hissed and snapped at him, and he sensed its golden scales grinding around his arm, but he fought through the illusion, ignored the phantom fangs digging into the hand that grasped its hilt.

The daemonettes shrieked in sympathy with the bound daemon's hatred, and S'aai's eyes widened. Though he tried to mask it, he could not conceal the expression of awe when his eyes caught sight of the barbed, mirror-black blade or the serpents that coiled, golden and gleaming, around the hilt and crosspiece.

'You know this sword, don't you, Lord S'aai?' Vanik asked, permitting himself a smile. S'aai simply glared, aware that the pilgrim had seen through his disdain.

'Tell me of it,' Vanik urged.

'You are its wielder,' S'aai said bitterly. 'You need not be told.'

'Regardless,' Vanik said. 'Tell me.'

S'aai was silent before speaking again.

'It has... six names I could recount from memory, but in the Eightpoints it is known most commonly as Nakali.'

'Go on,' Vanik said.

'Its origins are not known with any certainty. Some say it was birthed when the first lovers that murdered one another in jealousy died in each other's arms. Others say it was mortal once, but ascended to the Realm of Chaos when it turned a whole Free City upon itself with its teachings, daughter against father, husband against wife. There are many such stories. What we do know is that once Nakali became daemonkin, a Knight of Ruin named Sijn bested it and bound it to his blade. Ever since Nakali has served the Varanguard, until it was lost in the realm of Shyish.'

'Lost, and recovered by my strength of arms,' Vanik added. 'I know how much you covet this weapon, Lord S'aai. I know its legend is told to this day amongst the followers of the Lost God. And I know that in exchange for it, you will give me Ulek.'

Silence followed the Black Pilgrim's words. S'aai's expression had become guarded once more, but still there was a hint of humour in his eyes. It made Vanik uncomfortable. So far everything had worked as he had hoped. Amusement, however, was not the response he had expected.

'For one who has progressed so far along the Path, Vanik, you are astonishingly stupid,' the Slaaneshi aelf said. 'You hardly stopped to question just how I was so sure you had come here for Ulek, or even how I knew he was one of your bonded champions. Perhaps if you truly appreciated how precarious your current state is, you would see the snare set in the undergrowth before you.'

Vanik's thoughts turned cold, and his grip tightened around Nakali. The daemon had gone unusually silent since it had been drawn, but now it whispered in his ear, a childish giggle.

Our time together has come to an end, little pilgrim.

'I was told to expect you, Vanik of the Splintered Coast,' S'aai continued, a smile breaking through his false stoicism as he fought and failed to disguise his pleasure. 'A dear friend of yours, another Black Pilgrim, knows your bondsmen, knew you would seek out old allies, and came here specifically before he continued on his travels because he knew you, or one dear to you, would come seeking Ulek. And in exchange for seizing you, I will be allowed to reclaim Nakali for the rapturous Prince of Pleasure. From your disembowelled corpse.'

Vanik stood rooted to the spot, paralysed by hate and rage as S'aai's treachery became clear.

Die, Vanik, hissed Nakali.

PART EIGHT

THE BLOOD BOON

The killing began. The chamber's remaining veils were ripped down and pallid Slaaneshi warriors in slender purple armour sprang forward, joining the daemonettes as they threw themselves at the Eightguard. The creatures howled, their perfect beauty twisting into hideous visages of hunger and lust. Thoughts fogged by the sickly perfumes of Lord S'aai's court, the retinue barely raised swords and axes in time to meet the claws of their attackers.

None came for Vanik. He had already been chosen by the castellum's master. With the lithe grace of his race, S'aai rose from his reclined position and drew a curved scimitar, its hilt fashioned like the silver twin of Nakali's golden serpent haft. The champion of the Lost God saluted Vanik. He didn't return the gesture.

Nakali crashed against S'aai's silver steel. The daemonblade was keening its reluctance in Vanik's head, desperate not to be turned against a servant of its own God. Vanik crushed its protestations, projecting his own anger and hate into it like a

139

rod of white-hot iron, taming the serpent. S'aai dropped back towards the fireplace as Vanik's heavy blows rained down, using his greater speed to arch and dart out of the way of the strikes that hammered through his guard. It was rage and brute strength against the instinctive grace of the aelf, further tempered by the Lost God's blessings – S'aai was faster than any opponent Vanik had ever faced before.

The prince regent had allowed Vanik's initial attacks to fall home merely because they amused him. Vanik realised as much the second S'aai went from defence to offence. Almost before he realised what was happening, the aelf had spun into his guard and slashed his scimitar down across his body. Steel jarred against steel and Vanik found himself thrown back, the runes carved into his black plate blazing with a fiery light as they absorbed a blow that would have cleaved even an armoured mortal knight in half. He recovered his balance just in time to half turn and take the next slash against his pauldron, grunting as the razored steel drew blood. His breastplate was mangled, almost cleft in half by the force of the first blow.

'I had hoped for better sport than this,' S'aai sneered, giving Vanik time to recover his guard. The Slaaneshi champion gestured contemptuously with his blade at the melee behind Vanik. A glance told him it wasn't going well – the Eightguard were beset, unable to match the darting speed of S'aai's daemonettes in their befuddled state. Out of the corner of his eye, he saw one of the Chaos knights, Lanval, on his knees, staring dull-eyed at a daemonette as it clamped its snapping claws around his throat and, with a delighted sneer, sheared the knight's head off. Beside him, S'aai's herald, Shor'qual, had buried its glaive in Aktar's breastplate and now pirouetted with deadly speed, disembowelling him in a spray of blood that splattered the room's veils.

'And your soul will never leave this manse–' S'aai began to say.

The crash of splitting timber and a roar of pure fury interrupted the aelf before he could go on. The melee in the chamber disintegrated as a battering ram of muscle and spiked armour smashed into the midst of the combatants. Vanik turned in time to see half of the remaining Eightguard being pitched from their feet, and an axe falling in a blurring arc to cleave a howling daemonette from horn to groin in a gout of purple ichor.

The whole mansion seemed to shudder at the new arrival's war cry.

'*For the Seventh Circle!*'

Sir Caradoc had arrived, and he had not come alone. The Varanguard's konroi were at his back, smashing in through the broken archway, each one a brute mountain of black battleplate and throbbing musculature. They ignored the Eightguard who, for all their own armour and prowess, looked like stunned children caught up amid a nightmare as the Varanguard barrelled past them. Caradoc and his brothers seemed focused on nothing but the slaughter of S'aai's harem.

Vanik turned back to the aelf just as he leapt once more. Gone was his mocking expression, replaced by a twisted visage of pure hatred. Vanik was far too slow to parry the scimitar blow to his scalp, and could only trust in his Azgorh-forged helm to withstand the ringing impact. He stumbled, narrowly bringing up Nakali in time to fend off another strike to his neck, then grunting as S'aai's blade thumped into his flank, slicing away a length of his Dracoth-scale cape.

For all the violence and bloodshed, there was a terrible efficiency about the fighting style of Caradoc's knights. They attacked S'aai's court with a reliance on their plate armour and their own brute strength, making little effort to parry or match the speed of the Slaaneshi blows. Instead, they let their warp-steel take each hit, ignoring those that drew blood, focusing their every vicious effort on hacking down enemy warriors and daemons with their axes.

Vanik had seen such bloodshed before, but to experience it in the confines of S'aai's hall at the hands of a konroi of the Varanguard was another matter entirely. The eight knights moved through the Slaanesh worshippers like a blade storm, axes rising and falling relentlessly.

Regardless of the skill and prowess of the numberless champions of the Four, none made war quite like the Knights of Ruin.

Sir Caradoc swept up behind Vanik. The Black Pilgrim tried to turn while keeping S'aai to his front, desperate not to be attacked from both sides. Instead, Caradoc simply smashed his heavy warpsteel shield into Vanik's shoulder, sending him stumbling out of his path.

The Varanguard was going directly for S'aai.

The prince regent tried to dodge back out of reach, but when it instead became obvious the Varanguard would charge him all the way to the wall, he sidestepped to the left. It was a moment of sublime grace, the aelf ducking beneath Caradoc's axe swing then sliding past the battering ram of the knight's shield. As he spun, his scimitar slashed down, and it seemed as though the blow, perfectly timed, would split Caradoc's skull.

But for all his brute strength and bulk, the Varanguard was almost as fast. As his charge brought him past S'aai, he lunged left, missing him with both axe and shield but ensuring the downward slash jarred off his helmet's crest rather than slice it in half. S'aai was left unbalanced, and that was all the opportunity Caradoc needed.

He smashed his shield into the aelf. The prince regent was

hurled back with a hideous crunch, slamming into the insanely wrought fireplace beyond his overturned chaise longue. While it was a blow that would have pulverised most mortals, S'aai recovered quickly, scrambling back to his feet, but he was not quick enough to escape either the flames that leapt from the disturbed ashes of the fire or the sawtoothed axe that came hurtling for his head.

'Blood-mad savage,' was all he was able to spit at Sir Caradoc before the blow landed. His skull left his shoulders, and the pale, toned skin of his naked upper body turned suddenly red as blood shot across the chamber. The decapitated torso swayed, as if it were still seeking to duck and weave out of harm's reach, before Caradoc thrust it contemptuously back into the open fireplace.

Caradoc bent and retrieved Saai's head, as the remaining daemonettes let up a chilling wail. They backed away from the Varanguard, hissing in distress and snapping their wicked claws. Their corporeal forms flickered, like a candle in a breeze, struggling to retain their grasp on material existence as whatever blessings the Lost God had once bestowed upon the Castellum of the Virtues started to unravel.

The konroi did not pause their assault. Vanik lowered his blade as the eight knights fought their way to the corners of the upstairs chamber, cutting down everything they found. Amidst it all though, Vanik could see no sign of Skoren. He doubted the rival pilgrim had stayed for long after laying his trap.

S'aai's herald, Shor'qual, was the last to die. It actually managed to strike a deep wound on one of the knights, ploughing its glaive into the warrior's guts. The Varanguard responded as though he had barely been pricked, disembowelling the lithe Slaaneshi warrior with one cleaving blow before wrenching the glaive free and tossing it scornfully to the floor.

As Shor'qual's corpse slumped, a sudden, terrible stillness descended. As one, the Varanguard konroi turned, in silence, to look at Vanik and the remains of the Eightguard.

'Sir Caradoc,' Vanik said, trying to keep his tone level. His heart was still hammering out the rapid rhythms of combat, and his grip on Nakali shook, as though he were wrestling to hold on to a writhing serpent.

'Have you come to kill me yourself?' he asked the Varanguard knight.

Sir Caradoc did not answer. Instead, he had reached down and picked up S'aai's severed head. Vanik expected Caradoc to tie the gore-slick hair around his belt, claiming it as a trophy, but instead he raised it in both hands to his lips. Then the knight bared his bestial teeth and, with a snarl, bit.

The other warriors seemed to take the sudden savagery as their signal to emulate it. They fell upon the corpses of S'aai's mortal warriors; unyielding, spiked gauntlets ripping apart their pale bodies in welters of corrupt blood. They sank their fangs into the torn flesh and meat, gorging themselves like animals, gore spattering their armour. Vanik couldn't keep a grimace from his face.

Caradoc wrenched away S'aai's face with great, vicious bites. Soon the head had been reduced to a glistening sphere of muscle and cartilage, Caradoc's gauntlets painted bright red.

The grisly feast continued for long minutes. The Eightguard gathered around Vanik, still wary of their apparent saviours.

'Do you not honour him by consuming his flesh?' Vanik asked.

'No,' Caradoc said bluntly, still swallowing. 'That is a common mistake. We consume the flesh of our enemies because in doing so it destroys them utterly. Victory cannot be won until the enemies of Archaon have been torn and ripped and crushed and burned to nothing. Anything less is no victory at all.'

'Are all knights of the Seventh Circle so base?'

Caradoc offered Vanik a bloody smile.

'Most.'

'Do you really believe such a display will convince me to turn from the Fifth?'

'No,' Caradoc grunted, swallowing another gobbet of S'aai's flesh.

'If you don't seek to convert me, and if you have not come here to kill me, then why are you here at all?'

The knight bared his teeth in a red smile.

'For the Varanguard, boy. For an oath long-sworn between my konroi and your mentor.'

'Karex sent you?'

'She did, after a fashion. We have followed you at a distance since you departed the Varanspire. For my own part, I prayed in blood that your path would take you to the Castellum of the Virtues. Long have I sought leave to butcher this pathetic nest of vice.'

'I am a pawn again in your games,' Vanik surmised. 'You will use me as an excuse, to explain why you have slaughtered an anointed servant of the Gods.'

'Your cynicism is couched in idiocy,' Caradoc responded, ripping away the last remains of S'aai's face, leaving only his bloody hair intact. 'How the Daemonflayer has not yet carved your skull from your spine is beyond me. Butchering S'aai was a joy, but our first task was to protect you.'

'So you still covet me for your lord Arken?'

'No, and we never did. Though she belongs to a different circle, Karex respects our order. She is a sister to us.'

'She tasked you with stopping me in the Varanspire?' Vanik said slowly, beginning to understand.

'She did. It was a test, another step on your pilgrimage. Had you accepted our offer and betrayed the Fifth Circle, I would have cut you down there and then. Praise the True Gods, but even you are not that much of an idiot.'

'I am a Scourge of Fate,' Vanik said firmly. 'I will never turn my back on the Fifth.'

'That is well,' Caradoc said, absent-mindedly tossing aside the torn remains of S'aai's head and shaking strings of gore from his serrated axe. 'All knights of the Fifth are sworn not to meddle in the quests of their own pilgrims, your mistress included. No such oath binds those of the other circles, though, at least not when one pilgrim is interfering in another's quest. She has renewed an old pact with my Bane Sons brethren to see you safe from the Varanspire. She expected treachery from your rival before you even left.'

'Zubaz,' Vanik said. 'He will stop at nothing in his thirst for advancement.'

'Perhaps,' Caradoc allowed. 'But enough of this. Servants of Khorne remain trapped in dishonourable bondage. Let us go and see what remains of your Bloodbound.'

Caradoc led the way back down the stairs to the castellum's entrance hall. Only there did the full extent of the Bane Sons' horrific, glorious proficiency with axe and shield become apparent.

The revelry of S'aai's mansion was most definitely at an end. After the whirling madness of the dance that Vanik had forced his way through, the totality of the stillness and silence was all the more shocking. The hallway was carpeted with corpses, semi-clad and drenched in gore. Blood had painted every surface of the chamber, coating the panelling, the paintings and tapestries, even drizzling down from the rafters. The bodies of the Slaaneshi revellers were indistinguishable, unrecognisable, a mulch of ripped meat and skin, opened organs and brain matter, half submerged in a flood of viscera. Vanik had seen the handiwork of the Varanguard before, but never had he encountered it in such a small, concentrated space. The charnel stench was almost overwhelming.

Several of Caradoc's knights followed him through a corridor to the left of the hall, and down a flight of stone steps. Here the bloodshed was less intense, though dismembered bodies still littered the floor, and the stink of blood and spilt innards was mixed with the sulphuric tang of banished daemonkin.

Vanik followed Caradoc down the steps, into candlelit shadow. He was still on edge, his thoughts running hot and angry over S'aai's betrayal, Skoren's presence and the trickery of the Varanguard. Once again it seemed as though he'd been plucked up by events and carried along, helpless to decide his own fate. For a warlord who had trodden the Path to Glory almost to completion, helplessness was an unnatural and disturbing concept. He would not be beholden to any other, man, God or daemon – and yet here he was, his life in the hands of this frenzy-knight, and Karex, and Lord Neveroth, and a Gaunt Summoner no less.

He tried to shrug off the toxic mix of anger and unease, tried to keep his thoughts in the present. Regardless of how it had happened, he'd still achieved his aim in coming to the castellum. All that remained was to find Ulek.

Caradoc seemed content to assist in that matter. The stone steps ended in a long, chill corridor of cut stone, crudely chiselled from the bedrock upon which the manse was sited. Bracketed torches illuminated half a dozen timber doors, set into the walls on either side. There were no signs of any guards or gaolers – those who had once inhabited S'aai's dreadhold had either fled or been killed already by Caradoc.

'He is here,' the blood-soaked Varanguard said, tapping one of the metal-studded doors with the edge of his axe. 'Can you smell his blood-greed?'

Vanik couldn't, but he didn't intend to question the brutal knight.

Caradoc stopped before the door and slammed his boot into its timber frame. It took three strikes, but finally the wood splintered around the lock, and the darkness of the cell within was revealed.

Now Vanik could smell the blood, even over the charnel reek coming down from the hall. He snatched one of the torches from its bracket and stepped inside.

The cell was barely big enough to stand in. Its floor was matted, rotten straw, old bones and indiscernible filth. The torchlight illuminated its only occupant, standing fastened to the far wall. His upper torso was a great mass of muscle and scar tissue, bare and streaked with blood from Slaaneshi runes that had been carved into his skin. His trunk-like arms were splayed to either side, pinned directly to the stone behind by metal nails that had been hammered into his flesh. His lower body was clad in plate armour – red-raw, banded with bronze and brass. His head was bowed, features obscured by a thick drape of greasy black hair, streaked with grey.

The figure didn't move as Vanik entered, followed by Caradoc, but he did speak, his voice a dry rasp.

'I thought the sounds of slaughter came from the Blood God's hounds, come to end my existence.'

'You are not far wrong,' Caradoc said. 'We are not Khorne's servants, though, but Archaon's.'

The figure looked up. His hair fell away from his face, revealing a bristling white-and-grey beard and eyes wild with the blood-forge fires of Khorne's furnace.

'Ulek,' Vanik said. The exalted deathbringer of Khorne did not respond to him. His mad gaze was on Caradoc.

'You are a knight of the Gods?' he asked slowly.

'I am Sir Caradoc of the Bane Sons, Varanguard of the Seventh Circle,' Caradoc replied.

'Kill me,' Ulek said.

'No.'

'I have failed my God,' Ulek snarled, baring his teeth at Caradoc. 'I have dishonoured him first with my defeat, and then by allowing the Lost God's slaves to mock me here, like this. I should have torn my arms from these nails and let the blood leave me as a final atonement.'

'Yet you did not,' Caradoc said, standing before Ulek. For all the size and strength of the deathbringer, he still appeared small compared to the armoured bulk of the Varanguard.

'If the shame was so great, why do you yet live?' Caradoc demanded.

'I was… commanded not to shed my own blood,' Ulek said, his dry voice equal parts shame and uncertainty.

'By what?'

'A vision.'

His burning gaze wandered to Vanik, and he started, as though only noticing him for the first time.

'Pilgrim,' he said, a degree of clarity returning to his gaze. 'So this is not a dream after all.'

'How do you know it isn't?' Vanik asked.

'Because you only appear when you want something, and what could you want with a madman or a corpse?'

'In a place like this, both have their value. But you are neither. I have come here seeking you for your sword arm.'

'The Red Path was gloriously refreshed when last we fought together,' the deathbringer admitted, his voice grudging. 'I will not bend my knee before you, pilgrim, but if you seek the butchering of the enemies of Khorne then we have common cause once more.'

'You owe me your freedom,' Vanik pointed out.

'Do I?' Ulek asked, eyes returning to Sir Caradoc. 'Or do I owe it to the Knight of Ruin?'

'Vanik has our favour,' Caradoc said. 'At least for now.'

'Then he also has my spear,' Ulek said. 'Warhound willing.'

'Why have you not pulled yourself free yet?' Vanik asked, looking at the nails that had been driven through Ulek's arms and into the wall at his back.

'Both nails sit beside a life-vein,' Ulek said. 'If I rip them free, they will rupture. Even if I broke from this cell, I would perish long before I left this mansion.'

'But now you are free,' Caradoc said. 'Prove your faith, Ulek. Atone for your failings by putting your trust in the great Warhound. If he has further uses for you, he will preserve you. If not, what use is living anyway? Offer him your blood.'

Ulek considered the Varanguard's words, then nodded. He tensed, his body like forged iron, and then, with one great roar, tore his arms free from the long nails holding him in place.

Fresh blood, red and vital, splattered the cell, and Ulek's lower arms were turned red. The deathbringer stood panting and trembling, his eyes ablaze once more, like a feral beast freed from its cage.

'Do any of them yet live?' he demanded. 'Any of the Lost God's cowards?'

'None within the walls of this place,' Vanik admitted. 'But if you seek blood to spill and flesh to rend, a whole forest awaits us outside.'

Ulek took a half-step to steady himself. Blood was still pulsing from his ripped arms, yet he made no effort to stymie it. Vanik knew there was no point in advising him to – every drop spilled, friend's or foe's, was a prayer to the Warhound for the servants of Khorne. It mattered not to them from where the blood flowed.

'My spear,' Ulek said. 'The bastard Slaaneshi took it from me when I was struck unconscious.'

'It is likely in S'aai's trophy room,' Vanik said. 'We will reclaim it.'

'What became of that cowering aelf?'

'I cut his head off,' Caradoc said.

Ulek growled.

'I prayed night and day that I could be the one to do so. Great Khorne is already punishing me.'

'There will be heads enough to cleave where we are bound,' Vanik said.

'Where?'

'Chamon. Did any of your Bloodsworn live through your last battle with S'aai?'

'If they did I would kill them myself,' Ulek said. His skin had gone deathly pale, but still he stood. There were few servants of the Four more resilient than the Blood God's brutes.

'You are less use to me without a warband, deathbringer,' Vanik said.

'I will bring others. Many have waited on the slaughtering of the castellum. News of it will bring fresh warriors to your black standard, pilgrim. Do not fear.'

'I fear nothing,' Vanik said. 'Bar you bleeding to death before we leave this accursed place. Come.'

They left the Castellum of the Virtues. Caradoc had returned upstairs before they departed and spread the flames from the upper chamber's hearth to the rest of the room. Black smoke was beginning to billow from the windows as they stepped out of the main doorway.

Vanik had expected to find Modred, Jarll and Forvin dead and the horses scattered or consumed by the forest. Instead they were all alive. At first, Vanik thought they'd been surrounded and hemmed in with the Eightguard's steeds by the snarling mounts of Caradoc's knights. Then he saw Tzatzo among the latter and realised that in fact the beasts were protecting the humans and horses from the forest beyond. It seemed Tzatzo was getting along with her fellow steeds for once. Their maws and claws were splattered with blood and ichor, and the flesh forest near to the doorway had been ripped apart, including the great trunks of muscle and bone that had stood either side of the entrance arch. The other steeds snarled as Vanik stepped out of the manse, but relented when Caradoc appeared at his side.

'W-we didn't know what to do,' Modred stammered, cringing in Vanik's shadow. 'The forest came for us, then the knights appeared, killing everything.'

'Bring Tzatzo,' Vanik ordered brusquely. 'Forvin, Jarll, lead Lanval's and Aktar's steeds. Ulek will take Ginesh's.'

'They are fallen, sire?' Forvin asked.

'They are. May the Eightstar guide their souls.'

'May it guide us out of here,' Kulthuk added darkly. The forest beyond the space shredded by the Varanguard's mounts was in a state of writhing pain, its screams seemingly connected to the fire slowly eating up the castellum.

'We cut our way in, and we shall cut our way out also,' Caradoc said, mounting his great warhound. He sounded pleased at the prospect. 'Keep your little knights close, pilgrim, and trust in the blessings of Archaon.'

PART NINE

THE THIRD EYE

'We thought you dead,' Jevcha said.

Vanik smiled, but the expression had little warmth.

'Did you, or only Mother Yogoth?'

'She prophesied,' Jevcha said, her tone uncertain.

'She lied,' Vanik replied simply. 'You have such little faith in me, sister.'

Jevcha did not respond. They stood side by side on the edge of the ruined shrine's hilltop, the warband's encampment spread beneath them. It had almost doubled in size since Vanik had ridden out for the castellum. Wagons, caravans and mobile warshrines stood in clusters around the standards and lodge poles of disparate tribes, and the air was hazed with the smoke of campfires and the tang of cooking meat, the musk of cattle and horses, and the stink of unwashed bodies.

'How many have come?' he asked.

'Five separate war parties,' Jevcha replied, her voice firm once more as the discussion turned to more certain ground.

'Their leaders are known?'

'They are. Each has been vouched for by one of your champions.'

'And did any of those champions believe Mother Yogoth's so-called prophecy?'

'You know which ones,' Jevcha said. Vanik laughed darkly.

'Were we not riding for war, I'd have them flayed and hung alive from the walls of this pathetic church.'

'I would do that regardless. They have no respect.'

'But that is why I lead this warband, Jevcha, and not you. I will take the blood-oaths of the new war parties tonight. Tomorrow we travel for the Third Eye.'

'We don't wait for more bands to join us? A Yekken scout rode into camp last night saying his kindred are three days' march away, and what of Ulek's Bloodbound?'

'If any more are to join us it will have to be on the march,' Vanik said. 'I have sent half a dozen of Faug's riders to tribes and warbands spoken of by Ulek. They have instructions to make for the Third Eye and await us there. If we arrive before them, what we have will need to be enough.'

He could sense disagreement from the warqueen, but she mastered herself, looking away from Vanik and out across the sprawling camp.

'There are tensions,' she said. 'Between the new war parties and the old. Between some of the champions.'

'Champions who doubt my abilities to lead them into favoured battle,' Vanik surmised. 'Who think we will sit here for weeks more, consuming our cattle, draining the well dry, boring the Gods with our indolence. They are imbeciles, but I would expect nothing less from them. That is half the reason we must strike camp and make for the Third Eye tomorrow. No warband of this size can stay idle without tearing itself apart.'

'The Knights of Ruin will quell doubts, for now,' Jevcha added.

Sir Caradoc and his knights had remained with the warband since carving a path out of S'aai's warped fiefdom, vowing to guard Vanik from any retaliation from the servants of the Lost God until the Black Pilgrim crossed over into the Realm of Metal. Their presence had inspired equal awe and fear among the gathering horde – scarred warriors, bearing the visible blessings of the Gods, cringed away when they passed, or paled visibly at the snarling of their hound mounts. They remained on the edge of the encampment, keeping their own counsel. Vanik had not spoken with them since he had returned.

'The Bane Sons will do as they wish,' he said. 'I owe them nothing. Karex sent them.'

The two lapsed into silence. Evening was drawing on, a great, baleful crimson orb – the blood moon – rising into the darkening firmament, throwing a ruddy golden light across the plains and deepening the shadows cast by the shrine's ruins. A tusker somewhere in the camp below bellowed as it was slaughtered, fresh meat for the cooking pits. Vanik realised he hadn't eaten for days. His hunger seemed like a distant concern now. Mortal needs felt as though they were slipping away. That, he thought, was a blessing indeed.

'I did not believe her,' Jevcha said abruptly. 'Yogoth. But every time you ride, I feel as though the Gods themselves are telling me I will not see you again. It is as though you tempt their hand with each new quest. How long before they grow bored with the odds you give them?'

He turned to look at her, frowning slightly. The sunset gave her an even more fierce appearance, her red hair like flame, the bloody light glinting from the jagged edges of her war crown and the runeshield strapped across her back. Her gaze smouldered with the same quick, cunning gleam Vanik knew his own eyes possessed.

'Would you mourn if I did not return?' he asked her.

'No,' she said, and there was honesty in her voice. 'All is as the Four will. But nor do I wish to see you fail. I would not have you become just another heap of rusting armour and bones, strewn somewhere in the wastes.'

Vanik said nothing for a while. Then he shook his head. 'I must pray. Return to your people, warqueen, and see they are ready. The road to the Realmgate will not be short.'

Jevcha bowed and made the sign of the Eightstar. Then, without speaking, she left. Vanik waited until she was gone down the slope and was back in amongst the encampment's crowds before turning his back. He paced into the long, deepening shadows of the old shrine, boots grating on broken stone. He let the darkness swallow him, and only then, when he knew there were no mortal eyes on him, did he allow himself to slump against a shattered pillar.

He had to keep going. He had come so far. He had sacrificed so much. Kindred slain, warbands abandoned, honour and glory spurned. Still the final victory seemed so distant, so unreachable, like one of the Inevitable Citadel's damnable endless corridors.

You will never be a Knight of Ruin, Nakali hissed. He did not have the strength to reply.

He had seen death in the darkling gaze of Lord Neveroth, when the Fifth Marshal had sat in judgement. He had seen it again when the flesh forest had closed in around him, and when he had stood before S'aai, surrounded and betrayed. He had seen it when Caradoc's relentless butchers had killed everyone. He was a warrior and a champion of the Eightfold, far advanced along the Path to Glory, but he knew he could not match what he had seen the Varanguard do. He was like a child before them, and that weakness – the thing he despised more than anything – ate away within. He feared it, though it took long seconds in the broken shrine's silence to admit it.

'Another heap of rusting armour and bones, strewn somewhere in the wastes,' he repeated quietly.

She speaks the truth. That is your fate, and nothing you can do will deny it, little pilgrim.

'*Truth*,' he snarled aloud. 'I am surprised you know the word, serpent.'

A thud followed his words, then another. He realised that he could hear a drumbeat, distant, its tempo steadily rising. It was joined by another playing counterpoint. Shouts and roars followed. He snarled with rage, wrenching himself from the shadows and striding out onto the shrine's slope.

Silence and solitude were never gifts the Gods granted for long.

'Modred,' he snapped. His retainer was sat on a moss-covered stone just beyond the shrine's broken archway, separate as usual from the Eightguard nearby, gnawing on the cooked wing of a fowl. He started as Vanik appeared, almost falling from his perch as he scrambled to stand and swallow his last mouthful at the same time.

'Sire,' he stammered, mouth still half full.

'What is happening?' the pilgrim demanded, glaring at the encampment below. 'If Moll has challenged another of the newcomers I swear by Archaon's third eye that I will skin him myself.'

A look of confusion crossed Modred's face, one which Vanik recognised. He'd missed something, and the boy was too afraid to point it out to him.

'Speak,' he barked.

'The oath-binding, sire,' the retainer stammered. 'You had commanded it for tonight. The war parties are preparing themselves.'

Vanik's anger cooled. Of course. The new warrior bands were gathering at the foot of the shrine's slope, preparing to swear themselves to his black banner. His own exhaustion was making him forgetful.

The drumbeats and the chanting below intensified, swelling into a roar as the old war parties joined in with the new. Vanik felt his spirits rekindle, and a smile ghosted across his thin lips.

He was a champion of the True Gods, and more than that, a Black Pilgrim. A swelling warband awaited his command, eager to do as he willed. He need but strike.

'Come,' he said, handing Modred his helm to carry. 'Summon the Eightguard, and have Kulthuk unfurl the banner. It is time to take the allegiance of the host.'

It took three and a half weeks, as Vanik counted it, to reach the Realmgate known as the Third Eye. In the Chaos-blessed landscape of the Eightpoints, it may only have been a few days, or perhaps it was a lifetime – it certainly felt like the latter to Vanik. He urged speed, but there was only so much haste even a modest warband could display. Each night, as he sought sleep, he considered taking just Faug's cavalry, Sir Caradoc's knights and the Eightguard and riding ahead. He suggested it twice to Caradoc. Both times the knight shrugged his thoughts and half-questions off.

'It is your warband, pilgrim,' he said. 'And your quest.' The Varanguard remained aloof in general, eating beyond the fires of the main encampment each night and riding forward in the vanguard each day. Vanik's followers, warriors and camp folk alike, stayed clear of them, though Renki's warhounds seemed to share a kinship with the Varanguard's terrible mounts. They would lope ahead with them each day, and howl mournfully whenever Renki demanded their obedience.

Vanik stayed with the main host. As much as he wished to leave the trundling caravan of carts and wagons behind, he knew that to do so would be an act of foolishness. He had assembled such a force for a reason; he would not abandon his plans by riding into the lands of their enemies without his full strength. Besides, the disparate war parties had yet to settle alongside one another. Despite the blood-oaths they had sworn on the slopes of the broken shrine, every night scraps and brawls broke out, usually between bands of newly arrived warriors not yet accepting of one another's customs and practices. Vanik had Kulthuk conduct executions each daybreak, the corpses left behind for the carrion. He'd threatened more painful measures if the unrest continued.

He knew that in truth the simmering violence was not necessarily a bad thing. They were all hungry, hungry with the battle-lust that had first drawn them to Vanik's banner. In his experience, a warband that was not fractious had no spirit, and no purpose.

After the first week another war party caught up with them. They were Kileki mountain tribesmen, a hardy, stout breed of warriors with distinctive stylised maw tattoos encircling their heads and arms. They brought with them two ogors, lumbering, squinting beasts with crooked noses and broken teeth. They had heard word of the Black Pilgrim's quest, their leader, a huge man named Tach'ach, told Vanik. They had heard, too, of the rich plunder to be had beyond the Third Eye. Vanik took the mountain champion's blood-oath, and accepted his party into the warband.

Tach'ach, according to the rumours that quickly filled the camp, was half-ogor himself. Vanik had to kill two of Dravga's corsairs the first night after the Kileki had joined, both guilty of attempting to start a fight with the mountain ogors.

There had been a third offending corsair, but apparently he'd been eaten.

Besides the arrival of the Kileki, they encountered few other travellers on the road to the Realmgate. This part of the Eight-points was barren, far from the main gates that lay near the Varanspire and the vast hordes and armies that travelled between them.

Red Steppe outriders sighted the Third Eye just after dawn on the twenty-fifth day since the warband had broken camp around the hilltop shrine. It was as Vanik had heard it described – three stone arches atop a rocky knoll, fashioned like lidless eyes, the third greater than its two sisters.

There was also, according to Faug's scouts, a battle raging around them.

Vanik mounted Tzatzo and took her, the Eightguard and Caradoc's konroi on ahead, while Jevcha took over leadership of the main column.

'Past this next ridge, lord-hetman,' the rider who had first made the discovery told Vanik, motioning up the rocky slope. The land had become ever more bleak the further they had pro-gressed, a tundra of baked stone and dead, dusty valleys. It was not the Gods-blessed desolation of the Chaos Wastes – there were no shrines, no sacred battlefields, no spawn or rival champions to test the favour of the Four against. The barren lands here were beyond the attention of any God or daemon, abandoned by all.

All except the warriors that fought one another beneath the gaze of the Third Eye and her siblings. Vanik saw them as Tza-tzo crested the rise, and saw the Realmgate on its knoll laid out below.

The melee was a general swirl of carnage, any order or

formation indiscernible amidst the heaving mass of bodies. Burly warriors hacked and beat one another with axes and maces, the clatter of steel and the screams of the dying rising up to Vanik. He spent a few seconds surveying the scene, then snapped to Aramor, his herald.

'Ride back and bring Ulek here, now.' Then, without waiting for a response, he touched his heels to Tzatzo's flanks.

'Sire?' Modred called after him, uncertain whether or not the retinue was supposed to follow or not. Vanik ignored them. Instead, he drew Nakali and rode hard for the edge of the battle.

'Bloodbound!' he roared, Tzatzo adding her shriek to his voice. 'Cease!'

The two nearest warriors broke apart, stumbling back from one another as they turned towards Vanik. Both were wounded, sheeted in blood. He stopped a dozen yards short of the combat, Nakali held high.

'In the name of your Blood God, cease!' he shouted with all his strength.

Slowly, the melee began to break apart. Warriors who had been hacking and cleaving one another to pieces just moments earlier tore themselves away or were ripped back by others. The frenzy fell apart in a heartbeat, to be replaced by a cold, dripping quiet, punctuated only by the moans of the wounded.

The Eightguard thundered up behind Vanik, hurrying to defend their lord. He waved them back irritably, then pointed Nakali at one of the two nearest warriors.

'You! Who are you, and who do you serve?'

'Golman, of the Brazen Skull,' the Bloodbound said. He wore a horned crimson helm and greaves, but his torso and arms were bared, the thick, scarred muscles slashed with blood from half a dozen cuts.

'And you?' Vanik demanded of the other. He was taller and

leaner, his skin white as corpseflesh, clad in rough pelts and scale hides.

'I do not know my name,' the warrior admitted, his accent thick and harsh. 'But I serve the Rawhide, great Vjalmir.'

'And why do the Brazen Skull and the Rawhide fight in this forgotten place? You would not have ceased at my command were it over a deserving matter.'

'We fight for sport, and to keep great Kharneth's favour,' a new voice said. The warriors close to Vanik parted, and the taller of the two directly in front of him fell to his knees before a towering, gaunt man. Like the one kneeling, he was white-skinned and draped in heavy furs, sticky with freshly spilled blood. A long, slender axe was grasped in one hand. His eyes, sunk deep into the sockets of his deathly face, were like ice, and his lips had been twisted into a skull-like grimace by ritual scarring.

'We did not know how long it would be before you came, Black Pilgrim,' the man continued.

'Well, I am here now,' Vanik said. 'You do no service to Khorne by carrying on your feuding.'

'All blood spilled is service to great Kharneth,' the pale warrior snarled.

'Not while there are servants of the Lightning God to be slaughtered,' Vanik said, pointing Nakali towards the Third Eye. 'Beyond the gate.'

'It is inactive,' the pale warrior said.

'Not for long. Clean your blades and stand ready.'

'Where is Ulek?' the pale one demanded, ignoring Vanik's words. 'Your rider swore the deathbringer was pledged to your host? Yet all I see are a few knights cowering behind their black armour.'

Vanik began to snap back a retort, but the drumming of

hooves on the stony earth stopped him. Aramor had returned, and he rode alongside Ulek.

'Here is your deathbringer,' Vanik said, gesturing at the Blood-bound as he dismounted before the pale warrior and untied his great spear from his back.

'Vjalmir,' Ulek snarled, striding forward.

With a scream, the pale warrior swung his long axe for Ulek's head.

Vanik was too slow to intervene, but he didn't need to – with a speed belying his size, Ulek's spear swept round to knock the blow aside. There was a clang of daemon-forged steel, and the Bloodbound's axe flew from his grasp, embedding itself in the stony earth at Ulek's feet. The deathbringer's spear tip quivered, an inch from the pale one's throat. The warrior froze, though he trembled, as if having to resist the urge to thrust forward and decapitate himself in a bout of bloody madness.

'Did you truly think you could claim my skull so easily, Vjalmir?' Ulek growled, his own arm shaking, eyes blazing behind the greasy strands of his grey-shot hair.

'You would have me yield without any test?' Vjalmir responded, his throat pressing up against the spear's notched edge. Ulek seemed to consider the answer before, slowly, lowering the weapon.

'No,' he said. Vjalmir let out the slightest groan, as though disappointed to feel the spear's wicked kiss leave the bare flesh of his throat.

'Submit,' Ulek ordered. Vjalmir fell to his knees before the deathbringer without hesitation. Ulek sneered.

'Not to me, you oaf,' he said, gesturing at Vanik. 'Him. He is your oath-lord now.'

Vjalmir inclined his head to the ground before Vanik, crouched double in the dirt. One by one, the rest of the Bloodbound around the Third Eye did likewise, their weapons lowered. Vanik cast his gaze over them, and nodded.

'We go beyond the Eye,' he said, his tone terse. 'You will serve Ulek as he serves me – without question. If you do not, I will see your skulls crushed and your blood used to water my cattle. If you do, you will find slaughter in abundance.'

There were no cheers for his words. He did not expect any. He had passed beyond mortal plaudits.

'Bring up the rest of the warband,' he ordered Kulthuk, as the Bloodbound began to make their oath in rasping, bestial voices. 'And prepare to ignite the Realmgate.'

The Third Eye came alive as Neveroth had said, with the strike of warpsteel against stone.

It ignited like a furnace, the empty space beneath its stone arch transformed into a roiling wall of white heat. The gateway throbbed and resounded with a roar like the striking of hundreds of hammers on anvils.

'At last,' Vanik murmured, a gauntlet raised against the forge-glow of the Realmgate. Beyond lay Chamon, the Realm of Metal and, if the Gaunt Summoner's words and visions were to be believed, the soft lands ruled over by Castellan Albermarl and the mountain city of Helmgard.

'This is where we part ways, pilgrim,' Sir Caradoc said, his konroi mustered behind him. 'To go further than this would be to meddle. May the Three-Eyed King watch over your path.'

'I hope someday to call you brother, Bane Son,' Vanik said, inclining his head to the Varanguard. Caradoc merely grunted, and turned his bestial mount away.

Vanik looked back to the portal. A multitude of doubts assailed him as he coaxed Tzatzo towards the gate, plucking at his thoughts like daemonic furies. What if Skoren had already passed through and tampered with the Realmgate? Worse, what if he passed over to find Helmgard already a burning necropolis and Albermarl slain by the Blackhand? What if Kar'gek'kell had misled him, and this was not the Realmgate he sought? What if the white heat cooked his armour and seared his flesh from his bones?

Tzatzo shied away from the blazing gateway, her dislike of the Realmgate only feeding Vanik's apprehension. He forced himself to dig his spurs in, to not glance back at his retinue or the warband gathered around the knoll with eyes wide and grips tight on their weapons. He would not show weakness. It was beneath him now.

Regardless of the gateway's nature, he was damned if he did not pass through.

'Come, Tzatzo,' he murmured, leaning low over his mount's neck so she could hear him over the ceaseless pounding of the gateway's unseen hammerers. 'All to gain and nothing to be lost. Ride.'

The Chaos steed shrilled and finally obeyed the spurs that dug at her scaled flanks. She sprang forward over the rocky, heat-blasted threshold and into the crackling iris.

The furnace engulfed Vanik. He drew breath to cry out, but could not – scalding heat invaded his body, and agony gripped him, as though molten metal were being poured down his throat. The white brilliance of the forge blinded him, and with his final thoughts he damned his quest, damned the Gods themselves for leading him to this simpleton's end.

Then, as though in answer, the heat was gone. The white light remained, burning away his sight, but the infernal temperature was suddenly only a memory. Tzatzo's claws were no longer clacking on rock, but swishing through long grass, and he could feel a breeze on his face. Finally, his vision started to return, blotches of white light still flaring across the scene that slowly resolved before him.

He was riding through a small, grassy valley, green beneath Hysh's light, the air heavy with pollen and dancing mayflies.

He pulled Tzatzo to a stop and ripped Nakali from its scabbard, snarling. It was a trap. It had to be. He turned his steed in a sharp circle, searching the long grass for creeping assassins, the valley sides for archers. But there were none. He looked back the way he had come. There, half lost amidst lichens and tall grass, the twins of the Third Eye stood, the central stone's core radiating the same furnace heat it had displayed on the other side.

He was through. The ancient Realmgate hadn't been a trap after all. The realisation, coupled with the unbidden relief, almost made him laugh aloud. He controlled the pathetic impulse.

'I should not have doubted you,' he said, looking to the azure heavens. 'I should not have doubted the Path. Gods forgive me.'

The Third Eye flared, and the tranquillity of the green valley was shattered by the neighing of horses and the clatter of armour as more figures burst through the portal. The Eightguard came first, the breeze snatching at Kulthuk's banner. They tore from the Realmgate as though the flesh hounds of Khorne themselves were pursuing them, scattering in confusion while they struggled through the same furnace-like experience of the gateway that Vanik had.

After them came Faug's steppe outriders. By that time the Eightguard had overcome the after-effects of the Realmgate's passage. They closed around Vanik, their weapons drawn. Still, however, no enemies presented themselves.

'Yovich, ride to the head of the valley – find out if we truly are alone,' Vanik ordered. The Chaos knight spurred off, while Vanik waited for Faug and his blinded horsemen to collect themselves.

He had grown accustomed to difficulty in everything he did. Such was life on the Path, and doubly so for one who had taken the vows of a Black Pilgrim. He had expected the Realmgate to burn his body and soul to ash, or if it did not, to be pitched out into the midst of a mortal host, posted to guard their lands from the servants of the True Gods. The quiet, fertile valley at the height of a summer season was the last thing he had anticipated.

Yovich returned. He had removed his helm, and his broad, dusky features and shaven skull were beaded with sweat.

'Nothing, sire,' he reported. 'Only smoke rising across the hills in that direction.' He pointed with his gauntlet. 'There seemed to be enough for a settlement, or perhaps a large encampment.'

'Faug!' Vanik called, summoning the steppe hetman. He'd been riding back and forth across the valley, collecting his scattered outriders as their vision returned and they came to their senses.

'Send scouts in all directions,' he ordered. 'And a rider back through the Realmgate. Tell Jevcha the Third Eye is secure. Bring the rest of the warband through.'

Faug made the sign of the Eightstar and started snapping orders to his tribesmen. Vanik turned back towards the valley. He realised he was smiling.

Once more the Mortal Realms lay before him, ripe for the attention of the favoured. Even better, there was no sign of Skoren. Despite his treachery, it appeared that the Blackhand had fallen behind. The realisation sent a surge of fresh determination through Vanik. He swore that by the time he reached Chamon, Zubaz's cur would find nothing but ashes.

PART TEN

CHAMON AFLAME

'Lord Ordinator? Lord Ordinator?'

The words brought him back. Too sharp, too hard. He gasped, his fists clenched, flinching as brilliant light invaded the darkness he had inhabited for so long. For a moment, he thought the heavens themselves were bursting and coming apart in their unassailable radiance, the simultaneous birth and death of a hundred million stars creating a kaleidoscope of infinite possibilities that shattered before him.

But he was mistaken. The constellations surrounding him disintegrated, replaced by the clear, bright light of the mountains. Hysh was high above the Ironroot peaks, beaming its illumination through the great telescopic lenses and mirror shields of Helmgard's star dome.

Marius, Lord Ordinator of the Celestial Knights, realised he had fallen to his knees. His orrery assistant, Matthias, was kneeling at his side in his dark blue, star-spangled robes, his aged face riven with concern.

'My lord,' he said, tentatively laying a hand on Marius' broad shoulder.

A shiver passed through the heavyset Stormcast Eternal as he remembered what he had seen. He accepted Matthias' help, the assistant bending double as he helped his master regain his feet.

Marius looked around. He stood at the centre of the star dome, his living quarters and seeing chamber, nestled amidst the craggy peaks of Helmgard's pinnacle. Around him was the grand orrery mechanism, a great device of arching brass orbit-lines and shimmerglass globes set into the clockwork mechanism that constituted the chamber's floor. The device, handcrafted by Marius when he had first risen from his apprenticeship to the position of Ordinator within the Celestial Knights Sacrosanct Chamber, mapped the movement of the Mortal Realms and the heavenly firmament. It was crucial to his divinations, providing him with point and reference in the difficult art of foretelling the future through the secrets of the stars. And now it was broken.

The cog plates he had been standing on were buckled and scorched as though by fire, and the closest orbit-lines of the great planetarium were bent out of shape. Smoke was rising from the whole mechanism, coiling languidly towards the ceiling arches. Even worse, a crack had appeared on the viewing lens of his celestial vision glass, the great telescopic device that stretched up and out of the main viewing port of the dome.

'Something tried to come back,' he murmured, rubbing his hand against his temples. His skull ached, and he shivered again. 'Something tried to come back with me.'

'From… the dark place?' Matthias whispered, eyes wide in the Stormcast's shadow. Marius nodded.

'We are being watched, studied by a creature of the Great Changer. A being whose power is matched only by its desire to inflict evil.'

It was Matthias' turn to shiver.

For weeks now the Lord Ordinator's visions had been disturbed, riven by unhallowed portents and the presence of foreboding figures. The tendrils of Chaos were stretching out over this part of Chamon again for the first time in many decades. Less than a month ago he had suffered a waking vision, and seen a dark daemon-champion stood within the very walls of Helmgard's high council chamber. While the apparition seemed to have been visible only to him, he could stand by no longer. Today he had resolved to star-walk, to travel the lightning paths and follow the solar energies to espy what was coming, try to divine some pattern, some warning, amidst the heavenly bodies he had spent his life reading.

It had not been as he had feared. It had been worse.

'The servants of the Dark Gods are abroad once more,' Marius said, gripping his arcanabulum and striding towards the sigil-warded door to the star chamber.

'Where are you going, lord?' Matthias asked, stumbling after his master.

'To the castellan,' Marius said, without turning back. 'He must be warned. The Varanguard are here.'

It began as Vanik intended it to go on – with fire and death. Faug's horsemen scouted a village four leagues from the old Realmgate a little after what Vanik assumed was midday. Some of the labourers working in the surrounding fields spotted the horsemen on the horizon, but didn't seem to think enough of it to run and tell the rest of the village. The people living within Castellan Albermarl's fiefdom had been strangers to war for years, since the last great Chaos invasion had been thrown back from Helmgard's peak-walls. The servants of the Dark Gods had been all but relegated to fishwives' tales and the ramblings of old beggars.

Vanik relished the thought of changing that. He sat upon Tzatzo, beneath the black banner and surrounded by the armoured phalanx of the Eightguard, watching from a grassy knoll as Faug's horsemen rode, shrieking, down upon the hamlet. It was little more than a dozen wattle-and-thatch dwellings, surrounded by a blanket of slowly ripening fields and clustered around a low, rickety shrine-place. It would do though, for a beginning.

The warband's marauding horsemen cut down those in the fields as they tried to flee towards their homesteads, and then took the killing on into the buildings. Doors were kicked in and torches were struck and thrust into thatch. The screaming drifted up to Vanik on the warm afternoon breeze, soon joined by the crackle of flames and the scent of burning.

He glanced over his shoulder, back in the direction of the Realmgate. The foot-bands were coming up, Jevcha's Darkoath at their fore, tramping beneath their banners and icons up over the rise and down towards the burning hamlet. Vanik could tell from the sullen expressions that none were pleased that Faug's riders had claimed first blood for the Gods, and first spoils from the village. Vanik didn't care for his infantry's displeasure – their time would come soon enough, and they knew it.

Vanik had ordered prisoners to be taken. As smoke from the hamlet began to billow more thickly, Faug and two of his horsemen returned from the village, dragging a man behind their mounts.

'He tried to bar us from the shrine,' Faug said, after dismounting and kneeling briefly in the dirt before Vanik. The hetman gestured, and his two riders hauled the man forward.

'I think he is a priest,' Faug added, sneering at him.

Vanik looked down at the prisoner. He was young, though it took a moment to realise it. A thick, bushy beard and unkempt hair obscured much of his face, and his eyes – glimpsed in that second he dared snatch a glance up at Vanik – were blue. He wore simple robes that had probably once been off-white, but were now torn and encrusted with dirt where he had fallen and been hauled along behind Faug's horses. His knees and elbows were bloodstained, and he was shaking violently.

Vanik dismounted. Faug snatched the priest and forced him roughly to his knees.

'What is your name?' Vanik asked.

The man stared at the ground.

'Answer the pilgrim!' Faug barked, cuffing him around the back of the head. He whimpered and said something. It didn't sound like a name.

'You know their tongue?' Vanik demanded of Faug. The hetman shrugged.

'I have never been to Chamon before today, lord. Besides, most of these human tongues sound like spawn gibber to me.'

Vanik sighed and motioned to Modred.

'Ride back to the camp folk, find Mother Yogoth and bring her here.'

Despite his usual subservience, Modred hesitated.

'Tell her I will splinter that walking stick of hers if she does not come,' Vanik added. 'Or feed her to Renki's dogs. Something like that. Go.'

Modred rode off on his nag. Vanik watched the prisoner for a while. He seemed uncertain about what was going on, casting occasional, furtive glances around, but never up at Vanik. He tried to appreciate the terror that was making the man quake in the Red Steppe tribesmen's grasp, but found he could not. All he saw was weakness, and it disgusted him.

'There is food in the village?' he asked Faug, turning his attention to the hetman.

'Some,' he responded.

'Some that your riders haven't yet eaten or stuffed into their saddlebags?'

'Some,' Faug repeated. 'There was a small granary, but this close to harvest it was not over-full. We've corralled livestock, but not many. This is a poor place.'

'There will be richer pickings to come,' Vanik said. 'Far richer. But we need enough food for the entire warband before we reach them.'

'Of course, lord,' Faug said. 'Do not be concerned. My outriders will have found half a dozen more places like this by tomorrow night. We will all eat well.'

'The shrine still stands?' Vanik asked, changing the subject.

'It does. Guri and Molkai are drawing water from the village well to ensure the flames do not spread to it.'

'Good,' Vanik responded.

At length, the thump of hooves announced Modred's return. He bore Mother Yogoth in front of him, bouncing like a half-empty sack of meat, her expression as wrathful as that of the Blood God himself.

'I cannot get down,' the crone announced shrilly as Modred brought his blowing mount to a stop. 'You will have to lift me down, Vanik.'

'If I butcher the horse and it collapses, what will you do?' Vanik demanded. Yogoth glared at him, but said nothing. She made a great show of dismounting unsteadily after Modred, shaking and groaning loudly. Vanik waited.

'Why?' she demanded as she finally found the ground and hobbled over, leaning on her stave. 'Why have you dragged an old woman from the slender comforts of the wagons to be with you and your mad warriors? It stinks of burning up here.'

'I need you to speak,' Vanik said brusquely, trying to keep his impatience at bay. Yogoth sneered.

'Speak? All you ever do is demand my silence, you brute. What strange irony have the True Gods forced upon you now?'

'You've travelled far throughout the Mortal Realms, crone,' Vanik said, pointing at the priest. 'Do you speak the tongue of these people?'

Mother Yogoth peered at the prisoner with her rheumy eyes, apparently noticing him for the first time.

'By the Changer's fins, where did you drag him from?' she demanded.

'The village,' Vanik said. 'Speak to him.'

Yogoth hobbled over to the prisoner, waving Vanik to one side. The man dared snatch a glance, and shuddered when he saw the old crone leering over him.

'Young, for one of the lightning priests,' Yogoth said, her age-ravaged face contorting in a rictus of a toothless grin. The next words she spoke, Vanik didn't understand.

The priest didn't react beyond a slight frown. Mother Yogoth's grin became a scowl. She said something else, the words sounding different this time to Vanik's ear. The priest cringed, but still stayed silent.

Leaning heavily on her stave, bony limbs shaking, Yogoth lowered herself almost to the priest's ear, the man's face contorting with disgust as her pestilential stench engulfed him. She murmured something. Finally, the priest responded, garbling a few hasty words back. Yogoth let out a screech of laughter and stood back up.

'What did you say to him?' Vanik demanded.

'I told him if he did not speak with me you would give him over to me as my new lover,' she said, leering down at the priest.

'You are a vile creature, Mother Yogoth.'

'And you are five short steps from spawndom, you pathetic excuse for a champion of the Gods.'

'I need you to question him,' Vanik said, fighting down the impulse to strike the old woman. 'And I need answers.'

'Why should I?' Yogoth demanded, her petulance returning.

Vanik drew Nakali. The sudden rasping of the barbed, black sword from its scabbard made Yogoth stumble backwards, her eyes wide. It took a few seconds for her to recover her veneer of matronly disdain.

You hate her, Nakali whispered, its voice filled with humour. *Let me rend her soul for you, Vanik.*

'Do you want to taste daemonsteel, witch?' Vanik snarled, ignoring his blade's suggestion. 'Someone is about to, so pray that it isn't you!'

The priest had begun whimpering. Yogoth glared at Vanik, but clearly thought better about another outburst.

'What do you want to say then, pilgrim?'

'Ask him his name, and the name of this place.'

Yogoth bent over the priest once more and spat a string of indecipherable words. The priest stammered a response, his eyes locked on Nakali, like a man facing down a coiling serpent, too afraid to move.

'His name is Egmund, and this village is called Anvilum. Or it was, before you torched it. He is a priest of Sigmar.' She spat the last word.

'Ask him the direction and distance to the nearest town. Ask him how large the garrison is.'

Yogoth snapped something at the priest. His reply made her cackle again.

'He says he will not tell you,' she said to Vanik. 'He says we are the spawn of daemons and madmen. I told him he is not wrong.'

'I threaten you often, do I not, Mother Yogoth?' Vanik said. 'Use some of those threats, and tell him what will happen to him if he does not yield the information I desire.'

Yogoth spoke to the priest again, this time rapping her stave on his shoulder for emphasis. The man appeared close to tears. Eventually he spoke.

'North,' Yogoth said. 'A day and a half's ride. It is a place called Ferrium. He says the garrison is strong, over a hundred Freeguild soldiers. He says they will be here soon to investigate the fires.'

'Tell him I pray to the Eightstar that he is correct,' Vanik said. 'And ask him who his lord is. Who controls these lands?'

The priest replied to Yogoth with just one word, a word Vanik didn't need translating.

'Albermarl.'

'Where is Albermarl?' Vanik demanded.

'He claims he does not know,' Yogoth said, smacking her stave into the quivering priest once more. 'He says he assumes in Helmgard, but he has not been there for nearly three years. He is a simple parish priest and bookseller.'

'One more thing then, Mother Yogoth,' Vanik said. 'Ask him how he wants to die?'

The priest gritted his teeth, clearly trying to master his shaking body. Yogoth answered Vanik while he was still speaking.

'He is calling curses down upon us all with his prayers,' she said. Faug made the sign of the Eightstar across his chest, four fingers from each hand interlocked. Vanik laughed.

'On his feet,' he ordered the two steppe riders holding the priest. They dragged him up. The man's prayers faltered, the words dying in his throat like the ash on the wind as he found himself staring up at Vanik. The pilgrim again wondered what the man saw. His doom, surely.

He held out Nakali, and the priest whimpered.

'You were my bargaining price at the castellum, and I said I would reward you,' Vanik declared, addressing Nakali out loud. The priest's wide eyes darted from Vanik to the blade, confusion warring with terror on his face.

You lied, Nakali hissed, the daemon's tone surly.

'I didn't,' Vanik said. 'Your kind love the blood of innocents, do you not?'

The daemon only hissed louder.

'Well, here is one,' Vanik continued.

The priest seemed to have finally grasped what was about to happen. With a strangled cry, he managed to twist his scrawny body free and throw himself desperately at Vanik.

He snarled and thrust Nakali into the oncoming priest, the man screaming as the daemon sunk its serpent's fangs into his soul and began to feed.

He forced Nakali to drink slowly. The priest struggled against him, but slowly the screams died. The man's eyes had rolled back, and his breaths now came in pained rasps. After a while even Mother Yogoth turned away.

Nakali took its time, savouring the man's essence. Vanik wondered how much of the desire to cleave the human apart was his own, and how much belonged to Nakali. A bound daemon was at its most dangerous when its will blended with that of its master, rather than simply resisted it.

He pulled the sword free, teeth gritted against the resistance the daemon offered.

'Enough,' he growled. 'You've had your fill. And you will have more, much more, if you cut swift and true for me next time I wield you.'

I am not one of your dolt warrior-servants, to be bribed and cajoled, the daemon responded, but Vanik could tell from its heavy tone that it had enjoyed itself. It was still recovering. Even better, it knew that he now understood its weakness.

'Bribery and cajoling are the essence of our faith, daemon,' Vanik responded. 'And, sometimes, brute force. You are an immortal creature, so I'm sure you can appreciate so simple a solution. Serve me, or suffer.'

The daemon said nothing, but Vanik could feel its slow acquiescence, pulsing up through his palm. He sheathed it.

'It is time to move on,' he said, addressing the retinue. 'Faug, send your vanguard forward to the next village, and circle the column. Watch for other settlements, or stragglers from the foot-bands.'

'Should I seek a place to encamp too, lord?' the hetman asked.

'Not until you have torched the next settlement. We cannot afford any delay.'

'Yes, lord.'

'Disembowel all the bodies below and leave them inside the shrine,' Vanik said, indicating the burning hamlet with Naka-li's tip, then dropping it to point at the priest's drained husk lying at his feet. 'Then nail this one to the front doors. Let us make sure all know that the Lightning God has no power here. Not any more.'

'Yes, lord.'

The corpse of the man named Egmund was strapped over the back of Faug's saddle. As the horsemen rode back down to the burning village, Vanik allowed his eyes to wander over the landscape beyond. The hills were rolling and gentle, and the countryside green and gold with a ripening summer harvest. This was a fertile corner of Chamon, watched over by the Lightning God's minions and forgotten by the armies that waged war elsewhere throughout the Mortal Realms.

Peace made men rich and fat, and rich, fat men were easy pickings for Vanik's warband. News of the slaughter would spread, and more warriors of the True Gods would come. Then there would be a reckoning. Vanik's eyes focused on the mountain peaks, visible as a jagged outline against the blue sky, far beyond the hills.

Helmgard lay astride those mountains. It would burn, but not before every town and village that lay between it and Vanik's host.

'We carry on,' he said to the Eightguard, eyes still on the mountains. 'Follow the track on the other side of the hamlet. Faug's outriders will reach it soon. Look for the smoke.'

They mounted and departed, bellowing orders at the foot column tramping down into the valley beneath. Vanik realised he was smiling.

It had been a long time since he had carried the True Gods' blessings to the Mortal Realms. As the breeze blew black smoke and ash back across the hilltop, he offered a prayer of thanks, then spurred Tzatzo after the passing warband.

The next village was called Rockroot. Like Anvilum, it burned. Evening was approaching as the main column came upon it, casting the surrounding country into a golden twilight that backlit the clouds rising from the village's remains.

Vanik rode in among the flames, feeling the heat through his black armour, revelling in the choking ash and the eye-stinging smoke. Bodies littered the dirt track before him, strewn where they'd fallen beneath the hatchets of Faug's riders.

Jevcha's Darkoath tribesmen were in among the buildings, prising livestock from their pens to be herded into the main column. Jevcha was overseeing them, stalking between the burning homesteads like a wolf, lean and deadly.

'Have the outriders sighted anything?' she asked as she caught sight of Vanik coming in the opposite direction. He paused Tzatzo, letting the warqueen run her fingers over the creature's spines.

'No,' he replied. He knew what she was hoping for – resistance, a column of soldiers from the town the priest had spoken of, anything more than pathetic village folk to slaughter.

'Helmgard will not offer battle,' he went on. 'Its master, Albermarl, is too precious to be risked.'

'How can you be so sure?'

'It is the reason I have come here to slay him. There is a prophecy concerning his future. He will be a curse to the servants of the True Gods if he ascends to the lightning realm. The Summoner showed me.'

'The Summoner?' Jevcha asked, frowning.

'Yes,' Vanik replied. 'A creature of the inner spire. It journeyed to Neveroth's court specifically to tell him of its visions concerning me. Its counsel was what saw me sent out here, to Chamon. I am the one who must slay Albermarl, to earn my place within the Fifth Circle.'

'A Gaunt Summoner?' Jevcha reiterated, her expression growing grimmer. 'One of the Nine great sorcerers of Tzeentch singled you out for this?'

'Yes.'

'Why didn't you tell me?'

'I have never encountered a creature like it,' Vanik said. 'Were it not for Karex's words, I would have assumed it was a daemon.'

'I do not know if this means we are blessed or cursed,' the Darkoath queen said heavily. 'I have heard many tales and riddles about the Nine. Few end well, even for the most favoured mortals.'

'I will not be lured into its games,' Vanik responded.

'Then why are we undertaking this quest for it?'

'We do this for Karex Daemonflayer, and the Varanspire. She believes there is a daemonic plot being hatched, and I will help uncover it.'

'Perhaps she is using you too.'

Vanik scowled, but said nothing. Jevcha didn't continue.

They burned another village before nightfall. This one had been forewarned, presumably by the smoke still pluming from Rockroot. Even so, a dozen villagers were still in their dwellings, either too slow or too stubborn to leave. Vanik had them nailed up, alive, to the boundary markers that surrounded the hamlet. Hopefully some would still be living by the time outriders arrived from Helmgard to investigate the reports Vanik was sure would now be on their way to the mountain city.

Marius was awake when the city outriders brought the survivor to the high council chamber.

'Rise, Matthias,' he commanded. The orrery assistant started awake from his cot bed in the sleeping cell across from the star chamber. He opened his mouth as if to speak, then paused when he heard the grinding of cogs and gears. The planetarium, broken since Marius' last star vision, was active once more.

'What I feared has come to pass,' the Lord Ordinator said, standing in the doorway like a graven statue as his bleary-eyed assistant hurried to get dressed. 'I must go immediately to the high council chamber. Watch over the planetarium while I am gone.'

He had worked almost unceasingly since his last vision had shattered and burned the seeing orrery, consulting his arcanabulum as he pieced it back together part by part. It had still refused to function, though, no matter how he recalibrated the base cogs or measured out, with precise detail, the correct arcs of the celestial bodies represented by the arcane mechanism.

Then, as darkness had stretched out across Helmgard, the orrery lurched and engaged. Marius had spent the rest of the night mapping and measuring the new orbits of the reassembled heavens, checking them against the firmament above using the dome chamber's repaired scope.

The projections had been unambiguous. Chaos had returned to the Ironroots and the plains below.

Leaving Matthias, he marched for Helmgard's high council chamber. Movement was already disturbing the inner rooms of the city's spire, servants hurrying backward and forward, guards standing by. Clearly Marius was not alone in recognising the approaching threat.

'My lord Fulbricht,' he said as he strode down the stone-clad entrance hall leading to the council chamber. Lord Vulf Fulbricht, one of the foremost of Helmgard's human lords and Castellan Albermarl's cousin, grimaced as he fell into step beside the Stormcast. He had clearly only just been awoken. His eyes looked heavy and his doublet, emblazoned with his hawk heraldry, was askew. Marius was surprised to see him without his son, Rodik, tailing him – lately the youth had been tasked with learning the ways of the nobility by following his father around relentlessly.

'Lord Ordinator,' Vulf said, stifling a yawn. 'What is afoot? The damned boy sent to wake me would say nothing, only that the castellan required us immediately.'

'Why he has summoned you, I know not,' Marius replied.

'But I come with my own tidings. The celestial heavens have sent us a warning. The servants of the Dark Gods worry at our doorstep once more.'

'By the lightning,' Fulbricht murmured. His step faltered, but Marius strode on. He caught up.

'Can it be true, after all these years?' he asked.

'I suspect we are about to find out,' Marius responded.

They passed between the hammer-armed duardin longbeards guarding the council chamber's high doors, and into the long, echoing room. Graven statues, their grim features thrown into flickering contrast by hastily lit torches, glared down at them. The combined work of human and duardin masons and artisans, they displayed generations of the joint kindreds of Helmgard. For over an age, the human and duardin populace of the mountain city had striven side by side. Never had that been truer than under the stewardship of the city's latest castellan, Albermarl.

He sat now at the far end of the stone council table, in a high-backed throne decorated with silver sigils. He was clad in deep-blue robes, inlaid with gold banding. Despite the lateness of the hour, his heavy auburn beard was combed and pleated, and a golden circlet rested on his brow. His great warhammer, crafted in the likeness of a twin-tailed comet, lay in one strong, scarred fist, its head resting against the stone-flagged floor.

'Lord Ordinator,' he said as Marius and Fulbricht entered. 'You come with haste. I had only just dispatched a messenger to the Star Chamber.'

'I come bearing my own portents,' Marius responded, stopping at the far side of the council table and sketching the sign of the lightning bolt. 'Though I suspect you already know of them.'

There was a murmur among those already assembled around

the table. There were six of them, two duardin and four humans, now including Fulbricht.

'Who else are we waiting for?' Grunbad, the duardin warden king, demanded. He was the most senior member of the clan council that looked to the interests of Helmgard's duardin guilds, alongside the other duardin present, the Runelord whitebeard Norri Smeltmaster.

'I have yet to hear from the other lords and thanes,' Albermarl said. 'And time presses. We here will have to be enough to debate the matter at hand.'

'Is it true?' Garrin Leo, human high priest of the city's Sigmarite cult, asked hesitantly. 'Have they returned?'

'According to one young man, Theobold, from the village of Anvilum, yes,' Albermarl said. He carried on over the shocked words of the council. 'He was brought in by riders from the town guard of Ferrium, near dead. The horsemen spoke of more refugees, many more, on their way.'

'And where is the boy now?' Grunbad demanded, his gravelly tones cutting through the protestations of the human council.

'With my personal physicians. He is not expected to live long enough to see the dawn.'

More shock and outrage. Marius said nothing. A cold, dark mood had settled over him, one that was only exacerbated by the panic among the council members before him. Before he had come to the chamber, a part of him had wanted to deny the truth behind the orrery's warning, to believe his precious planetarium was still broken and malfunctioning. There was no doubt in his mind any longer, though.

'Marius,' Albermarl said, stifling the conversation around him and drawing the Stormcast's attention once more. 'What does the firmament say of these tidings?'

'There is a storm coming,' Marius responded.

'Is that not a blessing? The lightning brings your kindred, and the tidings of the God-King, does it not?'

'Not this time,' Marius responded grimly. 'This is a thing of blood and shadows. Fell creatures have turned their attention towards us. I have felt their gaze upon your very court. A fledgling champion of the Dark Gods has been dispatched here. He comes now with all his speed and might.'

'To what purpose?' Albermarl responded. 'The last Chaos incursion in this part of Chamon was many decades ago. What has drawn the attention of their foul breed?'

'You,' Marius answered simply. 'I have told you before, the grand courts of Azyr follow your progress closely, lord castellan. You have ruled the duardin and men of Helmgard and its surrounding fiefdoms wisely for over twenty years, and you proved your mettle against the orruks not three summers past. Few men in all the realms command the ancestral respect of the duardin the way you do.'

Albermarl grunted, but said nothing to deny the Lord Ordinator's words.

'If your favour is being discussed from Azyrheim to Sigmaron, it should be no surprise that your name has reached less exalted places,' Marius went on.

'You assume much, stargazer,' Grunbad, the warden king, said, fixing Marius with his iron stare. 'But I'd rather hear what this boy from Anvilum has to say.'

'He says the same as Marius. Riders came to his village, and began killing and burning. He abandoned his family and ran.'

'A boy without honour,' Grunbad growled. 'They could be simple bandits, thieves. How do we know they are the servants of the dark ones?'

'They took nothing but livestock, and spared no one. Even if he is mistaken about their nature, they are a threat to the stability of the Ironroots. I will not allow that to stand. With the agreement of the council, I am assembling the Freeguild regiments and marching to stop them.'

'No.'

Marius said the word clearly and firmly. Silence settled over the council chamber.

'They want you to do precisely what you have just suggested,' the Lord Ordinator continued. 'Helmgard is an unassailable fastness. The forces of Chaos have broken themselves against its walls before. Let them do so again.'

Albermarl's expression throughout the meeting had been stoic, but Marius' words caused displeasure to tug down on the corners of his mouth. He leaned forward in his throne.

'What you suggest is abject cowardice, Lord Ordinator. How many thousands in the villages and townships beyond the wall will be massacred if I remain here? I would be eternally dishonoured, a worthless thing, no longer fit to rule.'

'The servants of Chaos have not come to raid and pillage,' Marius said. 'They have come here for you, castellan, and you alone. They seek to kill you and unbind the forces of the duardin and mankind in Chamon. They seek to stifle the potential you still have in the eyes of the God-King. Why specifically they seek you beyond this is not yet clear, but if you risk yourself in open battle, you offer the Dark Gods a great victory. They can be broken with far less loss of life on Helmgard's slopes and ramparts.'

'We could send riders to the townships,' Leo ventured. 'Have them brought within the walls.'

'And how long will that take?' Albermarl demanded. 'How many would fall victim to these savages in the meantime? The army of Helmgard stands ready. To not repel the invaders would be a dereliction of all my duties.'

'And how many of the brave men and duardin of Helmgard will fall when you bring them to battle?' Marius asked. 'There is a better way. I will send word to my chamber, to great Azyrheim itself. A cohort of my brethren will be dispatched to aide us. They come with the lightning.'

'Who knows when that will be,' Grunbad grumbled. 'Your golden legions fight a war across Eight Realms – how soon can we expect them here in any number?'

'I do not know,' Marius admitted. 'But with their arrival, victory will be assured. Between our two forces we will crush the slaves to darkness utterly. If we march forth now, we risk defeat, and should that befall us, what then? Helmgard left defenceless? What carnage would be inflicted if the daemon worshippers storm the mountain city?'

There were low mutters among the other council members. Albermarl was silent, his expression dour. Fulbricht was the first to speak up.

'I agree with the Lord Ordinator. Regardless of the risk to your own person, the risk to the city is too great. Besides, there are logistics to consider. A full muster will take time, and supplies will have to be amassed. If we march with only the core regiments of the guard, we place an even greater risk on ourselves.'

'The manling speaks the truth,' Norri Smeltmaster said, the Runelord speaking for the first time. 'We must find out more about this threat, more than just a boy's ramblings and the signs of the stars.'

He inclined his head to Marius, who returned the acknowledgement. The Runelord went on.

'We must call the thanes and convene the clan council before discussing anything more. To not do so would be an unthinkable insult.'

Albermarl nodded.

'Riders must be dispatched now, to every township,' the castellan said. 'And all regiments are to begin mustering at dawn. Fulbricht, you will see to that. Lord Elgrim and Constable Holduren, you will clear the westslope quarter in anticipation of the arrival of refugees. Likewise, Leo, your eminence. The halls of your shrines may have to play host to the dispossessed come the week's end.'

Leo bowed. Elgrim and Holduren had already fallen to discussing the difficulties of clearing space in the westslope.

'Lord Ordinator,' Albermarl said, turning his attention to Marius. 'Summon your kindred, and watch the heavens for us. We will need the guidance of your portents. If there is indeed a storm coming, you will see it break first.'

PART ELEVEN

A RECKONING OF PILGRIMS

Nearly three weeks passed before an outrider came seeking Vanik with the news he had been waiting for. He was standing amidst the ash and blackened timbers of a townhouse, smoke still coiling from its scorched foundations. The warband had fallen upon the place – Merkurium, according to the prisoners taken from the neighbouring hamlet – the night before. They had found precious little beyond abandoned homes and empty barns and outhouses. If the town had once had a garrison it had departed, and had clearly taken the townsfolk and their goods with it. Vanik had ordered the place torched, the fires rising in sympathy with his own temper.

'One of Hetman Faug's scouts, sire,' Modred said, leading the dismounted Red Steppe tribesman cautiously past the Eight-guard standing vigil around the townhouse's smouldering ruins. Vanik did not respond, eyes on the smoke rising lazily into the warm summer air.

Almost a month had gone by since he had first ridden into Chamon. Day by day, the warband had worked its way deeper into the misbegotten realm, burning every settlement they found, staking prisoners by the roadsides and torturing priests of the False God. Still, though, there was no sign of any organised resistance. They were halfway to the Ironroots, the great mountains soaring on the skyline. Helmgard was all but in sight, and still the city's castellan and its army had not sallied out to protect the inhabitants of the realm. Vanik had started to question the very purpose of his quest – if Albermarl did not have the courage to march out and face him, what great threat could he possibly pose? Perhaps it was all a trick, a plot to banish him from the Varanspire to some soft-bellied backwater?

'What news?' he demanded of the steppe rider, finally looking at him. He was a squinting, toothless man, squat like all of his kin, seemingly uncomfortable and ungainly unless he was mounted on the back of his savage little steed. He bowed hastily before Vanik, not daring to look up at the black-armoured champion.

'The Third Eye is active once more, great hetman,' the man said. 'Warriors of the Gods have passed through, as Hysh rose three days ago.'

'Whose warriors?' Vanik demanded. 'What was their sigil?'

'Their main party rode beneath a black banner, great hetman,' the scout said. 'And their outriders were Uk-Chen halfbreeds.'

He paused to spit amidst the ash and charred timber at his feet. There were none the horsemen of the Red Steppe hated more than the Uk-Chen, their great, ancient tribal rivals.

'So, he has come at last,' Vanik said. If the black standard was not enough, the presence of Uk-Chen was – he knew Skoren possessed a party of the horsemen in his warband. 'How great was the host?' he demanded. 'Did you count their icons?'

'No, great hetman. The halfbreeds protecting their column were too many. We lost two saddle-brothers before we could escape them and bring word.'

'Go to Faug,' Vanik told the scout. 'Tell him to ride in person for the Third Eye. Find the host that has passed through, and bring me word on their numbers and the direction they are marching in with all the haste you can muster.'

The scout offered a scraping bow and, eyes still averted, loped away. Vanik spoke to Modred.

'Bring me Tzatzo.'

It was the Blackhand. Faug confirmed as much when he returned with his detachment towards evening two days later, their horses lathered white with sweat.

'You saw him?' Vanik demanded as the hetman drew his steed warily alongside Tzatzo, at the front of the warband's column. They had been marching for the Realmgate since departing Merkurium, skirting a rare patch of woodland nestled amidst the tilled and cultivated countryside, then following a stream as it meandered through a series of shallow valleys.

'Yes, I saw him, great hetman,' Faug replied. 'His entire retinue was about him. His warband is strong.'

'How strong?'

'I counted nine icons, and there were likely more I did not see. The scum Uk-Chen shield his numbers from our eyes.'

'Nine icons,' Vanik repeated. 'Whose?'

'Takchar's Anointed, and the Fifth Scar of Ogoth. Those were the only ones I recognised.'

'Bloodbound?'

'I do not think so. The only skull standard I saw was Ogoth's.'

'Very well,' Vanik said. A shout from one of the horsemen accompanying Faug drew his eyes to the near horizon.

There were riders on the brow of the low hill to his right. They sat and watched the column, silhouetted against Hysh's dying light.

'Not yours?' he asked Faug.

'No, great hetman,' he replied, grimacing. 'Uk-Chen.'

'Come to count as well,' Vanik said. 'You must do as they have done for the Blackhand, Faug. Bring your outriders in, we no longer seek hovels to burn. Stay close about the warband and keep Skoren's dogs from scenting us.'

'Yes, great champion,' Faug said, before spurring his tired steed off again, his horsemen whooping as they closed around him.

'You think he will fight?' Kulthuk asked. Had the two warbands encountered one another in the wastes there would have been little reason to hesitate. Here, though, there were servants of the False God to slay. Vanik doubted they would make a difference to the Blackhand.

'We shall see soon enough,' he said.

Whether the Blackhand came to kill Vanik, or to continue their joint quest to slay the castellan, his Uk-Chen certainly seemed in no doubt about their purpose. Through the next day, as the two warbands drew close to one another, they clashed in a dozen short but savage skirmishes with Faug's cavalry, fighting in the gentle valleys and along the rolling hills traversed by both parties as they focused their attention and kept their scouting efforts away from the main warband. Vanik gave Faug's warriors free rein to strike as they saw fit, knowing that they would have done so anyway. Some enmities ran too deep for even the commands of the champions of Chaos to have much effect. By evening, over a dozen Red Steppe riders had presented fresh scalps to Vanik. He suspected a similar number were being displayed to Skoren by the Uk-Chen.

'A little over half a day's march, if they keep their baggage and camp followers close,' Faug estimated. 'They're at the far end of the next valley.'

'Keep harrying them,' Vanik ordered. 'Rotate your riders. Keep them fresh and do not overcommit. I will not sacrifice warriors for the sake of your feud with the Uk-Chen.'

'Yes, great hetman,' Faug said. Vanik dismissed him, and he rode off with a primal whoop.

There were few pleasures the Gods delighted in more than seeing hated foes strike at one another. Vanik promised to delight them further.

As darkness fell, the warband carried on. Vanik directed them up onto the crest of the valleys they had been following all day. It was slow, tiring work in the darkness, and for a while they lost all contact with their outriders. Vanik ordered a halt on a stony bluff protruding out over a sparse woodland. No fires were to be lit. The families huddled together in the darkness, while Vanik sat astride Tzatzo on the edge of the slope, looking out into the night. He wasn't tired. He wasn't sure how many times he'd slept since reaching Chamon. Occasionally he caught sounds carried on the wind – the shrieks of horses and the screams of men, and the war whoops of the Red Steppe.

Eventually, he heard the clipping of hooves amidst the rocks of the slope below. His gauntlet strayed to Nakali's hilt, but stopped – the horsemen were Faug's. The hetman himself appeared moments later, a shadow picked out by the sickle moon that had risen over the mountains during the night, blood from a fresh scalp hanging from his saddle glistening across his horse's flank.

'They're in the trees,' he reported to Vanik. 'Uk-Chen, in numbers. Their warband is close behind, but they have not moved for at least an hour. I think they've stopped for the night.'

'Their outriders lost contact with us earlier?' Vanik asked. Faug nodded, little more than a silhouette in the moon-shot darkness.

'We met them in the valley below, but they've withdrawn. They likely think we are protecting an encampment down there.'

Vanik looked past Faug, into the darkness that he knew was a treeline beyond the foot of the slope. He had taken to the valley sides initially as a precaution – high ground was always valuable. Now, however, the humid night air was heavy with possibility. Skoren's halfbreeds had lost contact with Faug's protective screen, and in the darkness had quite possibly mistaken the location of Vanik's entire warband.

That, or they were feigning their position and seeking to lure him into a trap.

'The forest below, it is open?' he asked Faug.

'Yes, great hetman. Little undergrowth. We passed through it with ease.'

'And you are certain the Blackhand's host is encamped beyond?'

Faug hesitated. Vanik could not make out his face in the darkness, but he could feel the tension. He knew how much rested on his report. He knew, also, that Vanik did not look kindly on any indecision or lack of decisiveness from his scouts.

'The camp is there,' he said.

'And prepared for an attack?'

'None could get close enough to be sure.'

Vanik fondled Tzatzo's quills, his thoughts racing. It was a foolish thing for the servants of the Eightfold to do battle in the Mortal Realms, deep into the fiefdoms of the enemies of the Gods. A Black Pilgrim, aspiring to the brotherhood of the Varanguard, should know better than any how to set aside the divisiveness that so often beset the warriors of Chaos. Yet he also had few doubts that Skoren had come to kill him. There had been no messengers in the days since he had passed through the Realmgate, no offer of parley. That did not surprise him. There would be no truce between fellow servants.

The Blackhand had just entered Chamon, but Vanik had been roaming this land for weeks, burning homesteads and salting fields. He knew better than Skoren how to take advantage of his surroundings. He knew that the ruins of a village once named Ironfield lay past the forest at the foot of the slope before him. He had watched it burn a little over a week previously. It would have made a good place for an encampment. Skoren would assume the woodland would shield him, not realising how light the forest was, not understanding that Vanik's host was not where he thought, at the bottom of the adjacent valley.

Or perhaps he was completely aware. Perhaps his warriors even now waited in the dark, armed and armoured, praying their enemies were mad enough to come rushing down on them seeking an easy victory. He summoned his retinue.

'The Blackhand's band is below,' he said. 'If we are to strike him, we will have no better opportunity than this.'

'You will not seek his aid?' Kulthuk replied.

'Oh, I will seek him,' Vanik said. 'And I will kill him.'

'Your quest is to slay Albermarl. That is Skoren's task as well. By turning on him you turn on the Gods as well.'

'Skoren will not kill the castellan,' Vanik replied. 'I will, and if I fail I will be cut down in the attempt. But regardless, the Blackhand or I will die this night.'

The Eightguard and Jevcha's Darkoath would lead the attack. Vanik had ordered the warband's champions to attend him in the dark. The plan was clear. The initial charge would have one task – killing Skoren. Once that was done, Vanik would demand the oaths and allegiance of his followers. If they refused, the rest of the warband would be summoned by Aramor's carnyx or the horns of the Darkoath. That would lead to a general slaughter, but if that was the will of the Four then so be it.

'We will have to move fast once their scouts see us,' Jevcha said. 'The forest will slow us.'

'Faug has ridden it,' Vanik said. 'He says it is open. It should not encumber us too greatly.'

Faug himself was absent, leading bands of his horsemen along the valley floor. If the plan worked, they would tease at the far edge of the Blackhand's encampment, keeping the attention of their sentries and outriders throughout the few remaining hours of darkness without doing enough to raise a full alarm. When the attack went in, they would throw themselves into the Uk-Chen, finally free to strike as they pleased.

'Return to your war parties,' Vanik ordered the other chieftains and champions. 'And stand ready. At the triple-blow of the carnyx or the oath-horns, bring your warriors with all speed.'

The gathering dispersed. Jevcha returned to the Darkoath, amassed in two wings either side of the Eightguard. A screen of a dozen Red Steppe riders stood mounted a little way down the slope, waiting on Vanik's signal. He paused, inhaling the warm air, feeling the light breeze coming through the valley. Was that burning he could smell? The scents of cooked tuskers? An encampment nearby, at rest, weary warriors awaiting the bloodshed they thought they would find only with the dawn? Or was he being deceived? Did they wait ready in the darkness, shields locked, axes already to hand?

There was only one way to be sure. Vanik pulled on his helm, his world suddenly reduced to near total darkness. He took a second for his eyes to adjust, then raised a gauntlet, fingers splayed. Below, like pallid ghosts, the outriders took off. After a few seconds, Vanik let Tzatzo follow.

He had promised a slow death for any warrior who let out a shout or cheer before they were in amongst Skoren's campfires. Despite this, it still seemed as though they may as well have announced their approach with drums pounding and horns braying. The thudding of hooves, the swish of branches, the rattle of bridles and saddles and the clatter of armour, it seemed to fill up the entire world. Vanik's own breathing rasped in his helmet, and his heart slammed in his chest, an alarm to wake every sleeping man and beast for miles around. It made him grip Tzatzo's chains a little tighter, battling the urge to draw Nakali immediately.

Tzatzo, at least, seemed fully aware of the need for speed and silence. She descended the rocky slope easily enough even in the dark, and then moved among the trees beyond with a litheness the horses of the Eightguard were unable to match. He was forced to halt her on the edge of the wood to allow the retinue to catch up.

The camp is unprepared, Nakali whispered.

'Be silent, treacherous snake,' the Black Pilgrim hissed back, fretting once more at Tzatzo's crest.

Cursed if I help, cursed if I do not.

'Sire?' murmured Kulthuk as the Eightguard finally arrived.

'Nothing,' Vanik muttered, signalling them to ride on.

Tzatzo took off once more, racing between the trees, her reptilian bulk unimpeded in the sparse undergrowth. Vanik leaned low in the saddle as trees whipped by, twigs and branches snapping and scraping more lacquer from his armour and barding. The darkness beneath the canopy was almost total, and he found himself relying solely on his mount's sight. He couldn't see the Red Steppe riders ahead any more.

He heard them though. A horse shrieked in the night. Moments later there was a crack, and a man screamed. He caught motion, not far ahead. Tzatzo's pace quickened. He dared not turn in the saddle to see how far behind the Eightguard were.

There was another scream, and he caught the telltale swish as something passed invisibly through the darkness overhead – an arrow, he was sure. Was that light ahead? A slight, ruddy glow? The flicker of a campfire, past the boughs of the furthest trees?

Shouts now, up ahead. Tzatzo vaulted something. At first Vanik took it to be a log, but as the steed landed back on her foreclaws, he realised it was the body of a horse and rider, their allegiance indiscernible in the dark. The flames ahead had become clearer – fires indeed, set just past the edge of the treeline, in the valley bottom. Dark shapes darted around them, and the wind carried more shouts to his ears.

The time for silence was over.

'For the Varanspire and the Eightstar!' he bellowed, and unsheathed Nakali. The daemon howled, and Tzatzo added her own cry. The Eightguard were still behind, but he no longer cared.

Skoren could have had ten thousand warriors standing in locked ranks, waiting for him beyond that treeline, and it wouldn't have mattered now. Vanik was a warrior. He had a mount beneath him, a blade in his hand and was riding to the slaughter. In that moment, his soul sang.

Skoren's encampment was unprepared. Vanik realised as much as Tzatzo burst from the treeline. Before him was a scene of carnage. Lit up by the hellish glow of fires, braziers and torches, warriors and camp followers scrambled back and forth between hide tents and hastily erected branch huts, seeking weapons or shelter. Those nearest to the treeline were a long-limbed breed of men, crying out in a rapid tongue that Vanik didn't recognise. They were armoured in golden scale mail and bore tall blue horsehair crests on their helms. Most were carrying daos, glaives or short spears.

Tzatzo ripped into the first man she reached without breaking stride. Blood gouted, dark in the firelight, splattering her quills and barding. Vanik urged her on and over the man as he fell, screaming and clutching at the red remains of his throat and shoulder.

Nakali sang. The daemon sword fell first on one of the gold-armoured men trying to intercept Vanik. The black steel carved straight through the marauder's dao, slicing into his collarbone and chest. Tzatzo carried him on, momentum sawing the man open while the steed's claws splintered a spear lunging at him from the other side.

'Drink,' Vanik commanded. Nakali needed no encouraging. The weapon struck with wicked, ravenous force, shearing through another blade and beheading its wielder, sending his plumed helm spiralling into the air. Vanik had no idea how close the Eightguard or Jevcha's Darkoath were behind him – the uproar ahead was all that mattered.

He applied his spurs to Tzatzo's flanks, directing her towards a man waving an eye-and-fin warpsteel icon that glimmered with magical potency. More of the golden-armoured warriors were rallying to him, struggling to form amidst the tussling bodies. Tzatzo vaulted a broken wall, a remnant of the village the camp had been pitched over, and burst among them like lightning, claws raking the face from one man while Nakali took the standard bearer's arms off. The icon toppled, its sorcerous energies snuffed out before they could burst into life.

Rider and mount pushed through the melee before their scattered enemies could recover. Vanik knew he had to keep moving. Speed and surprise were the only advantages he had. He was penetrating deep into the enemy camp, and he was massively outnumbered. He had to locate Skoren before the rival pilgrim's warriors rallied.

A brazier had toppled nearby, igniting one of the tents. Flames danced and licked hungrily, spreading to a larger shelter, adjacent. In the sudden blaze, Vanik saw order amidst the carnage. Ahead, through the press of fleeing bodies, a force of dark-armoured warriors had formed themselves before a black pavilion pitched amidst the charred foundations of what had once been the village's hall. He recognised them at once. They were the Blackhand, Skoren's personal guard.

Familiar slaughter-oaths and the crash of blades and shields from behind told him that Jevcha's Darkoath had arrived. A glance told him the Eightguard were closing on him, but too slowly. Even striking indiscriminately at all before them, the sheer press of bodies this deep into the encampment made progress difficult.

Vanik did not pause for them.

'On,' he shouted, urging Tzatzo into the Blackhand. Claws and fangs gouged the screaming camp followers in their path, and the Chaos warriors ahead hunched and locked shields as they saw the pilgrim coming.

It made little difference to Tzatzo. With a shrill cry, she launched herself directly at the shield-wall, her powerful hind-leg muscles bunching, spines bristling as her immense strength carried Vanik up and over the braced front rank.

'Skoren!' he roared, searching amidst the press for his rival. There was no sign of him. Tzatzo struck. There was an ear-splitting crash of steel, the thump of bodies and bone, the jarring impact that stole Vanik's breath away. He fell, flung from the saddle and into the crumpled bodies of the second and third ranks, who'd taken the full impact of steed and rider. He tried to grasp Tzatzo's chain, but his grip on the saddle was gone. He slammed hard into one of the Blackhands, feeling the warrior's shield buckle beneath him. His own shield had flown from his arm as he'd pitched over his saddle, but Nakali was still firmly clenched in his gauntlet.

Let me feed! the daemon sword screamed at him, making his skull ache. A will not of his own dragged his arm down, slamming his sword through the breastplate of the warrior he was sprawled atop even as he fought to right himself.

No time to consider the odds, no time to acknowledge that he must surely die here, surrounded by the Blackhand's guard.

Blows rained down, and pain flared as swords, axes and maces battered at his black plate. Nakali ripped itself free and swung in a wild arc, smashing aside half a dozen blades. The daemon was keening, no thought given any more to defying Vanik. It wanted the souls of each and every being surrounding him.

Tzatzo was back up, her barding split and broken but her muscular body unharmed. She twisted sharply about, thick tail sending one attacker flying while her claws raked the shield of another, protecting Vanik's back.

He found his balance, slamming Nakali clear through the shield of the next warrior to come at him, spearing his stomach and running him through. The daemon groaned with pleasure as its invisible fangs drank deep, rending the Blackhand's soul and flinging the body back off the blade. Those behind stumbled as it slammed into them, given pause by the sight of the towering, black-armoured knight whose sword screamed at them in their heads.

'Come on then, worms,' Vanik spat, regaining his breath. 'Can't you hear? My blade is still hungry.'

The first one to come at him died on Nakali's tip, but the armoured warrior's charge bore him onto his knees. He flung the body off him and surged back to his feet, ripping Nakali free from the corpse in the same motion. Around him, the press had become a general melee. The Eightguard had crashed home, breaking the Blackhand's ranks. Vanik stood in the midst of it all, Tzatzo panting heavily at his side, snapping whenever a combatant was thrust too close.

'Eightguard, on me,' Vanik bellowed, raising Nakali high. He pushed himself towards the entrance to the Blackhand's pavilion, none now moving to oppose him. He moved in, expecting darkness, expecting a sudden blow from the side, darting left once under the flap with Nakali up and questing for any opposition.

Instead, he found himself in daylight. It was streaming in through a great rent torn in the pavilion's back. Arms and armour lay scattered about, but of the Blackhand there was no sign. The tent was abandoned.

Vanik thrust through the rip, and found himself back in the melee that had engulfed the area all around the tent. The Blackhand's standard bearer was directly ahead of him, locked in combat with Zoth. The banner carried by the warrior was rippling black silk, the same as Vanik's, the pennant of a Black Pilgrim.

Vanik came upon the standard bearer from behind. He gripped him firmly by the pauldron and stepped in close, thrusting Nakali into the small of his back. The man screamed horribly as the daemonic serpent ripped him open, and the banner began to topple. Vanik snatched it, kicking the shuddering body off his sword and raising both high.

'Where is he?' he roared.

Around him, the Blackhand's guard were breaking. None answered.

'The Blackhand cannot save you,' he shouted. 'There is only one pilgrim demanding your allegiance here! Where is your coward master?'

The Eightguard had stopped cutting through the nearest warriors, but carnage continued throughout the camp. Vanik turned to Tzatzo. The steed had been gorging herself on the fallen standard bearer, gulping down flesh and plate armour indifferently. At a snapped command from Vanik she lowered her haunches, allowing him to bury the banner's haft in the dirt and mount her before snatching it back up again.

'Kulthuk, Aramor, attend me,' he barked. 'Keep the standard raised and sound the carnyx, single blasts. We must find the Blackhand!'

The hunt continued through the night and on into the morning. It took that long just to end the battle atop the ruins of what had once been the village of Ironfield. Hysh was high and bright in the sky when the remains of Skoren Blackhand's warband knelt amidst the dead and the dying and took the oath to Vanik.

Not all did so. Vanik permitted those who wished to die in Skoren's service to do it with weapons in their hands. He did not watch. His own desire to kill had drained away. There was no sign of the Blackhand. He had fled, or perhaps he had never even been with the encampment in the first place. The discovery made the victory a hollow one. By attacking the camp, he had allowed Skoren an opportunity to slip away and, presumably, draw closer to the castellan undetected. He had no doubt that the Blackhand was just as dangerous alone as he was with a warband. The need to draw Albermarl out was now even more acute.

Vanik summoned Jevcha as the last of Skoren's beaten war

parties rose up from their knees, forearms red with their fresh blood-oath. The Darkoath queen was busy having a pyre built for her war party's dead.

'Leave the dead where they fell. Not one is to be touched.'

Jevcha's expression darkened.

'If the bodies are not burned, the spirit and the flesh may both wander. The Great Necromancer's servants could defile them.'

'Then you must decide what you fear more, their unquiet spirits, or my wrath.'

Jevcha said nothing.

'Pass the word to the other chieftains,' Vanik continued. 'We are to march for the Third Eye within the hour.'

'The Realmgate,' Jevcha demanded, expression becoming angrier still. 'We are to return to the Eightpoints? But, brother, the warband is stronger than ever! The favour of the Four is upon us. Skoren cannot be far, if we–'

'Enough,' Vanik said. 'I am not a fool, Jevcha, and you should not take me as such. Obey my orders. Once we have pitched camp tonight I might deign to explain them.'

ACT III

SLAVES TO DARKNESS

PART TWELVE

HEAVEN'S SILENCE

Nothing.

Marius set his measuring callipers down on his arcanum rack and stifled an oath. Matthias, sensing his ill mood, bowed his head sorrowfully.

'Still nothing from your chamber, lord?' he ventured.

Marius shook his head. He didn't trust himself to speak without snapping at his assistant.

Nothing.

Almost a month had passed since he had first sent a summons to the Azyr, accompanied by a plea for aid. The Three-Eyed King's barbarians were once more loosed within this corner of Chamon. Albermarl, his great warden-post as castellan approved by Azyrheim, was directly threatened. Could not just a portion of one of the chambers of the Stormcast Eternals be spared from the great struggle elsewhere to come to their aid?

The message had been sent, chiselled upon an arc of lightning and launched with mathematical accuracy into the heavens. Since then Marius had watched and waited, studying the celestial bodies, measuring the great orrery, watching his arcanabulum.

To no avail. The arcanabulum lay dead and dormant, and the skies themselves were worse – they spoke of abandonment, desolation. Defeat. He had not the stomach to take such portents before Albermarl or Helmgard's ruling council. That realisation in itself shamed him.

A knock at the door disturbed his thoughts and made Matthias jump. He roused himself, disengaging the pattern-scribe of the slowly turning orrery and unmaking the warding sigils around the Star Chamber's entrance.

Beyond it, one of the council's young attendants stared up at him, wide-eyed before the Stormcast.

'A summons to the high council chamber, Lord Ordinator,' the boy said hastily, holding up a sealed message scroll. 'At noon today.'

He took the paper without speaking, waving the boy away. The message within was written in Albermarl's own hand, and demanded an immediate meeting of the council. There had been half a dozen such impromptu summons over the past week, as news of yet another fresh atrocity reached the mountain city. Each time Marius had been forced to call for restraint, and cajole human and duardin alike into resisting the urge to march out against the invader. Wait for word from Azyr, he had told them.

But there would be none. He had come to terms with that now.

Marius was the last to take his seat at the council table. Helmgard's rulers were assembled in full, human lords, guildmasters and priests, and the thanes, runesmiths and longbeards of their duardin counterparts. None but Albermarl would look him in the eye as he sat down to the castellan's left.

It was Albermarl who spoke first.

'I have received word from our outriders. You are all familiar with the village of Ironfield?'

There were a few grunts from around the table. Albermarl carried on.

'As you know, about two weeks ago the barbarian invaders burned Ironfield, a day before marching on Haeburn. Sometime in the past few days they returned there, before departing again. Our scouts followed their trail. They found this.'

The castellan snapped his fingers, and one of the doublet-clad servants standing around the corners of the chamber stepped forward. He was carrying a heavy object, which he set on the table before Albermarl, wrapped in cloth.

The castellan plucked the material aside to reveal a helmet. It was heavy and roughly wrought, its crude metal stamped and carved with sigils that made Marius' hands clench. It was also split, the crown carved open by what must have been a heavy, cleaving blow. Dried blood crusted the hideous gash.

There were gasps as the helm was revealed, and several duardin spat on the floor to avert the darkling spirits.

'You understand what this is,' Albermarl said.

'The helm of some *thaggaz*,' Grunbad snarled.

'The armour belonged to one of the bestial warriors that have invaded this realm,' Albermarl agreed. 'Its owner, you might surmise, is dead.'

'How?' Lord Fulbricht asked.

'Killed by his own kinsmen,' Albermarl said. The words made the duardin growl and grumble as he carried on. 'And not him alone. The scouts brought more trophies than just this. Hundreds of savages lie dead in and around the ruins of Ironfield.'

'Praise the lightning,' the high priest, Leo, exclaimed excitedly. 'They have turned on themselves! Such barbarism is well documented throughout the realms. The evil in their twisted hearts overcomes their minds, and they become animals that seek only to consume one another.'

'There's more,' Albermarl said before the priest of Sigmar could go on. 'The scouts have tracked the remains of the Chaos horde. Their savage horsemen continue to shield them, but the direction they have taken is clear. They are marching towards the Three Doors.'

The council fell to excited chatter. Marius cut through it.

'This is the first clear information our outriders have delivered since the daemon-worshippers first set foot in Chamon. Until now, their own light horsemen have masked their movements and harried our own riders. All we have had is supposition, the tales of fleeing survivors and the smoke rising up from our burning villages and towns. Yet now their horsemen ride close to their main column, and permit our scouts to see what has passed, while they make a path for the Realmgate for the first time since their invasion began.'

'I would assume so many died at Ironfield that their numbers are now depleted. They cannot keep our outriders at bay any longer,' Albermarl replied. 'Perhaps their leader is slain, and their warband has collapsed.'

'I predicted this,' Grunbad said, smacking a palm into the stone of the council table. 'The longer we deny them battle, the more whatever passes as discipline among their kind breaks apart. The madmen have defeated themselves. And now we have an opportunity to make sure of it.'

'I agree,' Lord Fulbricht said loudly. 'The hand of the God-King has clearly crafted this situation in our favour. The army of Helmgard is assembled and eager, and the savages are skulking back to their damned citadels. Now is our opportunity to avenge their many atrocities, and put an end to their threat once and for all.'

The council bellowed their approval, banging fists against the table in the duardin style. Only Marius stayed silent. Albermarl waited for the din to fade before addressing him.

'How do the stars perceive our current state, Lord Ordinator?' he asked. 'What fortunes do the turning orbs tell of? Do the halls of the Azyr answer your summons? Are we still to await the lightning blow of the Stormcast?'

Silence gripped the chamber. Eventually Marius answered.

'There will be no aid from Sigmaron. My request for assistance has gone unheeded, and the passage of the heavens confirms as much. My brethren are elsewhere.'

'Then it is settled, surely,' Grunbad exclaimed, thrusting his chair back and standing. 'There is no more reason to delay! The Stormcasts cannot help us, and the enemy are retreating before us. If they escape back to their infernal realm, they may carry word that the armies of Helmgard will not march from their fastness. More will come, and our lands and mines will never know peace again unless we show our strength, now.'

The council's agreement was unanimous. Marius felt Albermarl's eyes on him, waiting for him to intercede. He met the castellan's stony gaze with one of his own and, slowly, nodded.

'My lord, the warden king speaks the truth,' Albermarl said, his voice immediately commanding the council's attention. 'I myself have long felt that our vengeance is overdue. Send word to every Freeguild regiment and every duardin forge-band. Tomorrow, we march from Helmgard. We will not return until the last of the invaders have been put to the sword.'

* * *

There was a storm forming over the Ironroot Mountains. It framed the white peaks against a morass of broiling darkness, riven through with flashes of light. Thunder followed, echoing out across the plains.

'The Lightning God is watching,' Jevcha said quietly.

'I pray so,' Vanik responded, voice terse. 'He will see me sunder one of his champions this day.'

Nearly two weeks had passed since they had sprung Skoren's trap. Two weeks since the Blackhand had escaped them, apparently disappearing into the aether. Two weeks since the warband had turned back towards the Third Eye. Vanik had ordered Faug's riders to close on the main column, allowing the pathetic scouts sent from the mountain city to discover the scene of Skoren's defeat.

After weeks of waiting, it hadn't taken long for the army of Helmgard to march out, now that they believed Vanik's host was wounded and fleeing. He had led them slowly towards the Third Eye, but then turned away, trailing back in an arc and dragging the cumbersome army of the Free City after him. By now they must have begun to realise that the Black Pilgrim's warband was far from crippled, and certainly not retreating.

'They haven't turned back,' Jevcha wondered aloud. 'Have the lightning worshippers finally found their courage?'

'Or they simply fear turning back more than carrying on,' Vanik responded, turning his gaze from the horizon to the chieftains assembled nearby.

He had gathered his war party heads on the crest of the ridgeline, his old champions and the new influx of Skoren's former leaders standing stiffly apart. The combined warband lay below, currently formless as they waited Vanik's decision. Many sat and ate the last of what they had been able to scavenge from the villages and towns below Helmgard, rough gritbread, root vegetables and meat half cooked over small, hasty fires. Others knelt for blessings from Mother Yogoth or the half a dozen camp women known to bear the Eye of the Gods. They were anointed with blood from the last of the slaughtered goats and cattle, or their own. Vanik had permitted Faug's cavalry to forage for their steeds further out on the plains – most of the horsemen were walking their mounts beyond the edges of the combined warband, out amidst the long grass. One of the camp drummers was testing his skins not far from Vanik, a percussive thump to challenge the distant thunder.

'We face them here,' Vanik said. His old chieftains, Jevcha, Gulgrak, Moll, Svarbald, Dravga, Faug and Ulek, murmured growls of approval. The new ones echoed them. This was why they had come, keeping their feuding warrior bands united under the promise of shedding the blood of the Free City.

'This will be no simple slaughter,' Vanik went on. 'I have come here for the castellan's head, and I shall have it. Everything that we do must be bent towards that purpose. Albermarl should fall by my hand alone. If so, the glory will be great not only for me, but for every Gods-fearing warrior who has had a hand in his defeat.'

'We are with you, pilgrim,' Ulek snarled, the massive Bloodbound already shivering with a rising, Khorne-blessed frenzy. 'Just say the word.'

Vanik did not. Instead, he turned to survey the horizon again. The sound of a horn, pealing out low and distant over the rumbling of the thunder, reached his ears.

The army of the Free city of Helmgard was approaching. Currently, it was little more than a dark smear on the landscape, a slowly shifting expanse on the foothills leading from the towering mountain city. The vanguard was just passing into the sunlight beyond the edge of the gathering storm, and as they did so Vanik caught the gleam of Hysh's glory reflecting off helmets, breastplates and pike tips.

'They will have artillery,' Gulgrak said as the warband's chieftains likewise surveyed the enemy's approach. 'And plenty of it. The duardin will bring every damned gun in the city.'

'Those will not concern us,' Vanik said. Several of the assembled champions frowned.

'As much as I trust in the blessings of the Gods–' Moll began. Vanik cut him off.

'Blessings do not come into it. I will personally ensure that their weaponry is useless.'

'How?' Gulgrak asked.

'Don't you trust me?' Gulgrak glanced away, but said nothing.

'Do we know more about their host?' Svarbald asked. 'Guns aplenty, but what of horsemen? Warbeasts?'

'I have not heard tell of any beasts when the armies of the Gods last came to this place,' Jevcha said. 'The duardin do not keep horses, and the humans usually have only light cavalry to patrol the plains and see to the farm towns and villages.'

'Faug's riders will outmatch them,' Vanik said.

'You make it sound like victory is already assured, sire,' Moll said tersely.

'Victory is simply a matter of cutting the castellan's head from his body,' Vanik said.

'And the army between us and him?'

'If they stand, they will die to a man. It makes no difference.'

'So what would you have us do?' Moll demanded. 'Wait until they are prepared, then charge screaming into the teeth of their guns?'

'That sounds like a worthy plan to me,' Ulek said, baring his teeth in a savage grin. Moll grimaced.

'I would have you assemble your war parties,' Vanik said,

fixing the brute chieftain with his yellow eyes. 'Discipline them, tell them they are to follow your instructions exactly, and have them stay close to their banners. There will be no more infighting and no more defiance. They will do as you say, when you say, and you will do likewise with anything I command you to do.'

Vanik could sense the battle-lust among the assembled warriors, but all remained silent. He smiled at them.

'One more thing. Build the fires. Use the long grass if you have to. I want two dozen pyres lying ready to be lit within the next hour.'

'Should we bring forward the prisoners as well?' Dravga asked.

'No, not yet, but hold them in readiness. Go now, all of you. Glory to the Eightstar.'

The champions repeated the words and made the sign of the Gods, two sets of four fingers interlocked. They left the ridgetop, each returning to their own band of warriors. Only Jevcha lingered.

'You're playing a dangerous game,' she said.

'A necessary one,' Vanik corrected, looking out at the warband as it began to draw itself into shape.

'Keeping them from knowing even the most basic plans will only frustrate them further,' Jevcha continued. 'You can trust them. They will not turn on you with an army of the Free Cities bearing down on them.'

'Even our new allies? Am I also to entrust Skoren's bondsmen with my every thought, especially when we have not been able to find the Blackhand? I cannot afford to squander the reinforcements they bring, but I cannot fully trust them either, not until I have Skoren's head. He is still out there somewhere.'

'Dhol and Parmin have both sworn blood-oaths,' Jevcha

pointed out. 'For all we know the Blackhand may well have fled back through the Realmgate. What more do you want from his surviving warriors?'

'Skoren will not dare abandon this quest,' Vanik snapped. 'And his former warriors should be thankful I am not going to use them as fodder for the duardin cannons. Assemble your Darkoath, sister, and stack the fires high. You will see my reasons for yourself soon enough.'

Hysh was approaching its zenith as the army of Helmgard approached Vanik's warband. The storm had crept up with it, its shadow crawling across the plain. Though the thunder had ceased, the air was full of static charge and heavy with the promise of rain.

Slowly, Vanik's chieftains beat and cajoled their war parties into order. It was no simple thing, forming a host of the Gods for battle. Hours could be spent building a shield-wall or forcing bands of blood-hungry warriors together into a reserve. Some would gather, only to wander back to the baggage or into other groups when their champions moved on to another section of the line. Sometimes there would even be brawls between devotees of different Gods and daemons, though the threat of summary executions for all kept most in line.

Today, the warband shook itself out at a tolerable rate, likely in part because of the visible presence of the Free City army bearing down on them, and partly because of Vanik's baleful mood. He watched from the ridgetop as Jevcha's Darkoath took up their traditional post on the left of the line, Dravga and his corsairs on the right. The drummers had begun to work their skins, finding a rhythm that quickened the blood and summoned the attention of the deities and demigods of the Eightfold. The Darkoath had begun their binding chants, and Ulek's Bloodbound were working themselves into a fury, screaming and gibbering like beasts as they ingested the sacred root plants that allowed them to commune directly with the Warhound.

The army of the True Gods was making ready. Vanik finally felt his spirits start to stir.

The baggage had been moved back behind the crest. With it had gone the camp followers, and the remaining prisoners rounded up over the past month, the last hundred or so filthy, bedraggled farmers and townsfolk unlucky enough not to have died when the warband first reached their homesteads. Vanik glanced back, ensuring they were far enough away from the reverse side of the ridge.

The Lightning champion is coming, Nakali murmured in his head. *Your destiny is close at hand, little pilgrim.*

Vanik nodded but did not reply to the daemon, instead turning his attention back to the glittering, storm-shrouded host marching towards the ridge.

There was always something strangely fascinating about seeing an army of the so-called Free Cities arraying itself for battle. The defenders of Helmgard spread out on either side of their vanguard, which halted perhaps a little under a mile from the base of the ridgeline. Vanik could now discern the individual regiments and brigades constituting the long column. He could see pikemen and halberdiers beneath bright, waving battle flags, and cohorts of duardin stomping beneath their metal ancestor icons. After a while, the artillery became visible amidst the ranks and files, a long train of wagons and caissons dragged by shaggy mountain korgoths and tuskers.

'It is always the same,' Vanik mused out loud. Modred, the closest member of the retinue, looked at him questioningly.

'They fight the same way,' he elaborated, eyes still on the distant column as it peeled apart to form a line facing the ridge. 'So many of the Free Cities. They think of war as a profession. They view it as a job to be performed, like tilling a field or labouring in a forge. At the end of each day they collect their payment, and they go home. That is why they lose. That is why the Mortal Realms will fall. War is not a profession. It is the reason for existence itself. It gives us focus and purpose. It fixes the eyes of immortals on us, and brings us unimaginable rewards.'

Modred was silent for a while before responding. 'Sometimes I think I should like to go home, as these men do each night.'

'Do not,' Vanik said brusquely. 'Your opportunity to tread the Path will come someday, when you are older. Remember these lessons when you embark upon it. These servants of the False God are weak, coddled curs. Hate them for it.'

'They turned back the hosts of the Gods once before,' Modred said quietly. 'At least, that's what Jevcha said.'

'Their only strength is in their discipline,' Vanik said. 'With that a rabble or an ill-led horde can be halted. But we are neither. Remove their discipline, and what you see approaching now is a gathering of cowards. Look to the likes of Ulek. I doubt he sees any strength before him right now, only so many necks to be cleaved. That is all they really are.'

'But how?' Modred asked. 'How will you convince them to break their discipline before us?'

'Patience, boy,' Vanik responded. 'You will see soon enough.'

A wind blew from the mountains, making the tall grass bend and rustle. It carried with it the barked commands of the approaching army, and the rattle of their drums. Directly below Vanik the war parties were still shaking themselves into distinct blocks, the breeze twitching at their black pennants and hide banners. He felt his heartbeat quicken. The tempo of the daemonhide drums increased, as though in sympathy.

The fires were still being attended to. He had sent runners with orders that the grass ripped up by Faug's forage riders was to be stacked next to each blaze. They needed more time.

The Helmgard army had almost completed its initial deployments. The last artillery pieces were being wheeled forward, a conglomeration of great brass and iron weapons that glinted in the gathering gloom of the approaching storm. One of Jevcha's two Darkoath war parties were still chanting their oath praises, the guttural sound stirring up the battle line. The wind carried the blare of trumpets and bugles across the grassland, calling the soldiers of the mountain city to order.

'Tzatzo,' Vanik said, motioning to Modred. The retainer hurried forward, the Chaos steed chomping at her chains. Vanik mounted her. The Eightguard moved to surround him, but he raised one hand, warding them off.

'Remain here. If I do not return, Jevcha is to lead the host. Obey her as you would me.'

As the Eightguard murmured their agreement, Vanik held out a gauntlet towards Kulthuk.

'My banner.'

Kulthuk handed it to him, the black silk wrapped tight around the barbed haft. Without glancing back, Vanik spurred Tzatzo down the slope.

Heads turned at the thumping of the steed's claws, and chieftains and pack leaders barked at their men to make way. A cheer went up and spread like a changeling's lies – the warriors of Vanik's warband started to bellow his name and hammer sword edges and axe hafts against shield rims, sending up a clamour. Vanik passed between the parted ranks of Jevcha's Darkoaths, ignoring the swelling of mortal praise, his eyes on the open steppe beyond, and the dark line spread along the bottom of the foothills edging the distant mountainsides – the army of Helmgard.

His heart began to race as Tzatzo left the front ranks of the Darkoath and rode out into the grasslands, seemingly sensing her master's purpose. He was excited, he acknowledged, set on edge with the huntsman's yearning for the quarry he knew was nearby.

Failure had haunted him since he had set out from the Varanspire. He was testing the Gods' patience, of that he was certain. Each time he was merely taking a step towards a destination. Now, at last, the destination itself lay directly ahead of him. The knowledge that his fate was once again his own invigorated him, and it was all he could do not to cry out with joy as he rode, alone, towards the mortal host.

Your overconfidence will be your undoing. You forget you are still mortal too, Vanik.

He ignored Nakali's hiss. The daemon was tamed, and had been ever since the castellum. Nothing would cloud this moment, nothing could detract from the razor-edge excitement of being on the brink of either complete victory or absolute defeat.

He was leaving the warband behind. Ahead, across the open expanse, Castellan Albermarl's army was becoming ever clearer. He could make out the bright designs on the flags of the human regiments – griffons and anvils, lightning bolts, and their duardin allies' weaponry marked with ancestor masks. There was a battery of great cannons directly ahead, their uncapped muzzles like the gaping black maws of the spawn beasts dragged along in his warband's wake. The realisation that he was riding directly into their arc of fire only increased his own anticipation.

He was now closer to the Free City infantry than he was his

own host. Still he rode, Tzatzo panting and snarling beneath him, the wind whipping at his black standard as he let it fly free. Finally, just three or four hundred yards shy of the Helmgard front line, he dragged Tzatzo to a halt. She reared, forcing him to lock his knees tight to her flanks, and let out a piercing shriek that made the nearest men visibly flinch before him.

There were riders and runners racing between the nearest blocks of infantry, and the formation directly beside the artillery battery ahead of Vanik actually lowered their pikes towards him. The sight made him laugh out loud.

Eventually, a group of horsemen rode out past the halberdier reserve behind the great cannons. They were a cohort of fully plated knights, either side of a trio of horsemen. Two were dressed in the armour and finery affected by the leaders of the Free Cities, while the third carried a great banner of rippling silk, depicting a mountain crowned with lightning bolts. They passed by the cannons and rode out beyond the edge of the Helmgard host towards Vanik, moving from the gloom of the storm clouds out into the light of the plain. Their armour gleamed, and the banner became a bolt of flowing, liquid colour.

Vanik waited. His helmet was still at his hip, and he sneered at the horsemen as they rode up and pulled on their reins.

'You are bold, beast of darkness, to ride here alone,' said one of the riders. He wore a helm with the blue and yellow plumes of Helmgard's livery, its visor raised. The man's face was craggy and flinty-eyed, and he bore a thick auburn beard. It was a face Vanik had seen before. Kar'gek'kell had showed him it, in his visions during the Tournament of the Fly and the Fish.

'You are bold to come and face me, Castellan Albermarl,' he said. 'Even with your retinue of lackeys and armour-plated servants to try to protect you.'

'You ride out to parley, yet have only insults to offer,' Albermarl said, betraying no surprise at the fact that Vanik knew who he was.

'Insults are about all you are worth,' Vanik replied. 'I have a simple offer. Fight me, here and now, in single combat. If you triumph I will be slain, and my host will depart your miserable lands without further bloodshed. Likewise, if you fall by my blade, my host will depart, and not another village or farm will be razed. You have nothing to lose, nothing but your own life if you accept, and any pride you may have if you refuse.'

'You dare,' spat the rider next to Albermarl. He bore human-forged plate armour, and his raised visor betrayed younger features than the castellan's – a poor, wispy attempt at a moustache, and features unscarred by blade or disease. His blue eyes burned with hatred as he tried to drive his mount at Vanik, but Albermarl snatched his horse's bridle in time to stop him. Vanik laughed in his face.

'Is this child your get, castellan?' he demanded. 'I will find his mother in your mountain city and make her watch while I feed him alive to my steed.'

'You think me a fool,' Albermal said, casting a furious glance at the younger rider. 'Your warband of murderers and daemon-worshippers are outnumbered, undisciplined and ill-equipped. You seek to achieve your aims with a duel because you know that when full battle is joined your horde will be crushed and I will be victorious.'

'I see you have no pride to lose then,' Vanik said. 'You will never be one of the Lightning God's champions, Albermarl. You are a coward.'

'And you will never serve your dark king. Your bones and the bones of your rabble will moulder away on this plain, forgotten by even your own Gods.'

'By refusing to fight, you condemn thousands of your men to slaughter and death,' Vanik said. 'My Gods and masters will rejoice in each and every killing, regardless of who falls. To give battle here today is to make these grasslands a shrine to the inevitable glory of Chaos. That is what will never be forgotten.'

Albermarl opened his mouth to respond, but Vanik carried on over him.

'I see I am wasting words with you. For this, I will ensure every last one of your soldiers is slaughtered and your city burned in front of you, before I allow the final blow to fall.'

'When this battle is over I will have your remains staked out-side the Three Doors, as a warning to any more of your insane breed that tries to enter my realm,' Albermarl retorted. This time, Vanik did not respond – he was already wheeling Tzatzo away, back towards the ridgeline. As he rode, he heard a cheer going up from the ranks of the Helmgard soldiers, seemingly drawn by his retreat.

He realised he was smiling again. A part of him had been praying to the Eightfold that Albermarl would turn down the chance to duel.

Now he could slaughter them all.

The womenfolk were making their final blessings as Vanik rode back among the host. Those touched by the Eye passed along the front of each band in turn, wailing and tearing at their hair and clothes. Bannermen lowered their standards and icons to be touched by them, or slashed cuts along their fore-arms to anoint the poles. Some of the women were smeared in the blood of the last of the slaughtered livestock, shrieking for the attentions of their daemonic patrons. Mother Yogoth had found a mule somewhere and tied herself to its back, and was now riding up and down the line, her crooked staff aloft, attempting to appear dignified as she clung to the exhausted beast's back and screeched out gibberish blessings.

The drummers were reaching a crescendo, hammering their daemonhide skins, the primal beat calling Vanik back among his warriors. He rode through one of Skoren's former war parties, the dark-skinned Uluthu tribesmen of the champion Dhol. They bellowed praises in their own tongue at him as he passed, desperately reaching out to touch his armour or the flanks of his steed. Any antipathy towards their new lord was now gone, subsumed by the presence of the enemies of the True Gods.

It was his warband now, and the knowledge filled Vanik with a bloody, unexpected pride.

He rode through the rear of the main line and on up the ridge, past the fires still smouldering next to their stacked grass. The Eightguard were waiting for him on the crest, and rallied round as he pulled Tzatzo to a stop.

'The coward will not fight me,' he said, handing his banner back to Kulthuk.

'Praise the Gods,' Kulthuk responded, expression unreadable behind his black helm. 'I was beginning to wonder whether there would be a battle at all today.'

Vanik's answer was interrupted by a crash. He assumed he was hearing the sound of thunder, and twisted in his saddle in expectation of lightning strikes. Iron struck instead – one of the great cannons of the army of Helmgard had fired, lost now in a distant gout of dirty smoke. Vanik turned just in time to see mud and torn grass burst from the site of the round shot's impact. The cannonball bounced once, twice, then was lost in the grass as it skittered to a halt maybe fifty yards shy of Jevcha's Darkoaths. The Chaos marauders let up a great jeer that spread rapidly across the whole line.

'Ranging shot,' Vanik said. 'They will have to advance closer if their long guns cannot reach us.'

'And we attack while they are still setting their cannons in place?' Kulthuk asked.

'No.'

Another great cannon loosed its thunderclap discharge, and another round shot ploughed up a line of grass and dirt. More cheers followed its failure to find a target.

'You are to divide, brothers,' Vanik said, addressing the whole of the Eightguard. 'Ride now to the champions of each war party. Tell them to send warriors back to pile the grass upon the fires as soon as the next gun sounds. Then, when I send Modred among you, you are to follow the instructions he bears without hesitation. Kill any that refuse them. Am I clear?'

His retinue answered. He was.

'Then go.'

He watched, alone now apart from Modred as, like a great beast bristling with the spines of pikes and spears, the army of Helmgard began to drag itself forward.

The temptation was there, the urge to order an immediate attack. To charge screaming across the grassland, give Tzatzo her head, and crash heedlessly into the blocks of human and duardin soldiers while they pushed forward, struggling to hold their formations. It would be slaughter, it would be glorious, but at the end of it he would be dead, and he suspected Albermarl would not be. He would leave it to the likes of Ulek or lesser champions of the Gods to throw themselves madly into the fray. There would be a time for that, but it was not yet.

Albermarl's army completed its redeployment. Vanik watched the distant gunners as they hurried around their pieces, swabbing barrels, ramming down charges, spiking the powder bags and setting fuse cord. It seemed to take an age. Eventually, he saw artillerists stepping away from one of the great bronze instruments, clapping hands over their ears.

The gun roared. This time it was in range. Its shot hit a small rise just ahead of Dravga's corsairs and bounced up and over them, taking off the head of a single warrior in a splatter of brains and shattered skull before burying itself in the foot of the slope below Vanik.

'Eightstar guide me,' he murmured as the thunderous echo of the discharge clapped out over the plain. It had begun.

The rest of the battery opened fire. The crash was like the barring of the Varanspire's gates, an ear-straining report that seemed to make the whole grassy plain shiver. Impacts followed. Round shot whipped and slashed like great, invisible blades at Vanik's line, blood blossoming amidst the torn limbs and broken bodies that were flung back by the iron's passage. Worse followed – from his vantage point Vanik could see more blooms of smoke coming from behind the bristling front line of the Helmgard army. Moments later the mortar shells wailed down, like outraged daemons that burst themselves apart amidst fire and smoke, further shredding the Chaos line. One shell slammed into the earth directly below, halfway up the ridgeline, and Tzatzo reared with anger as great clods of steaming dirt came raining down around them.

He turned to Modred, the retainer even more pale-faced and wide-eyed than usual.

'Go to each of the Eightguard at the head of the war parties,' he ordered, as the echoes of the first salvo cracked out over the plain. 'And tell them to withdraw.'

The Godhammer battery was crashing its first salvo into the storm-heavy air as Marius approached Castellan Albermarl's retinue. The knights of his personal guard parted to allow the

Stormcast through, just as the wind blew smoke from the mortar batteries forward to briefly shroud them all in a pall of gunpowder-reeking smog.

'Lord castellan,' Marius said. Albermarl and the son of Lord Fulbricht, Rodik Fulbricht, had both dismounted, and the former was now utilising one of Marius' triscopes, gifted to him when he had first ascended to command of the city, to survey the work of his artillery's initial barrage. Grunbad was standing nearby with one of his runesmiths and a trio of grim-faced hammerer guards. He grimaced when he saw Marius, but said nothing to the Stormcast. Albermarl looked up from his tripod-mounted device as the smoke momentarily obscured his view, and noticed Marius' presence.

'Lord Ordinator,' he said, making the sign of the lightning bolt. 'Come to see our batteries compete?'

The artillery companies of Helmgard, split as they were between human and duardin pieces, enjoyed a healthy rivalry. It had been a long time since they had last tested one another anywhere except on the proving grounds and practice ranges. Rodik Fulbricht was grinning with excitement, and even Albermarl, usually as stoic as a duardin, appeared to be enjoying the ear-splitting roar of the heavy guns. They had been waiting weeks for this, Marius realised.

'You refused the daemon-worshipper, as we agreed?' he asked, ignoring Albermarl's question. The castellan frowned slightly but nodded.

'Yes. His hand has been made clear. He seeks only to slay me.'

'He is an arrogant beast,' Rodik added, his smile turned to anger.

'Your safety is paramount,' Marius said to Albermarl.

'We have had this discussion,' Albermarl said, expression now as dark as the storm clouds overhead.

'In the quiet of your halls, yes,' Marius said. 'The thunder of battle is a different matter. Even when the fighting is joined he will seek to tempt you into a personal challenge. You must continue to refuse. It does not matter if we are victorious this day – should you fall it will be a hollow triumph. You have made Helmgard a great city for all free peoples. That must continue.'

'Do not worry, Lord Ordinator,' Rodik said. 'If we see the beast in the melee, I will uphold my family's honour and slay him myself.'

'You will do no such thing,' Albermarl snapped. 'You will wait on my instructions and follow them to the letter, is that clear? We all have our part to play.'

Rodik looked crestfallen, but managed to nod.

Albermarl returned his gaze to the triscope's lens and cursed. Marius followed the direction of the triscope, and saw immediately what had drawn the oath.

The smoke from the mortars had lifted while the gunners reloaded, and Albermarl's retinue was afforded a clear view of the Chaos host arrayed below the ridgeline opposite. At first, Marius thought infighting had broken out in the midst of the heathen horde – the line was in motion. After a few seconds, however, it became apparent that there was a uniformity to the movement. They were going back. He realised there were thick plumes of smoke rising up from the rear ranks of the dark mass of bodies, shrouding the ridgeline that lay over them.

'They're withdrawing,' Albermarl said, eye still to the triscope. 'It's as I feared. They will refuse battle, and we will have to hunt them all the way back to the Three Doors again. This will take us weeks!'

'We must pursue immediately!' Rodik said. 'They are disorganised!'

'You will await my orders,' Albermarl snapped, then turned from the scope to Marius.

'It may be a trap,' he said.

'I agree,' Marius said. 'Haste is as much a danger right now as the daemon-worshippers themselves.'

'Nevertheless, we cannot allow them to refuse battle again,' Albermarl said. He began speaking to the half a dozen couriers clustered around his standard bearer. 'The main battle line will advance four hundred yards. The mortars are to remain sited, no units to break formation or get ahead of the great cannons. And send word to Lord Fulbricht to bring up his cavalry.'

The order was addressed not at Rodik, but for the benefit of his father.

'I will lead the vanguard,' the younger Fulbricht said eagerly.

'Tell Lord Fulbricht that his son is to remain at his side at all times,' Albermarl called after the messenger as he rode off. He turned to the young noble.

'Go to your father, and don't do anything rash,' he told him. Rodik mounted his horse and spurred after the courier, grinning.

'You trust him to keep his head?' Marius asked.

'No,' Albermarl admitted. 'But I do trust his father to keep him in check, certainly better than I can.'

'If it were my decision, I would have left him with the squires in the city.'

'With respect, Lord Ordinator, your station means you do not have to concern yourself with the favour or goodwill of noble lords. The Fulbricht family must be kept close if the harmony of Helmgard is to be maintained. And that means favouring the younger Fulbricht with a place on my retinue.'

'Your human customs will never make sense to me,' Grunbad growled, speaking up for the first time. 'If one of my clan kindred sought the favour of a leading lodge or guild, they would be honoured to have their offspring taught by one of the lowliest apprentices. A master of the craft has more important things to do than cleave to some high-born beardling.'

The cannon fire had ceased, replaced by the rattling of drums and the clatter of arms and armour as the regiments of human and duardin infantry across the Helmgard line stirred into motion.

'They're trying to screen their withdrawal using the smoke from the fires,' Albermarl said, looking once more through his scope. 'A wise move, for such savages.'

'Do not underestimate them,' Marius said. 'Not all servants of Chaos are blood-crazed madmen. The one leading them would not have risen to his current rank if he were.'

Rodik Fulbricht rode amidst the armoured might of Helmgard as they advanced. As a mountain city, the numbers of horsemen the noble houses could put in the field were not great. The duardin had no truck with mounts, and many of the human guilds and free associations sought to gain their favour by emulating them. Nevertheless, the open grasslands below the Ironroots made for excellent riding pastures, and Albermarl had cultivated heavy cavalry tactics among the human nobles of the Free City since the orruk horde had been repelled almost two decades earlier. The army of Helmgard boasted a host of light horsemen, reared on the plains, and a core of noblemen, the Knights of the Mountain.

Rodik was there with them beneath his father's hawk banner, ahead of the main body of the army. A wall of smoke was rising up before them, born out of the fires set in a vain attempt to cover the barbarians' retreat. The knowledge that they were in flight before the might of Helmgard filled Rodik with a fierce pride. He had been brought up on stories of the last time the beasts of the Dark Gods had been driven from Helmgard, of how his grandfather had fought in his youth in the great battle before the city walls. Even more importantly, he had seen the ruined townships of Weatherward and Caeston, seen the bodies staked out on the roadsides and smelled the charred flesh of those herded inside shrines and barns and burned to death. The memories made him clutch his lance a little tighter and dig his spurs in a little deeper.

Today they would all be avenged.

'Hold formation,' his father, Vulf, bellowed over the clatter of plate armour and the drumming of hooves. The phalanx of knights surrounding them was a wedge at the heart of an open mass of light horsemen, the steel fist that would crash through the barbarian's disorganised horde and turn their retreat into a total rout.

Rodik had already ensured he was in the front rank, by his father's side. His visor was still up, and the unrestricted view of their quarry and the rapidly narrowing ground between them was only fuelling his desire to rake his spurs back. The smoke was starting to obscure the main mass of the barbarian horde as they mobbed their way back past their fires, and the ridgeline beyond was now wholly shrouded. They couldn't be allowed to escape!

'Forward, knights of Helmgard!' he yelled over the thunder of hooves, digging in his spurs. He heard his father curse, but ignored him. His stallion, Morningstar, went over a thick tussock, and the jolt caused his visor to clatter down, plunging him into a world of panting, steel claustrophobia. The sudden restriction in his vision caused him to yank reflexively on Morningstar's reins, and the barded warhorse twisted awkwardly to one side, neighing shrilly.

He barely had time to spit an oath at the beast before something crashed into him from the right. He was vaguely aware, through the slit of light provided by his visor, of another knight partly colliding with him as he sought to compensate for the sudden movement of the younger Fulbricht's mount. Plate armour clattered, and he noticed more bodies – man and beast – riding past as the entire formation sought to shift in time to avoid unhorsing Rodik.

He cursed again, cheeks burning with embarrassment, snarling at Morningstar as he sought to wrestle the distressed horse back into line. Something rebounded off his left side, almost driving him from the saddle, and he twisted awkwardly as he tried to see who else had ridden into him. Reins gripped in one hand, he managed to get his visor back up, and gasped a lungful of the smoke-filled air.

'Sire, don't!' shouted a voice, a gauntlet clapping against his shoulder. He turned, squinting in the sudden light, trying to discern the identity of the knight desperately motioning at him.

'Lower your visor!' the man shouted, rapping the side of his own helmet for emphasis. The livery on the man's surcoat was a blazing comet, or was it a sun? Was that Sir Longmark? Or Sir Tlutz? For some reason he couldn't seem to think clearly. He could no longer differentiate between the thunder of hooves and the rush of blood in his ears.

Something struck him again, this time cracking off his breastplate, and he realised it wasn't some knight barrelling past in the smoke now swirling around him. An arrow had just hit his chest and rebounded from the duardin-forged steel of his cuirass.

They were all being struck. Arrows were slashing down through the smoke, hissing like mountain vipers as the wind dragged through their fletching. The sudden disruption in the formation hadn't just been because of Rodik's rash charge. Members of Fulbricht's elite were falling, struck through with black shafts.

Another arrow slashed past Rodik's head, and he smacked his visor back down. The knight he decided must be Sir Longmark had seized Morningstar's bridle and was turning the horse back after the rest of the formation. Only then did Rodik realise that Longmark had the broken stub of an arrow impaled in his right shoulder, blood staining his surcoat. The arrows had little individual hope of penetrating the thick plating of the Helmgard knights, but the weight of shafts darting through the smoke of the grass fires meant some were finding weak spots in joints and between barding plates. The attack, so certain of victory mere moments before, was suddenly in doubt.

A horn blared, three short, sharp notes. Through his mounting panic, Rodik recognised the command to rally. Another arrow clattered from Morningstar's armoured flank, and he realised that Sir Longmark was pointing. There was a banner amidst the smoke, his father's hawk standard. Grasping his mount's reins firmly, he urged the steed towards it.

'To me, Knights of the Mountain!' Vulf Fulbricht was bellowing. Rodik pushed his way through the press of horsemen to his father's side, glad suddenly that his lowered visor hid his expression.

'Sigmar's oath, boy,' Vulf spat. 'I thought you'd been struck.'

'He is well, sire,' Sir Longmark answered before Rodik could reply.

'Did you tell Sir Longmark to look after me?' Rodik demanded, his fear stoking a sudden anger.

'I told you to stay by my side, damn you!' Vulf shouted. An arrow had struck the hawk standard being carried by Sir Gerrin, and had snagged in its silken folds. Amidst the confusion, Rodik found the sight of it dangling there strangely incongruous.

'You stay with me or Sir Longmark!' Vulf was bellowing. 'And hold the damned formation! Torrin, sound the rally again!'

The horn blared once more. Slowly, the mass of knights around Rodik were beginning to order themselves, suffering beneath the incessant archery like men pushing through a hailstorm.

'That's enough,' Vulf snapped. 'Forward. Sound the advance, at the trot. And stay together!'

The mass around Rodik began to move, pushing him with it. He experienced the sudden, mad urge to lift his visor. He could hardly breathe. His heart felt as if it were going to dent his breastplate.

Then, abruptly, the smoke cleared. They were out, out and past the grass fires. Ahead, the ridge loomed up before them.

It was swarming with horsemen. Riders in pelts and rough leathers were wheeling like a swarm of bees across the near slope, loosing off arrows from short composite bows. They let out a wild, ululating wail as the first Helmgard knights cleared the smoke beneath them.

'Where are the damned hobelars?' Vulf shouted, referring to the light cavalry screen that was supposed to have shielded the knights. They had been ahead and on either side of the formation when they'd first entered the smoke, but now there was no sign of them. Not until Rodik realised Morningstar was riding over the humped shapes of men and animals, stuck like wild boars by dozens of fletched black shafts.

'Press on!' Vulf shouted, the horn sounding again. 'Up the damned slope!'

'Father!' Rodik shouted as Morningstar swerved around the body of another hobelar and his mount, forcing him away from

Vulf. The arrows were coming thick as rain now, a continuous deluge loosed by the ever-rotating barbarian cavalrymen just ahead. The Knights of the Mountain hit the foot of the slope and began to climb, their mounts blowing hard. Everyone around Rodik was stuck with arrows, their plate armour tested to its limits. Three were caught in Morningstar's barding, and another had lodged in his own thigh plate. He could feel its wicked tip nicking his skin.

The mounted archers ahead were going back. Their steeds, small and hardy, took the slope easily, while their riders continued to send arrow after arrow slashing down. Now that the knights were clear of the smoke, they were able to pick their targets as well. The knight to Rodik's left – he didn't see who – was suddenly gone as his horse went down with a crash of armour, his lance splintering as it dug into the slope's earth. Another arrow thwacked, quivering, into the boiled leather of his saddle. Sir Walin was to his left now, his lightning-bolt heraldry half obscured by his ripped surcoat. Sir Longmark was still to his right, then his father, arrows studding the front of his mount's barding. They were still going forward despite it all, still climbing, the crest drawing nearer, Morningstar striding out beneath Rodik. Sweat stung his eyes. He could hardly breathe. His entire existence, his very purpose in life, had been reduced to reaching the top of the ridge before one of those arrows punched home and stole his life away.

Then, abruptly, he realised the arrows were no longer flying. A braying horn was sounding an unfamiliar note, and the savage horsemen and their maddening bows were going back, back properly now, over the crest, disappearing from view.

They were going to escape.

'On!' he heard Vulf shouting. 'The bastards are running!'

A hundred yards, maybe less. The last of the horse archers

were vanishing over the crest. But something was taking their place. Between the sweat and the slit vision of his visor, Rodik could make out a black standard. Sunlight flashed from dark plate armour. Horsemen. Knights. Maybe a dozen, beneath the black flag that had been carried by the beast who led this horde. They were directly above him.

'Charge!' he heard his father screaming breathlessly. 'Sound the charge!'

The notes pealed out shrilly. The Knights of the Mountain tried to respond, digging their spurs in, but their steeds could no longer match their riders' fervour. They were blown, exhausted by the pursuit up the slope and wounded by the stings of dozens of arrows, their formation broken. Rodik raked Morningstar's flanks, but the white-slicked beast only slowed, neighing mournfully.

Above, another horn answered Sir Torrin's. The knights of Chaos charged.

PART THIRTEEN

OF BLOOD AND BROKEN LANCES

Vanik's blood sang with the promise of slaughter. Tzatzo needed no urging – she sprang down the slope, shrieking with hunger, her many-fanged maw agape. The Eightguard were either side of him, stirrup to stirrup, lances raised.

The human knights below were totally disordered, broken by the rain of arrows from Faug's light cavalry, the smoke and the slope of the ridge.

It had been a long time since Vanik had seen prey so ripe for the slaughter.

He chose the first to die. The man was standing in his stirrups, seemingly trying to direct those around him. A standard bearing a hawk was flying over him, the same symbol worn by the boy who had accompanied Albermarl. He wondered whether it was him beneath the burnished plate armour. He hoped so.

Tzatzo outpaced the steeds of the Eightguard. His target

seemed to have sensed his attention and was now desperately trying to urge his steed into a canter. The distance closed. He lowered the lance given to him by Modred, couched it under his arm, and screamed his praise to the Gods.

'For the Eightstar!'

The lance struck, square and true. It slammed through the hawk knight's breastplate and splintered, pulverising his heart and lungs, bursting his torso apart in a welter of blood that struck Vanik as he surged past.

He didn't see the knight lifted from his saddle by the impact – Tzatzo had already carried him by, leaping the last few yards down the slope. The mount of the knight beyond the first one tried to shy away, terrified by the unnatural sight and smell of the Chaos steed, but that only served to expose the unarmoured underside of its throat to Tzatzo's jaws. The beast latched itself around the horse's neck and twisted, her momentum and force of impact only adding to her strength. The horse's head came away in a spurt of bright arterial blood that doused both the human knight and Vanik, a second before Nakali flew from its scabbard and beheaded the falling nobleman.

Yes! the daemon howled as the blood drenched it, searing as it was absorbed into the black blade. There would be no complaints from Nakali today, of that Vanik was certain.

Tzatzo's collision with the horse arrested her charge, and she threw her head back to gulp down the great gobbet of flesh she'd ripped free. Vanik twisted and cut back with Nakali in time to parry a sword swing from the knight bearing the hawk standard, while a mace carried by another knight to his left crashed into his warpsteel shield. For a few seconds, he was alone, surrounded by the noblemen of Helmgard.

Then the Eightguard slammed home.

* * *

Riding full tilt against the Chaos knights, with their line well ordered, the human elite of the mountain city might have met the Eightguard on an even footing. But disorganised and with their mounts barely managing a trot uphill, it was never going to be anything other than a massacre. The Eightguard's lances took the front rank almost without exception, spitting riders or toppling their mounts amidst a storm of splintering shafts. Their steeds slammed against the falling wall of armoured man and horseflesh, while the riders drew swords, axes and maces. Then the real butchery began.

'Glory to the Four,' Vanik snarled, and thrust Nakali into the flank of the hawk standard bearer who'd turned in his saddle to strike him. The daemon sword bit through the burnished plate armour where a mortal's sword would have been jarred aside, and the knight's agonised scream faded as his soul was devoured by the thirsting daemon within. The hawk standard wavered and fell, snapped and trampled in the press.

Vanik searched the press for any sign of the castellan or his banner, but there was none – he had not joined his army's vanguard. He was a coward and a whelp, and the desire to see him slain made Vanik's anger surge.

'Stay together,' he shouted at his retinue, locking his stirrups to compensate for Tzatzo's sudden twist as she went after another rearing mount. The Free City cavalry outnumbered his retinue by at least three to one – let them rally or re-form and Vanik knew the battle could quickly turn.

But the knights of Helmgard weren't thinking about rallying. Vanik could already feel the pressure around him decrease as he tore Nakali free. He saw the rear ranks further down the slope turning their steeds away, back towards the smoke of the grass fires. He grinned savagely, urging Tzatzo on.

The Gods were watching, and their pilgrim would not disappoint them.

'What in the name of the God-King is happening?' Albermarl snapped. He turned away from his triscope in exasperation, but none of his retainers had an answer. Only Marius spoke.

'I suspect young Fulbricht has got ahead of himself.'

Albermarl grimaced, but didn't reply, turning back to his lenses. Marius watched the bank of smoke, even his own keen eyesight unable to detect what was happening beyond. A few dozen hobelars had come fleeing from it earlier. One, caught and dragged to Albermarl, offered little but a garbled description of a hail of arrows coming from the ridgeline. Later a riderless horse in the barding of the Knights of the Mountain had been seen clattering through the smoke, its armour bristling with black shafts. Since then the sounds of battle had been audible – Marius had recognised a horn sounding the charge, followed by the crash of steel and the shrieks of horses, but beyond that nothing.

'This is madness,' Albermarl said, eyes still pressed to his scope. 'I should be up there, going forward with the attack!'

'We all feel that way, castellan,' Marius growled. 'Do you think this is a simple matter for any of Sigmar's warrior-sons? I have been forged in lightning and cast in dazzling brilliance in order to crush the forces of Chaos. My every waking thought is bent towards that deed. But right now I must see to your own protection, and I cannot do that in the front ranks. That is the realisation I have been forced to come to terms with. You should make peace with your own position. You are the general of this army, not a young knight errant in the vanguard.'

Albermarl didn't reply.

The main body of the army of Helmgard had come to a halt

about three hundred paces from the grass fires that had covered the barbarians' retreat. The flames had spread, adding to the bank of smoke.

'Lord Fulbricht has engaged,' Marius said, trying to penetrate the uncertainty that seemed to have descended on the leaders of Helmgard's host. 'We should support him. If the savages have turned back in force, he will be quickly overwhelmed.'

'We can't know if they've turned or if they're just covering their retreat,' Albermarl said. 'If it's the former, the last thing I want to do is send the main battle line into that smoke without artillery support.'

'A brigade would be enough, surely,' Marius said.

'And risk them being overwhelmed?'

Marius forced himself to keep his voice respectful. 'Castellan, I have seen a great deal of war throughout the Eight Realms, and if it has taught me just one thing it's that any decision is better than no decision.'

Albermarl didn't reply immediately, setting his eye back to the triscope, as though hoping that a few more seconds would allow the smoke to dissipate. It didn't.

'Order,' he snapped, gesturing to a courier. 'To the Draz forgeband and the Gunbold brigade. Advance in close formation to the base of the ridgeline and support Lord Fulbricht's cavalry while they disengage. Pass word on to Lord Fulbricht as well, if he yet lives. And be sure to stress that they are to send runners back at regular intervals. I want to know what's happening in that smoke!'

'Tell the brigade to watch their flanks,' Marius added. 'They have light cavalry. Many horse tribes of the Chaos Wastes are deadly archers. We seem to have underestimated them at the start of this engagement, let us not do so again.'

The courier looked at Albermarl, who nodded firmly. The

man rode off, seeking out the correct flags and icons amongst the main battle line.

'Order to all other bands and regiments,' Albermarl said to the rest of his gaggle of messengers. 'Stand ready to advance. If they really haven't retreated, we are going to take that ridge.'

The Grimbald forgeband advanced, with the humans of the Hilfinger regiment following behind them. They marched with the customary slow, close-order step of Helmgard infantry, the heavily armoured duardin formed three deep ahead of the human pikemen, the musketeers hard on the flanks. They were at the centre of the Draz forgeband and the Gunbold brigade, flanked by their sister regiments – Hoffbad to their right and Franz to their left.

Hilfinger had captained his pike and musket regiment for over a decade. They had held the line against the orruks at Green Pasture, and their silk standard bore the coveted battle honour of Helmgard itself, earned when the last great Chaos incursion had been turned back. Hilfinger's grandfather had commanded the regiment then – Hilfinger had grown up on his strange, tall tales of the battle. He had yearned to honour the old man in battle for as long as he could remember. When the runner bearing the order for the Gunbold brigade to advance arrived, Hilfinger hadn't hesitated.

'Keep your ranks,' the slope-marshal snapped, instinctively returning to his days as a regimental sergeant by echoing their barked commands. 'Look to the standards!'

Hilfinger could hear Stromez, the duardin, barking the same orders to his warriors just ahead. United beneath the mountain and lightning bolt of Helmgard, men and duardin marched together into the smoke.

Hilfinger fought to master his own anticipation. The ash

caught in his lungs as the smoke shrouded the front ranks, coiling like a living creature around the regiment. Visibility dropped off instantly – all he could see were the helmets of the duardin ranks in front, and the dull glow of the grass fires that had spread across the front of the ridgeline. The duardin's iron-shod boots were soon kicking up ash and stamping out the flames still flickering around the charred stalks. Hilfinger coughed but kept going, a hand over his mouth.

While approaching the smoke, he'd been able to hear the sounds of a melee coming from ahead, but now there was nothing, nothing besides the tramp-tramp-tramp of feet and the rat-tat-tat of the drummers. He glanced left and right. He could make out the regiment's handgunners, advancing hard on the flanks of the pike block, but beyond them there was no sign of the other duardin warbands or human regiments. All was lost in a pall. He could only trust that they were still advancing side by side.

He noticed after another hundred yards that there were bodies. At first, he saw a row of half a dozen dark shapes off to the left, scattered around a furrow that had been ploughed in the dirt. He realised he was looking at the dismembered corpses of barbarian tribesmen, cut apart by a round shot that was now buried in the earth just ahead. A little further on and the duardin began to pass around the humped shapes of horses and riders. They were all stuck with wicked-looking arrows, their shafts turned black by a coating of tar.

He recognised the hauberks of hobelar light cavalry, and then the white plate armour of one of the Knights of the Mountain. The men behind him began murmuring among themselves as they passed around and over the arrow-riddled corpses of riders and mounts.

'Silence in the ranks,' Hilfinger snapped.

He'd barely spoken before one of the duardin in the forge-band bellowed.

'Movement ahead! A manling, just one!'

'Halt!' Hilfinger cried, moments after Stromez. The drums relayed the order with a rattle, and the regiment shuddered to a stop, arms and armour clattering.

Everything was still, everything bar the slowly coiling smoke that shrouded everything. His breathing seemed unnaturally loud, and he suppressed the foolish urge to hold it. He found himself wondering if the duardin were seeing things. One man? Should he have ordered the pikes to brace? Had Greich and Thron's handgunners presented? They were already primed and loaded, weren't they?

Then he saw it too. A figure came stumbling through the smog, clutching one arm. The slope-marshal recognised the armour of another Knight of the Mountain. He was alone, or at least he seemed to be. He was also drenched in blood.

'Grimbald, open ranks!' Stromez barked. The duardin unlocked their shields and allowed the knight to stumble in among them. One grabbed hold of the man's ripped surcoat and dragged him back through the formation towards Hilfinger's men.

'Eyes front!' Hilfinger barked at the Free City's soldiers, before taking hold of the knight from the grim-faced duardin. He could hear his panicked, wheezing breaths rattling about inside his helmet. He lifted the knight's visor, and found himself looking into the wide blue eyes of a terrified youth.

'They're coming,' the boy stammered, trying in vain to break free from Hilfinger's grasp.

'Who?' he demanded, holding firm.

'The black knights,' the boy said, casting a terrified look back the way he had come. 'Beasts riding beasts. It was a slaughter.'

'Who are you?' Hilfinger demanded, trying to hold together

the knight's ripped, blood-drenched surcoat with his free hand. The device looked like a hawk, and realisation struck the slope-marshal.

'You're Fulbricht the younger?' he said. 'Rodik Fulbricht, son of Lord Vulf Fulbricht?'

'They're coming!' the young knight repeated, voice rising shrilly.

'What happened?' Hilfinger demanded, drawing him in close and lowering his voice. 'Where is your father? Where are the Knights of the Mountain?'

'Manling,' Stromez shouted from ahead, his voice heavy with warning. A second later, Hilfinger realised why. The earth underfoot had started to tremor.

'Front ranks, shield-wall!' Stromez bellowed to his forgeband.

'Pikes, brace,' Hilfinger echoed to his own regiment, his orders followed by another rattle of the drums. 'Handgunners will fire on their officer's command only! Sergeant Gatz, take Lord Fulbricht to the rear ranks and remain there by his side, understood?'

'Yes, sir,' Gatz said, the burly soldier taking hold of the younger knight and guiding him firmly back through the interlocking ranks of blue-liveried pikemen.

'Courage, defenders of the mountain!' Hilfinger shouted, his body flushed with a heady rush of blood. 'Show these daemon-loving bastards how true men fight!'

The regiment's cheer was short-lived. From out of the mist, a terrible scream made Hilfinger's blood run cold.

Suddenly, he realised that all of his grandfather's stories had been true.

Ulek was blind. It was more than just sweat and the stinging smoke; it was the blood-blindness, the mindless savagery that descended upon Khorne's favoured when battle was joined. He and his Bloodbound had been chewing the butcher's roots, their lips and teeth now stained red with the maddening juices of the sacred wasteland plant. It had taken him beyond mortal concerns, beyond even the needs of sight, sound and smell. Everything was a hypersensitive blur, shot through with glimmers of steel.

There was a mass of bodies ahead, that much he knew. All unbutchered, fresh blood and unbaptised skulls. Heathens and unbelievers. Cowards. They had to die. The need made Ulek scream as he ran, scream until his throat was raw, scream until his face was red and his body shook. His muscles ached as he pounded down the slope, refusing to allow any other Bloodbound to reach the blasphemers ahead of him.

A part of his mind was dimly aware of a crash, and of more smoke joining the cloud that seemed to shroud everything. The air was suddenly full of zipping, cracking sounds. It didn't matter. They were close, so close. He screamed again, raising his great spear. He could not wait. He could not wait any longer.

He flung the spear as he ran, every ounce of his Khorne-blessed strength behind the throw. It crashed into the front of the mass ahead. He saw blood gout, sudden crimson across his vision, a blessing and a promise of more to come. He drew his axe from his belt without breaking stride and, with an ear-bursting bellow, threw himself at the gap his spear had ploughed.

'*Blood for the Blood God!*'

His vision blurred further. He saw a shield, its metal surface embossed with the icon of a glaring duardin. It crumpled. Blood spurted. He felt its warm droplets splatter his bare torso. He let out an incoherent roar of praise. A hammer struck his side. He registered pain. It only drove him harder into the mass before him. His muscles burned with exertion as his axe rose and fell, chopping metal and wood, then skin and bone. A helmet crumpled, jellied brain matter coating his forearm. A pike head scored along his side, drawing more blood.

More. There always had to be more. That was all that mattered.

His axe was stuck. It had carved halfway through the torso of whatever was impeding him, and now it was lodged there. He gripped the haft with both hands, slippery with blood, and ripped it out with another scream. He felt more blood strike him, this time from the side. A part of him was aware of the fact that the rest of the Bloodbound were cutting their way into the offering-herd, each striving to earn the attentions of the Warhound. They could not succeed. He was the only one worthy of great Kharneth. He had to kill more.

His spear was nearby, impaled through a still-twitching body, painted in blood. He ripped it free and swung it with his other hand, its broad-bladed tip clattering aside the pikes, axes and hammers coming at him. His side ached, and pain in his shoulder and left arm stung him whenever he moved. He was injured, he realised. Wounded in half a dozen places. All bled. He rejoiced.

'Khorne, witness me!' he roared and, thrusting his spear ahead, threw himself deeper into the endless press of screaming, struggling bodies.

Albermarl didn't wait for the runners. The howling that rose from the smoke was message enough – it was the bloodcurdling scream of thousands of beasts and savages, wed to Dark Gods and daemons.

They hadn't been retreating. They'd been luring the army of Helmgard in.

'The whole line will advance,' Albermarl barked. 'The reserve is to hold alongside the artillery. Battery commanders to choose targets at will, once the smoke clears. Watch our flanks!'

The castellan moved away from his triscope as he spoke, gesturing to one of his retainers to pack the delicate tool away. Marius didn't need to ask where he was going. He could tell he'd had enough of high command. He was going to follow the main battle line in.

'Castellan–' he began to say.

'Not now,' Albermarl said, glaring at Marius.

'If you go forward with the main line, you will place this entire battle in jeopardy.'

'How am I meant to command from back here?' Albermarl replied, untying his hammer from its straps across his back. 'None of us can see anything! If you wish to safeguard me constantly, Lord Ordinator, you can come with me.'

Marius began to unlatch his own twin, short-hafted astral hammers from his belt. In truth, he could no longer stand by himself. If Albermarl wished to go into the midst of the fray, he would at least be there at his side. That was where this battle would be won or lost.

'I am with you,' he said. 'And may the God-King guide us both.'

The monster killed Stromez.

Hilfinger saw it plough its great spear through the duardin's ancestor shield as though the gromril were mere parchment. It caught the duardin just beneath his silver ancestor mask, the stylised metal beard turning suddenly red as his head was half severed by the force of the blow.

The beast ripped its weapon free, howling incoherently. Stromez's blood gouted over his forge-kin packed in around him. The killing went on, the spear plunging down overarm, staving in another helm, its broad head carving through stout duardin steel. The animal wielding it had the appearance of a human in its thickly muscled, half-naked body, but Hilfinger was in no doubt about the fact that he was witnessing a beast tearing into his regiment's allies. Its features were lost in a thick mane of hair and beard that was heavy with blood, and its eyes, when he caught sight of them, were wide and white, like a feral dog contending with its pack mates for a few more scraps of flesh.

It kept on killing. It was unstoppable. Since it had come crashing out of the fog Hilfinger had seen it dealt half a dozen blows that would have been mortal to any man. It was bleeding from pike thrusts, axe cuts and the blunt trauma of hammer wounds, but not once had it slowed down its assault. It seemed to exist only to shed blood. The sight of it had paralysed Hilfinger and turned the hot flush of battle ice-cold.

And it was only one. One of dozens.

The melee was the worst he had ever seen. Muscle-bound savages clad only in scraps of red armour and gore-matted furs were carving through the front ranks of the regiment with the manic strength of madmen, axes and cleavers sending out a drizzle of bloody rain as they rose and fell over and over again. The duardin that constituted the front of the allied formation met the frenzied assault with every ounce of their race's iron stoicism. They locked shields and swung hammers and axes, and Hilfinger saw some of the barbarians go down, still screaming curses in their hideous language.

But none were like the first beast, the one that had led them down the slope and through the smoke, into the pikes and the slaughter. It was still carving a red path to Hilfinger's right. It had broken through the duardin now and was in among his pikemen, splintering hafts and bellowing with something that sounded distressingly like laughter.

'Push!' Hilfinger screamed. 'Push, you dogs! Kill it! For Sigmar!'

There was no concession to grace or finesse, to skill at arms or the hours spent on the drill square. Man and duardin were pressed against one another, no room to swing swords or axes, the air rent by screams and the crash of steel. The stink of blood, voided bowels and opened innards made Hilfinger choke. He saw Skeli, the duardin forge-tender who had fought alongside his father at Blackridge, hacked open like so much slaughterhouse offal. He saw Sergeant Kolk, the biggest man in the regiment, have his head torn off by the bare hands of one of the animals. He saw another half-naked barbarian, riddled with musket ball wounds and missing an arm, ramming a long, jagged knife through the body of a pikeman, the eldest Oberstmain brother. He was already dead, but the pressure of the melee was holding his body up while he was being disembowelled by the fatally wounded lunatic.

Amidst it all Hilfinger stood paralysed, stomach churning, body shaking. It wasn't supposed to be like this. What could he do? What could any of them do?

That was when he realised that the savage who had killed Stromez, the blood-drenched beast with the spear, was looking directly at him.

The sounds of battle were receding behind Vanik. It felt wrong, to be riding away from it. His whole body prickled and shivered, and his stomach knotted, as though the Gods themselves were watching him and reaching out, poised to punish the cowardice he was displaying.

He'd returned Nakali to its scabbard, ignoring the daemon's protestations. Now, right hand gripping Tzatzo's chains, he raised his left fist, clenched. After a dozen yards he turned Tzatzo left. Around him, the remnants of the Eightguard wheeled their mounts to follow his lead. Normally, Aramor would have given the order with the half-carnyx, but Vanik had demanded silence.

They continued on through the smoke. It was beginning to clear now, the original fires burning low, the flames that had spread to the rest of the grassland petering out. It had served them well, but they would have to be fast. A few minutes more and it would no longer conceal their movements.

He raised his left fist once more. Again, the Eightguard turned. They were now riding parallel to their original direction, following the foot of the ridge. He glanced either side, at the remains of his retinue. Only two had fallen in the first meeting with the human knights, so complete had the rout been. Still, barely half of the warriors he had first ridden into S'aai's flesh groves with still lived. A part of Vanik, the old part that still thought like a warlord of the Eightfold Path, felt an upwelling of pride as he glanced at Klexus and Zoth, Morrik and Jarll. He crushed the feeling, snarling at his own foolishness. They meant nothing now. He was not some wasteland champion struggling to band together a war party, not any more. He was one kill away from becoming a Knight of Ruin. His brothers and sisters would be his konroi, and his home would be the barbed walls of the Inevitable Citadel. He would serve the Three-Eyed King, the only being in creation worthy of his loyalty, and he would not fall back into the soft indolence of warrior-kinship or petty ambition.

Now that he was so close, he would not fail.

He gave Tzatzo her head, leaving his retinue behind once more. Albermarl had chosen duardin-like caution, sending a few sheep from his flock to test the slaughterer. Vanik would not disappoint him. Through the thinning smoke ahead, he saw his prey.

A dark mass of men and their duardin allies, tightly ranked and well ordered. They were fighting Dravga's corsairs, but it was an ill match. The combination of their shield-wall and pike block remained unbroken, and bar a few bold warriors still clashing with the duardin in the front ranks, most of the corsairs had withdrawn a few dozen paces and were launching javelins and slingshots. They had left behind a scattering of dead – the Helmgard formation seemed unbreakable, certainly from the front.

But Vanik and his retinue were not coming from the front.

Their route had taken them wide around the left-hand side of the blocks of Helmgard infantry. Now that they had cut back, the left flank of the first regiment lay directly ahead of the Chaos knights.

'Sound the charge,' Vanik snarled at Aramor, and raised Nakali once more.

'Remember your oaths!' Jevcha screamed, taking another hammer stroke on her infernal runeshield. Her axe hewed into the duardin's own shield once again, biting a deep notch in the upper rim but failing to connect with the helmet hunched just past it.

She thrust forward in rage and frustration, the two shields crashing, but she might as well have been trying to batter her way through a castle wall – the duardin didn't take a backward step, held in place by the ranks pressing behind him and by his own stubborn resolve.

The same thing was happening to Jevcha's left and right. Darkoath tribesmen were pounding at the front ranks of humans and duardin opposing them, swords and axes hewing steel and gromril. Rarely, however, were they finding flesh and bone.

'Eightstar blight your bastard existence – your shattered God will never be whole again,' Jevcha spat at the duardin before her, red-faced as she heaved on her shield. The duardin snarled something back in his own grating tongue, his expression lost behind the disapproving glare of his ancestor mask.

Jevcha had fought in the shield-wall over two dozen times before. Like so many tribes of the Gods, it was the traditional Darkoath method of war, adopted should the first wild charge fail to break apart the enemy line. She knew how to fight such battles. Warriors heaved and shoved at one another, close as lovers, boots slipping in the muck, shield to shield. Occasionally an axe or sword blade would come slashing over a rim, and a warrior would go down, skull split or shoulder carved open. There would be a sweating, driving effort to exploit the sudden gap. Sometimes it succeeded, but more often than not it failed.

Jevcha had broken enough walls in her time. To do so was to earn the favour of the Gods, to fulfil a dozen great oaths in one. Often her faith and her fury were enough, but if not then the hooked edge of her axe dragging the rim of her opponent's shield down to let the warrior behind her strike him was.

This fight was different, though. It was not the fact it was a duardin shield-wall – she had broken those before; they simply took more time and effort. It was the fact that it was also bristling with Free City pikes.

Druzvik went down a few yards to her right, his face horribly ripped by one of the long poles. He was dragged back, screaming, while another warrior thrust forward to take his place, but it was already too late. The duardin heaved, taking up a chant in their own language. Hammers and axes fell against the Darkoath in the gap, and the pikes thrust forward in unison. It had already happened twice before.

Jevcha was forced to bring her runeshield up to meet one of the pike tips driving over the duardin's shoulder, grunting as the Chaos-blessed steel absorbed the jarring impact. Contact broken, the duardin thrust forward. The ranks behind her had shifted as they tried to fill the gap to the right, and for a second there was nothing to hold her in place. She stumbled, cursing, bodies behind her steadying her just in time to knock aside the duardin's axe stroke.

Chanting, shields still locked, the entire Helmgard regiment was advancing. The Darkoath went back, as they had done twice before, their wall broken. Jevcha made to lunge at the duardin, a curse on her lips, but hands grasped her arm and shoulders and heaved her back.

'Do not test your blessings, my warqueen,' she heard Vochev say. She allowed herself to be hauled away with the receding tide, a few dozen yards up the ridge slope. As she went she saw Druzvik on his knees, face a bloody ruin. A duardin stepped past him and brought the rim of his shield slamming down onto his neck. He crumpled beneath stomping boots and disappeared. The wall came on, a row of grim duardin faces embossed on shields, scarred and dented but unbroken.

'Stand your ground!' Jevcha barked at those around her, raising her axe. The Darkoath stopped going back. With a final air-shuddering syllable and the crash of shields locking, the duardin line likewise came to a halt, less than two dozen paces away.

Another crash sounded, this time the rattle of a handgun volley. The second part of Jevcha's war party, led by her chieftain Vovich, had been trying to cut round the right of the Helmgard regiment. Its commander, however, had refused his flank with three ranks of musketeers. The acrid rotten-egg stench of gunpowder caught in Jevcha's throat, making her spit. The damnable lightning worshippers were no closer to breaking than when they had first set eyes on them through the smoke.

'Czevik,' she shouted, casting about for the fleet-footed tribesman. He pushed through the press of the Darkoath rallying around the warqueen, bowing his head. He'd taken a pike graze to the flank, his sinewy torso slicked with blood and sweat.

'Can you still run?' Jevcha demanded.

'Yes, my warqueen.'

'Go right, follow the base of the ridge. Find out if the Khorne-worshipping madman has made any headway. If you see the Black Pilgrim, tell him if he wants to win this fight, he won't do it on the left flank, unless he comes in person.'

'Yes, my warqueen,' Czevik said, bowing again and slinging his shield across his back before sprinting off into the smoke.

'We go again!' Jevcha shouted, her burning gaze sweeping the panting, bloodied warriors around her. 'I swear to you, we will break these lightning-loving dogs!'

She reached round to her cloak, ripping one of the small stone tablets strung about her tusker pelt free.

'Witness my oath!' she shouted. She pressed the tablet against a graze in her shoulder, drawn by a duardin axe blow, letting her blood stain it. Then she scraped the wet surface against the heel of her axe's bit, chiselling a rough line into it.

'With this mark, I swear I will not take a backward step again!' she screamed, holding the tablet up for all the war party to see. 'I make this oath before you and before the True Gods! Follow me, that I might not break it!'

The tribe let out a roar, hammering blades and axe heads against their shields.

'Zovich, Goll, raise the blessed icons,' Jevcha shouted. 'Tormev, sound the bray-horn!'

She dropped her axe, pointing again at the Helmgard battle line just ahead.

'Charge!'

The beast was dead.

Hilfinger saw the killing blow struck. A pike – he didn't know whose – caught the daemon-worshipping savage squarely in the gut. For a moment, it stood transfixed, as though unable to comprehend the fact that it had been impaled. Then, with a chilling howl, it lunged forward, driving itself further onto the long haft. Its gore-drenched spear carved through the man grasping the pike, and the one beside him. Hilfinger thought the thing would carry on for eternity, killing and killing, animated so long as it was capable of drawing blood.

Finally, though, its strength seemed to desert it. Still impaled and bellowing like a stuck boar, it sank to its knees. It was far ahead of the other animals still butchering the Grimbald forge-kin, and as it slumped, men and duardin closed in all around it, laying in with axes and short swords, striking with the feral glee that seemed to have infected the whole fight.

'Kill it!' Hilfinger found himself screaming. 'Cut it to pieces!'

It still wasn't dead. He wouldn't stop until he was sure.

It took a long time for him to realise that someone was snatching at his arm and screaming his name. He turned, blinking, as though just waking from a daze. It was Sergeant Rozner.

'Look, sir!' he was shouting, pointing into the smoke to the left of the regiment. The shroud was finally starting to clear, and as he followed Rozner's finger he saw figures running past the handgunner detachment that constituted their left flank. At first they were just indistinct shapes, but then more started to appear, running straight for the handgunners and the pike block beyond. Hilfinger realised they were soldiers of

Helmgard. Worse, he recognised their blue-and-red uniforms. They were from their sister regiment, Franz. The one that was supposed to be holding the formation's left flank.

'Run!' one of the men screamed as he broke in amongst the handgunners while they were trying to reload. He was a pike-man, though his weapon was long gone. A gash across his scalp had left his face a nightmarish mask of blood.

'They're coming,' he shouted, stumbling. 'For the love of the mountain, save yourselves!'

'Handgunners, left wheel,' Hilfinger bellowed. 'Pikemen, fifth division will incline left and brace!'

Only about half the men obeyed the orders. Some of the pikemen were still locked in the melee with the beasts throwing themselves against the regiment's front, and the handgunners' ranks were now being broken apart by the scattering of Franz survivors pushing through them. Whatever had hit them had hit them hard. They were completely broken.

'Incline left!' Hilfinger repeated, screaming now. He realised the earth underfoot had started to shake. He felt sick, pan-icked. He wanted to run, wanted to break ranks like whatever remained of the Franz regiment. Instead he gripped Sergeant Rozner by the gorget, dragging him in close.

'Run to Hoffbad. Tell them they're about to have their left flank turned. Tell them they should retreat, if they still can. Go!'

Rozner didn't bother to salute. He just ran. Hilfinger faced left. The formation was finally shaking itself into some sem-blance of order. The handgunners had re-formed, though the pikemen around the slope-marshal were still struggling to come about with their long poles. He resisted the urge to snap at them. It didn't matter any more.

He could hear Greich, the captain commanding the hand-gunners, shouting at them to prime and load. Wooden ramrods rose and fell, rattling in barrels. The smoke ahead swirled, and parted. Hilfinger's blood ran cold, and he realised that the sudden sense of resigned calm that had replaced his panic was well founded.

There was no point in running, no point in even being afraid. They were all going to die.

Greich was screaming for his men to present, but most still hadn't finished loading. A few muskets went off, snapping ineffectually at the oncoming wedge of black plate armour. Knights, conjured like some dark parody of the chivalrous horsemen of Lord Fulbricht, were thundering towards them. Their steeds were huge and red-eyed, and the visors of their dark helms blazed with unholy power. Worst of all was the thing that led them, mounted atop a quill-covered monster, its multiple jaws yawning like a butcher's vice. The monstrous rider seemed to look directly at Hilfinger as it plunged towards the regiment, the gaze behind its horned helm burning.

The Chaos knights barely broke stride as they struck the handgunners, trampling and goring them. The regiment had fallen into total disorder around Hilfinger – some men were still trying to form up to face the flanking attack, while others were struggling to hold back the bloody savages flinging themselves at the front ranks. Most were already starting to run. Hilfinger didn't try to stop them. He shoved his way to the edge of the formation, directly ahead of the avalanche of black steel thundering towards them.

'Come on then, you bastards,' he shouted, spreading his arms wide. The thunder engulfed him, filling his entire existence, drowning out the screams of those around him.

The black knight atop the spiked beast was at the fore. The mount's red jaws yawned, and it lunged.

Hilfinger's own scream didn't last long.

PART FOURTEEN

THE STORM BREAKS

The smoke had lifted. A part of Marius wished it hadn't. The ridgeline was a scene of carnage. Bodies were heaped in thick, dark mounds across the forward slope, poles and standards sticking up amidst the heaped bodies like bristling grave markers. Steppe vultures were already circling overhead, brought by the stench of blood and opened innards that hung heavy in the air. Marius knew they would descend the moment those figures clustered around the corpses departed.

The Chaos horde was intact and, seemingly, sated by the afternoon's slaughter. They covered the ridgeline, disparate groups of bloody warriors loosely gathered around standards and totems that made Marius' lip curl with disgust. Many were picking through the bodies, doubtless claiming trophies and loot.

'Have you found their range?' Albermarl asked of his Master of Cannon, a grey-bearded duardin engineer named Kreggan.

'Aye,' Kreggan growled, motioning for his gunners to make ready.

'Wait,' Marius snapped before they could ignite their fuses.

There were riders approaching. The Lord Ordinator counted four, all of them sallow-skinned steppe tribesmen mounted on small, hardy-looking steeds. One of them seemed to have a body strapped across his horse's rear, while the other three were carrying flags. The wind turned, and Marius recognised the rippling, torn silk in their fists as the regimental colours of the Gunbold brigade.

The riders stopped not far beyond the foot of the slope. The body was unstrapped and dumped off the horse. After a few seconds it rose, staggering. The riders with the flags tossed them to the ground and wheeled their horses, racing back to the ridge. The wind carried their triumphant, tribal yelps and shrieks to Albermarl and his retinue.

'Hold your fire,' Marius heard the captain of the nearest hand-gunner detachment bark. The dismounted figure was stumbling towards the Helmgard line. As he got closer, two artillerists from the nearest battery, stripped down to their shirtsleeves and hose, rushed out to help him.

'By the lightning,' Albermarl growled as the figure was brought over to the retinue, supported by the two gunners. It took Marius long seconds to recognise that the man was one of the Knights of the Mountain, so befouled by muck and blood was his plate armour. It took even longer to realise that it was Rodik, Vulf Fulbricht's son and heir.

'Lords,' the boy stammered. The gunners were on the brink of releasing him, but had to catch him again as he swayed.

'I take it your father is dead,' Albermarl said bluntly. Rodik didn't reply, just looked down at his shredded, soiled surcoat and sniffed.

'They gave you a message?' Albermarl demanded, voice uncompromising.

'It… it says you are a coward, lord,' the boy stammered. 'And your m-men doubly so. It says it will start killing prisoners if you still won't face it. It says it has many, not just from today. From the towns and villages also.'

'That's enough,' Albermarl said. Rodik looked up at the castellan, then abruptly burst into tears.

'Get him out of my sight,' Albermarl ordered. Two retainers took Rodik from the artillery men and led him away, still weeping.

'Do you still demand I avoid facing this beast?' Albermarl snapped, rounding on Marius. 'A brigade decimated and the nobility of my city slaughtered to a man, all because you keep insisting I abandon principles?'

'You force him into dishonour,' Grunbad added, the duardin's voice a stony growl. 'You will shame every clan in the city, Stormcast.'

'A city that stands on by the will of the God-King. The stars are clear, it came here with just one task–' Marius began to say.

Grunbad interrupted him. 'If the castellan is so important, let me kill the damned savage myself! He can no longer plague us if my hammer has staved his skull in!'

'If you wish to challenge him, I cannot stop you,' Marius said. 'But I doubt he will fight you. He is here for Albermarl.'

'Then he can have me,' the castellan snapped, making to stride towards the ridge. Marius snatched his shoulder. He turned sharply, and for a moment the Stormcast thought he was going to lash out. Instead he just grimaced, glaring at the maroon-armoured giant.

'This is what the beast wants,' Marius said, forcing his own voice to stay level. 'We still have the advantage. The first brigade to attack sold themselves dearly, and one of their regiments is still mostly intact. They have committed their best troops to the fight, and we outnumber them. Let the artillery break them, then crush whatever survives.'

'Assuming they stay where they are and let us shoot them down,' Albermarl said. 'If they disengage, we have no cavalry to press them.'

'And what alternatives are there?' Marius demanded. 'Withdraw to the city, and ensure the deaths this afternoon were all in vain? Or face the beast in single combat? You know that even if you slay it, the horde will likely throw itself at us with even greater frenzy. Not to mention the prisoners they will massacre. Men will die here regardless of your decisions, castellan. The best you can hope for is that they do not die in vain. Unleash the full weight of Helmgard on these barbarians, and we will end this before it becomes any bloodier.'

Vanik dismounted and threw Tzatzo's chains to Modred. The Chaos steed grumbled, but didn't protest – she was sated, for now, her maw crimson and drooling with thick strings of gore.

The Black Pilgrim was back where he had started, at the centre of the ridgeline's crest. The Eightguard formed behind him, arms and armour dripping. The black standard still fluttered, slashed in several places, stained with the blood of lesser men. A part of the castellan's host was broken and butchered, and a message had been delivered. It had been a good afternoon's work.

He dragged his horned helmet off, cuffing sweat from his brow and breathing in the humid air. The storm still hadn't broken, the clouds hanging low and heavy overhead. He wanted this to be over before it did. He knew what storms could bring.

'Call the champions in,' he ordered Aramor. The herald blew four notes on the carnyx, two short and two long, repeated twice. Vanik looked out across the ridge's slope.

The war parties were scattered below, disorganised in the bloody aftermath of the day's fighting, picking their way through the carnage that constituted the remnants of the Helmgard regiments. It had been glorious work, bloody and hard. It was not the end, though.

The main part of the army of Helmgard had come forward in belated support of their broken vanguard. They now sat barely five hundred paces from the foot of the ridgeline, arrayed in their lines and blocks beneath their fluttering standards. Their cannons, gleaming in the afternoon gloom, had not yet begun to fire again.

Vanik paced back along the crest, until he could see down the reverse slope. The warband's camp followers were clustered there, the children and those too old to fight. And the prisoners. They were guarded by a band of Faug's horsemen. Vanik watched them for a while. Many of the womenfolk had trudged back up the slope to join their men among the carnage, to tend wounds or grieve those taken by the Gods, or just to join in the looting.

If the lightning worshippers attacked now, he knew the warband was in no state to meet them.

'Covin,' he said to one of the Eightguard. 'Ride to the camp. Tell them to move back in the direction of the Realmgate. Tell them I will have anyone who tarries behind impaled. I cannot have their encumbrance here and now. The final clash draws near.'

He knew the threat wouldn't dissuade many – a warband was at its most difficult to control when it had just fought a battle.

Jevcha was the first champion to return. She was wounded, and furious. Her shoulder and side had been gouged, and a corner of her war crown had been dented. She said nothing as she arrived at Vanik's side.

'Vovich?' the Black Pilgrim asked. She shook her head.

'Dead. A coward's musket ball to his heart.' Vanik said nothing more. Eventually Jevcha spoke again.

'They wouldn't break. More stubborn than a steppe hound with the last scrap of meat.'

'They are well drilled,' Vanik said. 'They are soldiers of the Free Cities, you knew that. Fight on their terms and they will match you. Fight on your own and they will unravel. That was what we did. All you had to do was hold them in place.'

'I know,' Jevcha said, but her expression was dark. Vanik wondered how many fresh oaths she had made in her fury.

She began to speak again, but stopped as more of the warband's leaders approached. Faug, dismounted, led his horse up onto the crest, followed by Moll and a warrior Vanik recognised from Svarbald's dragonship reivers.

'Where is Svarbald?' he demanded.

'Dead,' the fur-clad warrior said. 'I am Ragnor. My brothers elected me to come in his place.'

Vanik nodded, but said nothing. One by one, the rest of the warband's leadership gathered round. They all bore the marks of glorious combat – fresh wounds, notched and bloodied blades, the Gods-blessed gleam of battle-lust in their eyes. Vanik addressed them all, looking from one to the other.

'We have pleased the Eightstar with today's slaughter. Your warriors followed my commands, and the slaves of the Lightning God have been humbled. But our work is not yet complete. The one called Albermarl yet lives.'

'Let us strike them now, while they look upon the corpses of their kin,' Dravga pleaded.

'Be silent,' Vanik replied, glaring at the corsair. 'Or I will butcher you myself, and save the mountain army the pleasure. They are ready for us now. The Gods do not reward idiocy.'

'But we cannot stay,' Faug said, his tone more cautious. 'Their guns must begin firing again soon.'

'That is why you will bring your war parties back over the ridgeline immediately. I have ordered the camp followers to return to the Third Eye.'

'You would have us retreat?' Gulgrak asked. Blood and pus were oozing from half a dozen wounds to his Nurgle-blessed gut, though he didn't seem to have noticed any of them. 'Leave this place after all the glory we have won here?'

'If your warriors disobey you, you will answer to me,' Vanik snapped. 'Your assumptions are ill-placed. The camp is returning to the Realmgate, but we are not. The Helmgard cavalry have been slaughtered – I no longer need to spare any of your riders to guard them, Faug. I have sent another ultimatum to the coward castellan. If he does not meet it, we will begin slaughtering the prisoners.'

A crash answered Vanik's words before any of the champions spoke. One of the Helmgard cannons had opened fire.

'Go,' Vanik ordered. Only Jevcha hesitated.

'Where is Ulek?' she asked, as the rest of the guns facing the ridgeline roared.

There was nothing but rage. It kept his dying flesh warm, kept his blood fresh and vital. It was the primordial reason for existence. Was not rage the first expression of every child, screamed into a new, uncaring world?

He screamed too. He heralded his arrival. The Warhound would know of his coming. He would know that there was no fear in Ulek, no pain in his cut-apart body, no shame in this final death. Only rage. Only such purity could be permitted within the Blood God's sacred slaughter-realm.

He tasted blood. It was glorious. He was drowning in it,

submerged in its invigorating essence. Rage and blood, the two most vital components of life.

Life that clung to him yet. He breathed. He was not drowning after all, though he barely tasted the air before more blood choked him with its coppery tang.

The agony returned, suffusing his whole body. He screamed again, to vent it. Something like fear reared up in his mind, accompanied by an addled, manic hope. He lived. The slaughter was not yet complete. His final tally of skulls had not yet been counted. He could add more, so many more.

He reared up. His body responded with an overwhelming surge of pain, but he ignored it now. It did not matter. He lived, his body still riven with blood, still drenched in it.

Ulek blinked. For the first time that day, he could see clearly. He was on his knees. Around him were his Bloodbound, scarred, bloodied. They were snarling like animals, their entreaties and words of worship incoherent but no less devout. They murmured as Ulek rose.

His body barely obeyed him any more. His flesh was ragged, carved open by swords and axes, pulverised by hammers. He felt broken bones grate, and spat the blood choking his throat – his blood, he realised. He was drenched in gore, from head to foot, his hair and beard matted, his entire body a raw, crimson spectre, like a very daemon of the Blood God.

And yet, he lived.

He stood. The Bloodbound roared. He answered them, raising both fists. He had been chosen to go on. Whether his body could or not did not matter.

The smoke had gone. He was standing amidst a litter of corpses, all of them dismembered, eviscerated or trampled. The ridge ahead was thick with more bodies. There was thunder, he realised, thunder that came not from the heavens. The earth of the ridge fifty yards to his left rose like some foul wizard's trick, bursting apart in a shower of dirt. Warriors fell. The cowards' guns were firing on them, he realised. The knowledge made him snarl.

The Bloodbound parted before him, their exultation fading as more shot and shells whipped past. Ulek wiped matted hair from his face. Before him stood Vanik. The Black Pilgrim had dismounted from his Chaos steed, his helm removed. His own black armour was bloodied, and the daemonblade at his hip was visibly shivering in its scabbard.

'You live,' Vanik said. 'The Warhound has work for you yet.' He spoke without relief or humour, as though he stated only facts. Ulek agreed.

'Where?' the exalted deathbringer growled.

'You will know soon enough,' Vanik replied, voice rising over the crash of cannons. 'Await my word.'

Ulek managed to nod, though his body shook, as much with the urge to rend and tear as with the pain that threatened to overwhelm him. One of the Bloodbound stepped forward to his right, offering a weapon. It was his impaling spear. He snatched it from the warrior's grasp, the mere contact with the brute weapon filling him with the urge to lash out.

'Assemble the remains of your war party,' Vanik said. 'Bring them back over the ridgeline, and wait. You will claim more skulls today. This battle has only just begun.'

Marius watched as the artillery of Helmgard spoke once more. This time there were no fires to obscure it, but the gunners found themselves with an even more complete problem – the ridgeline. The barbarians had withdrawn back over it, leaving behind the dead and dying.

There were no targets for the great cannons, but the mortar

batteries at least were unimpeded by the lack of line of sight. The engineers measured ranges and cut fuses, and the pot-bellied artillery pieces lobbed shells up and over the crest, evidence of their destructive potential relegated to the crump of their detonations and the smoke that rose up over the skyline.

'They might be disengaging,' Marius said.

'We thought that before,' Albermarl responded. 'We have no way of knowing unless we take the ridge.'

Marius conceded with a nod. Occasionally, small groups of riders would appear along the crest, the same light horse formation whose archery had first decimated the Helmgard cavalry. They were always moving, and always vanished back beyond the crest before the batteries below could fix on them, but Marius had no doubt they were monitoring the army's presence and standing ready to cut down any scouts Albermarl sent forward.

The only way they'd discover what was beyond was if they advanced. And Marius knew that Albermarl wasn't going to send forward any lone detachments again.

'The line will advance,' the castellan barked at his couriers, then turned to Marius.

'Will you accompany us, Stormcast?'

'I shall,' Marius responded. 'If the horde is still just beyond the crest, they will come for you, lord castellan.'

'They come, lord,' the Red Steppe horsewoman said. She bore two feathers, dipped in blood, in her leather headband, the mark of a hetman's child. Vanik wondered whether she was one of Faug's many bastards. He nodded to her, and she turned her stocky mount back towards the rest of her tribe.

He had remounted Tzatzo, once more at the fore of the Eightguard. She was hungry again, chomping at her chains and raking the earth underfoot. Vanik tousled a bunch of the spines just back from the plate armour guarding her skull, murmuring nothings at her.

You will die today, Vanik, Nakali said. The daemon had been almost incoherent since the fighting started, gorging itself on the blood its wielder had shed, drunk on the essence of butchered enemies. It spoke now without its usual mocking inflection or hiss, as though it merely relayed information it had been given. That, Vanik realised, was more chilling than its former hate and spite.

'As the Gods will it,' he muttered. The daemon said nothing more.

Something struck his armour, rebounding from his shoulder with a ticking sound. At first he thought it was a scrap of shell casing. The mortars had been lobbing their rounds over the ridge sheltering the warband for the better part of half an hour. He'd ordered that they move well back from the foot of the reverse slope, which was now a churned-up mass of dirt and smoking craters. Still, some shells did land among the warrior bands, ripping through lightly armoured bodies and hurling limbs and viscera out over the kindred of those struck. The warband bore the barrage with a dark patience, warriors from all across the realms fidgeting with tokens and charms and murmuring blessings. Each one prayed the Gods did not send the flying metal to give them an unworthy death. Vanik himself had taken two finger-length shards of twisted iron, both embedded in his warpsteel shield.

But it was not a shell fragment that had hit him, he realised, as more struck off his black plate. Raindrops. He looked skywards, as the clouds finally opened.

'That will dampen their powder,' growled Kulthuk.

'It will be of little use to them anyway,' Vanik said. 'Not once they cross over the ridge.'

He could imagine them now, the thick blocks of Helmgard infantry, bristling with their pikes, passing with difficulty over the dead heaped across the other side of the ridgeline, clambering slowly up towards the crest. They would be afraid and uncertain, bearing close witness to the butchery already meted out on their vanguard, wondering what awaited them in turn beyond the rise. And now the rain was drenching and demoralising them further, soaking through their uniforms and making the hafts of their weapons difficult to grasp.

Thunder rumbled, not the crash of the Helmgard artillery, but the true wrath of the heavens, stored up until now. The storm was about to break.

'Move the prisoners forward,' he said, turning and barking the command over another ominous rumble. More orders were bellowed and whips cracked as the mass of captives, who had been held back until now from the foot of the slope, were forced forward by Faug's horsemen. They were a sorry, pathetic lot, mostly villagers and townsfolk captured over the past month's raiding. There were a few members of Helmgard's soldiery among them in their bloody, dishevelled uniforms, those foolish enough to allow themselves to be taken alive during the day's fighting.

Vanik realised that the shells had stopped falling. Smoke drifted across the slope ahead, hugging the churned-up earth in the rain. It could only mean that the Helmgard battle line was reaching the crest, and the gunners below had ceased fire to avoid the danger of a short fuse bursting a shell above them.

'Faster!' Vanik snapped at the steppe riders. They whooped and shrieked at the prisoners, speeding up the stumbling, confused mass. Not for the first time, Vanik found himself thinking of a herd of brute-minded cattle. He hated them, hated their weakness, hated their fear. He offered a prayer to the Eightstar, asking that not one of their pathetic number be allowed to survive what was about to happen.

'Forward,' he repeated, signalling to Aramor. 'Everyone, now!'

This was the moment of decision. This was the part when the Gods cackled and wove what they would, and mortal man – no matter how blessed – could do nothing but carry on. Vanik urged Tzatzo forward, a snarl on his lips. Just ahead, the prisoners had broken into a run, their screams lost in the swelling roar of the warband now storming up the slope behind them. Some fell and were immediately trampled.

The crest was just before them. Vanik watched it, expecting to see the flags of the Lightning Mountain rise up over it, expecting to find himself faced with locked shields and a forest of pikes. For a few seconds, as the prisoners began to spill up across the crest, he knew doubt. What if the castellan hadn't brought his army forward at all? What if the warband crested it, only to find the great guns of the human and duardin host arrayed before them, waiting to belch forth a torrent of death? What if–

The doubts faded the same moment Tzatzo, snorting heavily, reached the crest. Immediately ahead he saw those prisoners still on their feet stumbling down the reverse slope. And beyond them, less than a hundred yards away – halfway towards the top of the ridge – he saw the regiments of Helmgard.

They'd timed it perfectly. The warband, fleeter than the cumbersome blocks of pikemen and musketeers, had won the race for the crest. Now they burst up over it. They found their enemy beneath them, drenched in the rain, struggling to form. One line of handgunners in between two of the pike blocks fired, their ragged, early volley only serving to cut down several of the terrified prisoners rushing at them. As they scrambled to reload, fighting to keep their powder dry, the Chaos horde swept up and over the crest.

Vanik knew he didn't need to issue any orders. With a shout that seemed to shake Chamon to its iron-bound roots, the entire warband charged.

The Black Pilgrim held his retinue back as Jevcha's Darkoath swept past. He stood in his stirrups, scanning the regiments below, searching the duardin icons and the human flags hanging limp in the rain. He was seeking a great square of silk, the device of a mountain crowned with lightning.

He was seeking Albermarl.

Hunting him.

And then he found him just as the warband crashed home. Near the centre-left of the Helmgard line, a knot of human and duardin warriors stood clustered around the flag he had seen earlier during the parley. Among them was a giant in maroon-and-silver armour, a lone Stormcast. Beside him stood Albermarl. The castellan was wielding a great warhammer as he engaged the first of Vanik's warriors to come crashing against his line. They were one of Skoren's former war parties, Parmin's marauders, their hands still bearing the black tattoos of their previous master. They fell beneath Albermarl's hammer, though they fought with a frenzy Vanik had rarely seen outside of Khorne's devotees.

He lowered Nakali towards the castellan.

'Albermarl!'

The champion of Sigmar caught sight of Vanik, and raised his hammer defiantly. Fangs bared, Vanik kicked Tzatzo down the slope.

The Eightguard were with him. As the Chaos knights thundered down on the castellan's retinue, there was a crash. The detachment of handgunners directly ahead had managed to reload. Renki's warhounds were ripping into them, but about a dozen of the second rank succeeded in getting off a ragged volley. Vanik heard a series of sickening thumps, and felt Tza-tzo twist beneath him as she was hit. At least one musket ball had struck her skull, punching through the barding plate. She screeched and went down on her forelegs, forcing Vanik to grasp her spiny crest to stay mounted. Around him the Eight-guard surged past, committed to the charge, his own black banner streaming from Kulthuk's fist.

He screamed with rage, and tried to urge Tzatzo up. The wounded steed huffed, dark ichor oozing from a vicious gash just below her left eye. Another ball had buried itself in her breast. Hissing a curse, Vanik threw a leg over and dropped to the ground.

'I will avenge you,' he said, placing a gauntlet on the beast's muzzle. She trilled back, claws scraping the dirt. There was a crash as the Eightguard struck home, ploughing indiscrim-inately through the marauders. Vanik turned and charged in their wake.

All ahead was carnage. Both retinues were locked in a death struggle. The weight of the Eightguard's initial charge had crushed the front rank of Albermarl's guards, but a wedge of duardin hammerers had rallied around the castellan. Already Aramor and Zoth had been unhorsed, and Klexus' skull had been split. The castellan himself fought in the midst of the melee, smashing his great hammer against Morrick's shield. The Stormcast was to his left, beyond the knot of duardin lifeguards.

Vanik strode over the trampled remains of several of Parmin's marauders, bellowing Albermarl's name. He was so engrossed in reaching the castellan that he didn't notice the figure running at him from his right side, through the press of Chaos warriors.

A body crashed into Vanik, checking his advance. He whipped around, snarling, expecting to find himself facing a duardin or some Free Cities soldier. Instead, he realised it was one of

Parmin's marauders who had rammed into him. The warrior was scantily clad, his sinewy body clothed in a furred loincloth and light leather armour, a scraggly beard hugging the man's gaunt face. It took a second for Vanik to recognise that face. It was the hate-filled eyes that did it.

'Blackhand,' he snarled. Skoren didn't respond. The rival Black Pilgrim howled and swung Vargen. Vanik stumbled back, the daemon sword cleaving the air inches from his gorget.

'Finally found the courage to face me then,' he spat at Blackhand. 'Have you been cowering like an unbloodied youth among the ranks of your former warriors all this time?'

'I am willing to do what must be done,' Skoren snarled manically. 'Did you truly believe all of my warriors would simply surrender themselves to you?'

Skoren lashed a blow at Vanik and the two pilgrims locked together, blades quivering and snarling at one another.

'You waited until now to strike,' Vanik spat through gritted teeth. 'You are not worthy of becoming a Scourge of Fate, Blackhand. We are not skulking assassins, we are the Three-Eyed King's huntmasters.'

'I knew your vanity would see you bring the castellan to open battle,' Skoren responded, managing to grin. 'Now he is mine for the taking.'

'He is mine alone to kill,' Vanik roared, and thrust himself at Skoren. The Blackhand was thrown back, stumbling but staying on his feet. Before Vanik could follow up, he realised Skoren was laughing. The unexpected reaction gave him pause.

'In your pathetic desperation to become a Knight of Ruin you have lost sight of my master's plans,' Skoren said, still full of dark mirth. 'You will never be a warrior of the Varanguard.'

'Your defeat has driven you mad,' Vanik snarled, but Skoren only laughed again.

'Perhaps it is best if you believe that. But know this before you die. I have not come here to kill the castellan. I have come here to bind him.'

Skoren lunged. As Vargen's saw blade scythed down, realisation hit Vanik. Skoren had never intended to kill the castellan, had never intended to even complete his quest. He was doing Zubaz's bidding, and his ambitions were far greater and darker than the Fifth Circle.

Skoren's sword met Nakali, the blow jarring. The black blade whipped out in riposte, fast as a striking serpent, Nakali stung by its rival's bite. Skoren's sword was smashed aside, and in the press of the melee he was barely able to dodge again. Though he had cast aside his armour in order to better hide among his former warriors, the Blackhand's light leathers had left him nimbler than Vanik.

There was no time for him to recover. Hits rained down, ringing from Vanik's shield and his black plate, the dark runes inscribed along its edges and seals smouldering. The marauders that had survived the battle between Albermarl's retinue and the Eightguard were attacking him, their treachery revealed. A mace struck him about the helm and it twisted, half obscuring his view and driving him back.

He lashed out blindly with Nakali, sweat stinging his eyes, feeling the daemon sword bite, but missing Skoren. He was swinging for Vanik, eyes wide and wild with the same feral madness that had seemed to grip him in the unsanguinary duel. No thought given to defence, he smashed Vargen down over and over, hacking into Vanik's shoulder as he tried to turn and shield himself. The steel buckled and crumpled, and Vanik screamed as the saw-edge found flesh. An icy cold shot to his very core, and his vision flickered. Gone was the heaving, unyielding mass of weapons and armour, gone was the skewed, claustrophobic pressure of his helmet. Even Skoren's hate-twisted face had disintegrated.

In place of it, all was darkness and cold, the snow-bound chill he knew from a childhood spent on the Splintered Coast. A new face loomed from the frigid shadows, skin stretched too tight over bestial bones, a skull-like visage whose brow bristled with horns and whose maw leered with wicked fangs. It was grinning at him, he realised, grinning with ravenous hunger. Its eyes were like infinity spun into a whirlpool.

VANIK.

The daemonic face was unmade, replaced by a flurry of images. He saw Skoren kneeling and being granted Vargen by Zubaz – not claiming it on his quest, as a Black Pilgrim should. He saw the Blackhand locked in battle against Albermarl on the very bloody slope on which he now stood. He saw the serrated daemon sword cleave the castellan's body, saw the champion of Sigmar fall. Flesh distended, and what should have been a corpse arose once more as the power of Chaos riddled Albermarl. His scream became deep, dark laughter, his features split apart as he rose into the air. Great bat-like pinions tore themselves free from his back, a halo of black light surrounding the horns that burst from his brow.

I AM VARGEN, PRINCE OF THE APOCALYPSE, AND I WILL BE FREE.

The visions dragged him to the court of the Fifth Circle. Warriors lay scattered upon the floor, bloody and broken. Varanguard. The great throne of broken Stormcast armour still stood, but Neveroth's banner had been ripped in half behind it, and upon it now sat Zubaz, splattered with the blood of the Knights of Ruin. At his left stood Skoren, clad in his armour once more, and to his right was the great, muscle-bound creature of darkness that had once been Albermarl.

THE ASCENDANCY OF MORTALS IN THE REALMS OF THE GODS IS AT AN END.

The throne room crumbled. The Varanspire lay before Vanik, riven with destruction. Its walls were broken, its lava quenched with the bodies of the once-faithful. Daemons cavorted through its streets, slaughtering the mortals that had formerly held its eight circles, gorging themselves on flesh and soulfire. Its foundations split, the Varanspire itself began to topple. Just as he had seen it when Kar'gek'kell had plunged into his mind, so it was repeated here.

THE VARANSPIRE WILL FALL, AND THE THREE-EYED KING WILL KNEEL BEFORE TRUE POWER.

Pain exploded through Vanik's mind. He could not force it out, nor drown out the laughter in his skull.

The screams returned him to reality. The screams of warriors, fighting and dying all around him. The scream of Skoren, issued in triumph. Most of all, his own screams.

The Blackhand gave Vargen one last twist, and dragged the daemon sword free from the gouged flesh and blood of Vanik's shoulder. He felt himself falling, Nakali slipping from his grasp, still drinking deep from the warrior it was buried in. He hit the dirt, on his knees, hands grasping at him from all sides. A fist clenched around his helmet's horns and wrenched it free. He blinked, tasting the blood and smoke in the air.

'Daemon,' he gasped, panting and shivering. 'You are going to use Albermarl's flesh as a host.'

'At last you begin to understand,' Skoren admitted, standing over Vanik. 'The vision the lie-whisperer saw was true. But it will not be the Lightning God who sunders the Varanspire. It will be my Lord Zubaz, with me at his side and the power of Vargen, Prince of the Apocalypse, bound to his command. So it has been foretold.'

'Your blade will meld the daemon with the castellan's flesh,' Vanik said, his rage beginning to overcome the sickening after-effects of the visions.

'Kar'gek'kell has been suspicious,' Skoren said, clearly relishing the moment of his master's triumph. 'It has been stalking Neveroth's chosen for some time, looking to pick up the scent it caught.'

'Karex Daemonflayer knows of Zubaz's scheming,' Vanik snarled.

'But not enough to stop us,' Skoren spat. 'My master will end your petty citadel, and when Archaon is broken the defiance weaklings like you show towards the True Gods will finally be at an end. Chaos will no longer be beholden to the whims of mortal flesh, and the orders of the great pantheon will never again be questioned. We shall answer directly to the Gods themselves, and no longer cower in the shadow of mere fellow mortals like the Knights of Ruin.'

'Karex will stop you,' Vanik said, his vision blurring once more as memories of Vargen's terrible ambitions returned. Skoren laughed.

'Time to die, Vanik,' he said, and clamped his fist around the pilgrim's throat. He tried to fight back, to bring the shield still strapped to his left arm up to smash against Skoren's side, but Vargen had left him weak and drained, able only to clutch Skoren's wrist as he clenched tighter.

'I will feed your soul to my master,' Skoren hissed, leaning closer, face contorted with strain. 'He will flay you for eternity, weakling.'

There was a clatter from behind Vanik, and a rapid, thudding tattoo. The crushing pressure around his throat was making his ears keen and thunder to the sound of his own racing heart. He kept his eyes locked with Skoren's, forcing words through his grip.

'You made just one mistake, Blackhand,' he hissed. 'You should have brought your own steed.'

A shape flung itself through the melee, shrieking like a newly summoned daemon. Skoren didn't have time to look up before Tzatzo's jaws slammed shut over his head and upper chest. The steed was hideously wounded, but feral rage and the dark essence that sustained her had driven her back into the battle. Vanik was afforded a direct view of the monstrous muscles in her neck and jaw as they clamped like a vice. There was a crunch, and blood flooded down the front of Skoren's chest before the Chaos steed twisted her head and wrenched the Blackhand's head and part of his upper torso away.

Skoren's body remained upright, anchored by the unyielding grip on Vanik's throat. He reached up, vision a blur, prising away the hand one finger at a time. As Tzatzo threw her head back to swallow Skoren's upper half, the death grip finally relaxed, and air, fresh and vital, flooded Vanik's lungs. Skoren's remains slumped against him, awash with blood.

One quest, at least, was at an end.

PART FIFTEEN

THE PROPHECY OF THE KNIGHT AND THE LIGHTNING

Vanik thrust Skoren's bloody corpse off him and rose to his feet, panting. Around him the battle continued. The Eightguard had been joined by a rush of Darkoath tribesmen, and were locked in a death-struggle with Albermarl's stalwart retinue. Tzatzo was tearing apart the last of the marauders who had stood beside Skoren. She was still bleeding from the musket balls that had scarred her hide, but a terrible frenzy seemed to have taken hold of her. She ignored Vanik as she gorged herself on the Blackhand's screaming warriors.

He turned his eyes to the trampled dirt at his feet, looking for Skoren's fallen daemon sword. Vargen was far too powerful to allow any other to claim it. He had to find it before someone else did.

The pilgrim bent among Skoren's ripped remains, wincing at

the pain in his shoulder. He could feel blood from the wound dripping down inside his armour, and most of his left arm felt numb. His shield was like a leaden weight.

'Beast!' A voice arrested his search. He looked up to see Albermarl thrusting his way through the melee towards him, his hammer and armour smeared with the viscera of the broken servants of Chaos.

'The bold castellan,' Vanik snarled mockingly, rising back to his feet. The human champion's visor was raised, and his expression was dark and grim as a cliff face.

'Monster,' he spat, hefting his hammer, lightning snapping around its edges. 'I'm going to break you into a hundred pieces and impale them in every town and village you burned.'

'Enough,' Vanik snarled. 'Your corpse belongs to Lord Neveroth, and your soul to the True Gods.'

Albermarl roared and swung. Vanik took the strike on his shield. Any other form of protection would have been shattered by the great hammer, but the Eightfold-blessed warpsteel rebounded the blow with an ear-splitting clang, its runes pulsating as they repelled the hammer's magical power.

The impact left Vanik's arm numb and made his wound flare agonisingly, but there was no time to recover. He drove Nakali in low and hard, up through Albermarl's guard and into his guts. The human's plate turned the thrust, magic-infused runes gleaming with a silvery light as they checked Nakali's hunger.

Another great overhead swing by Albermarl, another blow like a lightning strike against Vanik's shield. He attempted to thrust forward into the castellan's guard again, but Albermarl was nearly as tall and broad, and his stance was good. He brought his hammer back in time to use the haft to parry Nakali, the two weapons rebounding with teeth-jarring force.

Vanik couldn't find an opening. Albermarl would not yield

an inch, trusting in his heavy armour to preserve him while he rained down blow after blow, an unrelenting thunderstorm that left Vanik's body numb. He was planted like a mountain, unassailable, immovable.

'They cursed you with their last breaths,' he snarled at the castellan as he turned another blow with his battered shield. 'All the pathetic cowards in your little towns and villages. All the weakling prisoners now trampled here between our armies. They called you an honourless whelp, a disgraced cur who hid behind his mountain walls. Even were I not to slay you this day, your actions have ensured that you will never be one of your God-King's Chosen.'

Albermarl roared and threw himself at Vanik. Another strike crashed against his shield, but this time Nakali slid between the castellan's defences. The daemon sword didn't waste the opportunity, biting deep into Albermarl's side and penetrating his steel plate. He grunted with pain, and slammed the butt of his two-handed hammer up against the side of Vanik's head, forcing him back and dragging Nakali free.

'My daemon sword has tasted you now, castellan,' Vanik taunted, as they both recovered their stances. 'It will rend your soul to pieces.'

'Not if I break yours first,' Albermarl snarled.

Overhead, it was the storm that finally broke. Rain began sheeting down even harder than before, a deluge that pattered from armour plates, slicked weapon hafts and churned the dirt underfoot. The crash of thunder directly above made both warriors look up instinctively.

'My God is with me,' Albermarl said, brandishing his hammer.

'I do not need mine,' Vanik responded, a smile splitting his face. 'If I were so weak that I always required their gaze, I would not be worthy of them.'

Thunder split the heavens once more, and amidst the rain and the lightning, the daemon sword and the warhammer clashed once again.

'Castellan!' Marius shouted. It was useless. The thunder and the clash of arms drowned him out. Another barbarian threw itself at the Stormcast, screaming some garbled oath or praise to its insane Gods. Marius' astral hammers splintered the brute's eightstar shield with one blow and snapped its neck with the second. The half-naked savage was dragged down in the press, trampled as more of its kind threw themselves at the human and duardin ranks.

'Look to the castellan,' Marius shouted, directing his words at the hammerers guarding Albermarl. They were no more able to heed him than Albermarl himself. The Chaos knights that had come storming over the ridge had broken their lines, iron-shod hooves trampling indiscriminately over duardin warriors while their riders hacked and slashed manically with swords, axes and maces. Marius lunged through the press at one while it battled with a hammerer on its other side. He went for its steed as it snapped its fangs at him, smashing the side of its skull with one hammer and slamming the other into its hind quarters. It went down with a screech, and the black-armoured rider bellowed with fury as he was unseated, his axe cleaving through the hammerer's helmet and skull even as he toppled into the cloying dirt. Before he could recover, Marius placed a boot on his dying steed's flank and brought his hammer down, crushing the knight's skull in turn and discolouring the mud around him with a thick wad of blood and brain matter that burst from his ruptured helm.

The Lord Ordinator stood, panting, as he glared through the sheeting rain and the crush of bodies. The Chaos horde had overrun the regiment directly to his left. He saw their standard bearer hauled down by a mewling, tentacle-limbed creature while wiry marauders in white pelts attacked the duardin front ranks, the sheer force of their downhill charge driving them on. Those impaled on pikes or hacked by axes and hammers were thrust against the Helmgard regiment, the dead and the dying locked together while the living continued to fight over and around them.

The regiment to the right was faring better. They had held their ranks in the face of the rush of prisoners that had preceded the barbarian charge. Now the duardin in the fore were holding firm against a fierce wedge of dark-skinned, golden-armoured warriors, led by a gigantic shaven-headed brute wielding a pole arm almost as long as Marius was tall. The regiment's musketeer detachment was faring less well – they had been overrun by huge, baying hounds, and the dogs were now ripping into the fragile left flank of the main infantry block.

All along the ridgeline the battle ground back and forth amidst the rain and the muck. Further to his right, Marius could see a malformed ogor laying waste to the regiment with huge swings of an iron-studded tree trunk, each blow flinging broken bodies and splintered weapons into the air. On the opposite side, a trio of spawn beasts had dragged their blubbery, spiny bodies into the midst of a pike wall. Though run through by dozens of shafts, they continued to claw and tear at the screaming men before them, their prey driven half mad by the sight of their Chaos-tainted bodies.

And in the middle of it all, the castellan and the Chaos lord fought. Marius thrust towards them once again, struggling to cross the thrashing body of another Chaos steed that had been brought down by one of Albermarl's hammerers. The castellan was raining blows on the champion of the Dark Gods, but his shield seemed equal to the pounding, and Marius realised Albermarl was bleeding from a gash in his side.

He had to reach him, before it was too late. The master of Helmgard had to be preserved.

Lightning struck, earthing into the crest of the ridgeline above the fighting. It was no normal bolt, though, not a spear of the Azyr's brilliance. It was discoloured, a sickening spike of purple and pink, warped by the power of Chaos. The rain came down all the harder, and for a second Marius thought he caught the distant braying of horns over the battle's tumult.

'Sigmar, give me strength,' he roared, raising one of his astral hammers towards the broiling heavens.

The God-King was his only hope now.

But it wasn't the God-King who answered him.

The end came when the Stormcast slammed into Vanik from the left. He was smashed from his feet, bellowing with fury as he crashed against one of the hammerers grappling with a screaming Bloodbound. A blow fell against his splintering shield, catching him while he was still off balance and forcing him to his knees. Through it he could hear Albermarl bellowing.

'Grant me the final blow, Marius!'

Vanik's body ached. Hammer blows had crushed and smashed most of his breastplate and pauldrons. Broken ribs grated in his side, and his left arm was shattered, kept locked in place only by the straps of his shield. He swallowed blood, snarling as he fought up from the mud.

He would not fail. He could not.

He lunged up out of the dirt, roaring, driving Nakali at the castellan. The damned Stormcast struck him from the side again, one of his hammers jarring against Nakali's black steel and knocking it aside. Vanik's scream of frustration melded with his daemon sword's.

'It's over, slave to darkness,' the Stormcast declared, interposing himself between Vanik and Albermarl. He was without a helmet, his rain-drenched expression grim. 'You have failed.'

'Out of my way, you lightning-forged scum,' Vanik spat. 'If you wish to be returned to your False God to be reforged, I will oblige you next.'

A noise interrupted the Stormcast as he replied, rising up over the cacophony of the surrounding battle. Vanik saw the Stormcast's grim face change. His eyes widened, and he growled an oath that was lost in the crash of another purple-tainted thunderbolt.

Vanik wrenched the buckled remains of his shield from his arm, bones grating, and dropped it in the mud, then threw his head back in the rain and laughed.

'What?' he heard Albermarl demand, trying to thrust past the Stormcast. 'What's happening?'

'Get back,' the Stormcast replied, shoving Albermarl away. 'Take the reserve and go back to Helmgard! Now!'

'You are too late, Stormcast,' Vanik said, spreading his arms wide as the rain hammered down. 'My master is here.'

A terrible shriek filled Vanik's ears, like the wailing of a thousand damned souls being flensed in the Varanspire's depths. The air began to vibrate, and a sickly-sweet stench overpowered the reek of blood and bowels.

The ridgeline behind Vanik disintegrated. Dozens of armoured shapes ploughed over it, a wall of black-and-silver warpsteel, streaming with dark pennants. The screaming came from the maws of bestial steeds and a hundred unsheathed daemonblades, howling for blood.

The Varanguard had come.

* * *

The wedge of dark knights swept down the slope and into the heart of the battle. They crashed indiscriminately over any warrior not quick enough to get out of the way, and tore into the army of the mountain city as though the ranks of hardened duardin and well-drilled humans were small children. Pikes snapped and splintered uselessly, and swords, hammers and axes rebounded like wooden toys from black armour and barding.

The Knights of Ruin reaped a terrible toll. Glaives, lances, mauls and swords butchered the front ranks of the army of the Free Cities, the ripping fangs and claws of their savage mounts adding to the dismemberment. Another bolt of pink lightning earthed itself amidst the artillery in reserve, the bolt dancing between cannon barrels and cooking the flesh of their crews, as though the heavens themselves now conspired on behalf of the True Gods. Flags and banners were snapped and trampled, and the rain-drenched air became misted with a pink haze of viscera and pulverised bodies. In only a few minutes, the pride of Helmgard had been cut to pieces and ground into the mud by the onslaught of the Knights of Ruin. Vanik looked past the lone Stormcast, at Albermarl, a serrated grin splitting his thin lips.

'Where is your False God's lightning, chosen one? Where is Sigmar now?'

The carnage engulfed them. Heavy, armoured shapes slammed past Vanik, goring and dismembering the castellan's retinue. He recognised them. It was Sir Caradoc's konroi.

Another thundered past, focused on the castellan's great flag, carving open the core of the Helmgard battle line. Vanik saw Sir Caradoc himself chopping apart the standard bearer and grasping the ripped, bloody silk in one fist. Then something hurtled in from the left, causing Vanik to stumble.

It crashed against the Stormcast – a great daemon sword that rebounded from one of his raised hammers. The black knight twisted its hulking, spine-bristled mount around and struck again, forcing the Stormcast to raise both hammers, interlocked, to block the blow.

The warrior's visor was raised. Vanik realised it was Karex Daemonflayer.

'The castellan,' she barked at him as she struck once more at the Stormcast. 'Don't just stand there, boy!'

The moment was now. Vanik drove past the embattled Stormcast, lunging for Albermarl. The haft of the castellan's warhammer once more met the thrust, knocking it down and to the side, but Vanik followed up with his left fist, thrusting the gauntlet up and into the castellan's face.

There was a crack as Vanik's broken arm connected with Albermarl, splitting his nose and knocking him back. Pain from his broken bones jarred his body, but he ignored it. All that mattered now was finishing this.

He slashed across Albermarl's torso before he could recover his defensive stance, left shoulder to right hip, fast as a viper. Nakali sensed its moment. The bound daemon screeched as it bit through steel plate armour, leather, cloth and finally flesh. Vanik put all of his failing strength behind the blow, leaving his own guard completely open. When the savage swing stopped, Nakali shivering in the wet air, Albermarl's torso was in ruins. The blow had cleaved open his chest, exposing split ribs and sliced organs. The castellan looked at Vanik, his expression still grim as the mountain peaks at his back. Then a wave of blood burst from his mouth to soak his beard, and he fell with a clatter of armour.

Existence itself seemed to slow. Every part of Vanik tensed. The rain paused, each droplet held in place. In that instant he was certain the body of the slain champion would dissolve in light despite his earlier words, that energy would earth from the black heavens and drag him to the God-King's embrace.

But there was nothing. Albermarl's bloody corpse slumped and lay still. The rain fell. There was no lightning, no ascension. Vanik had changed the castellan's fate, and his own in the same instant.

The Black Pilgrim screamed in triumph. He raised Nakali, a boot planted on the castellan's corpse. Overhead, thunder crashed and another bolt of warp-infused lightning cracked downwards. It struck Nakali's tip amidst a hail of sparks and earthed down through Vanik's body.

His screaming ended. The lightning was gone. Slowly the Black Pilgrim lowered his sword, electricity dancing and sparking across his weapon and armour, steam rising into the air.

'It is done,' he rasped, his voice deep and riven with the power of the storm. 'Glory to Chaos. Glory to the Varanguard, and the Three-Eyed King.'

Karex Daemonflayer dismounted and cast her cloak back over her shoulder, her daemon sword, Lak'korr, grasped in one fist. A few feet away, a giant in maroon-and-silver plate armour knelt in the mud, surrounded by trampled and disembowelled bodies, head lowered and eyes on the corpse of the castellan beneath Vanik's foot.

Karex had dealt two wounds to the Stormcast's torso. The rain was slowly washing the blood and mud from his sigmarite plate, leaving it gleaming. His eyes didn't leave the castellan's body as Karex stood over him, and he made no move to raise the hammers at his side. She recognised the weapons and tools of one of the Azyr's star seers.

'Time for you to return to your False God, Stormcast,' Karex said. The Lord Ordinator did not look up, but when he spoke his voice bore the fire of a newborn star.

'When I am reforged I will find your champion, daemon-worshipper, and I will break him asunder with hammer and lightning.'

'Do not be so sure,' Karex said. 'The lightning is his now.'

She swung Lak'korr. The Stormcast's head fell. Before it struck the ground there was an ear-splitting crack. One last peal of thunder rolled out across the bloody ridgeline, accompanied by an arc of brilliance that lanced up into the tumultuous heavens. Karex snarled as its light blinded her. When her vision returned, the Lord Ordinator was gone.

The storm had moved on. Its black clouds and lightning travelled with the Varanguard as they rode down the army of Helmgard and swept onwards, towards the mountain city itself. In their wake the rain had become a dull drizzle that pattered down on the carnage that remained of the ridgeline.

The army of Helmgard was no more. The blocks and lines where once their formations had stood were now squares of butchered meat and dismembered bodies, indiscernible amidst the churned-up muck.

The survivors of Vanik's warband picked their way through the wreckage, even the most seasoned of marauders left stunned and slow in the wake of the Varanguard's fury. They were not alone. Sir Caradoc's konroi had remained behind, as had Karex's. The Bane Sons had already begun to feast on the dead.

Sir Caradoc himself, dismounted, approached Vanik. The Black Pilgrim stood in silence amidst the butchered remains of Albermarl's retinue, surrounded by the surviving members of the Eightguard as Modred bound splints about his forearm.

The retainer had stripped away much of his master's armour, revealing flesh bruised and purpled by the relentless blows it had endured. The wound in his shoulder had also reopened, blood staining pink in the rain.

'Are you sure you don't want a piece?' Sir Caradoc said, holding out a wad of gristle to Vanik. He was consuming Albermarl's corpse, one strip of flesh at a time. Vanik shook his head, saying nothing.

Caradoc grunted and shoved more meat into his fanged maw.

'It has been a long time since the Seventh Circle rode with the Fifth,' he said, voice thick with the raw feast. 'The Bane Sons and the Scourge of Fate. May it herald further conquests together, side by side.'

'As the Eightstar wills it,' Vanik murmured, his voice low. Sir Caradoc shrugged his broad shoulders and moved back to the castellan's grisly remains.

Tzatzo lived. Vanik could see Jevcha kneeling at her side a little further up the slope, murmuring to her as she worked the musket balls from her tough hide. The Chaos steed would allow no one else to approach her. In truth, he was even more relieved Jevcha had made it through. Amidst the fury of the Varanguard's charge it had seemed as though no one would survive, from either side. As though sensing her brother's gaze, the warqueen looked up from his steed, and nodded to him.

The clatter of armour turned Vanik's attention away from the Darkoath and his mount. Karex, on foot, was climbing the slope towards him. She had retrieved Vargen, the daemon sword gripped in her right fist.

'You have not gone on to burn Helmgard,' he called to her as she approached.

'Lord Neveroth granted the honour to Sandruil Halfborn,' she replied, coming to a halt before Vanik and looking him up and down. 'Besides, I have achieved what I came here to do. The daemon sword has been retrieved and tamed.'

'Am I really worth such a display of might from the Varanspire?'

'No,' Karex answered. 'But the presence of the castellan was more of a problem than any of us had anticipated. Had his flesh been wedded to Vargen's, the great threat that the Gaunt Summoner foresaw to the Varanspire would have transpired. That much is obvious now. The Three-Eyed King could not risk failure in this matter. That is why we were sent.'

'We have served Archaon well this day then,' Vanik said, nodding. 'None will usurp the eight circles, nor the Three-Eyed King's rule.' As though in sympathy with his words, a flicker of electricity darted along his sword arm.

'I have never known the lightning to strike like that,' Karex said, recalling the moment he had cut down Albermarl. 'It is a strange gift for the True Gods to grant. I cannot tell what these portents mean. I am not a seer or some thrice-cursed Summoner, but I know enough to be certain that the Four have won a great victory here today.'

'You have won a great victory,' Vanik corrected. 'Even after all my efforts, I would have fallen here and my warband would have been routed had you not come.'

'It was not some weak favouritism on my part,' Karex assured him. 'We are here at the orders of Lord Neveroth himself.'

'He knows of Zubaz's treachery?'

'He does, and may have done all along. Zubaz was consorting with daemonkin to sunder the hierarchy of the Varanspire and turn it over to them. The Three-Eyed King's power could have been broken at a stroke.'

'Vargen,' Vanik murmured, the mere name conjuring up an icy chill that seemed to settle within his bones.

'A powerful daemon prince,' Karex said. 'Raised up during

the last great struggles of the World-That-Was. It is but one of many daemonkin who would subvert the power of our king. As his bondsmen and guards, we can never allow that to happen.'

'Vargen might have succeeded,' Vanik said. 'But it made one mistake that undid all its work. It set itself against your Black Pilgrim.'

Karex smiled at that.

'And now it is tamed within this blade and its ally, Zubaz, languishes bound and confined beneath the very Varanspire itself, awaiting Archaon's pleasure. Kar'gek'kell ensured as much.'

'The Gaunt Summoner's prophecies were well founded,' Vanik said. 'But now I must fulfil my own.'

'You already have,' Karex said. She unclasped her cloak pin, bearing the sigil of Archaon's Third Eye, and pinned it to the hem of Vanik's ragged Dracoth-pelt cape. Then she turned to Kulthuk. The standard bearer made no effort to resist the Varanguard as she ripped away the tattered black silk of Vanik's banner.

'You are a Black Pilgrim no longer, Vanik Stormstrike. You are a warrior of the Varanguard and a Knight of Ruin. And, if you will it, a rider in my own konroi.'

Vanik inclined his head.

'It would be my honour, Daemonflayer.'

'Bring your warband,' Karex said, surveying the disparate marauders still scattered along the ridge. Those closest to Vanik had heard the exchange, and had begun to cheer. The noise spread across the battlefield, swelling in the wake of the storm.

'We ride for the Inevitable Citadel, where you will take the oath to Lord Neveroth and the Varanguard,' Karex continued. 'After that, you will embark on your first quest as a Knight of Ruin. You will journey through the Mortal Realms until you kneel before mighty Archaon himself. Only then will you receive his own sigil from the blessed Slayer of Kings, seared into your flesh.'

Vanik smiled, raising Nakali. In the reflection of its black surface, he saw lightning flickering in his gaze.

'Let it be so,' he said, raising the daemon sword higher. 'All the Mortal Realms are my hunting ground. I am a champion of the Eightfold Path, a servant of the Exalted Grand Marshal, and a knight of the Fifth Circle. I am a Scourge of Fate.'

ABOUT THE AUTHOR

Robbie MacNiven is a Highlands-born History
graduate from the University of Edinburgh. He
has written the Warhammer Age of Sigmar novel
Scourge of Fate and novella *The Bone Desert*, as well
as the Warhammer 40,000 novels *Blood of Iax, The
Last Hunt, Carcharodons: Red Tithe, Carcharodons:
Outer Dark* and *Legacy of Russ*. His short stories
include 'Redblade', 'A Song for the Lost' and 'Blood
and Iron'. His hobbies include re-enacting, football
and obsessing over Warhammer 40,000.

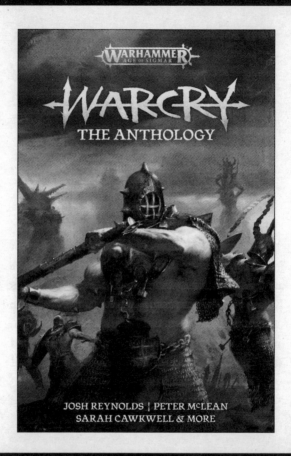

An extract from
'Eight-Tailed Naga'
by David Guymer
taken from the *Warcry* anthology

The snake moved across Marik's cheek, hard muscle and horribly dry skin holding on to his flesh like the tender hand of a corpse. It was as hideous a way to be woken as anything that Marik could have imagined.

With a reflexive jerk of the wrist he flicked the reptile from his face and pushed himself upright. An angry hiss and a rattle sounded from the ground beside him. He pulled his hand away.

A knot of serpents lay tangled over the dark sand.

Black. White. Orange. Red. Writhing together like a flesh tapestry. Bronze mambas. Bush dragons. Splinterworms. Double-headed Neb-Ka, feuding lords of the Varanspire, bound to a single entity by the sorcery of the Nine in punishment for holding the enmity of their Gods over the writ of Archaon. The vision had the eerie quality of a nightmare. His limbs felt swollen and heavy, as though he would find himself unable to fight or flee even if he could understand why he needed to. His head was woolly, confused by dry reptilian scents, the squirm of colours and a throbbing serpent *hsssss* of almost-human voices.

'*Papayagapapayagapapayaga…*'

What was he doing here?

Part on impulse, part on memory, he looked down.

His stomach was as thin and hard as old rope, sandy, dry and coarse with dark hair. He felt his attention pulled to the shallow cut across his navel. It was a vivid, blurry pink, but was no longer bleeding.

An attack.

The steading had been attacked in the night.

'*Papayagapapayagapapayaga…*'

He looked up.

He was in a hole in the ground. The sky was red and smoky, and tasted of recent death. In spite of their offerings, the God of Blood and Brass had come down on the Deepsplinter this night. He tried to get his eyes to focus on the walls of the pit. Its depth seemed to vary depending on how long he spent looking at it. A shimmering reptile with dark skin and silvered scales bobbed and danced around the circumference of the pit, and from its hissing aggregate of nearly human voices came the chant.

'*Papayagapapayagapapayaga…*'

Marik stared at the daemonic blur in open-mouthed horror.

'Husband!'

Marik's gaze swam to the left.

A bird-thin woman in an armoured bodice sewn together from cactus rinds slashed at a snake with a knife. In temperament and appearance there was something of the vulture about her. Never more so than now, the edges sharpened, the world around her blurred. Jarissa. His wife. At the sight of her, Marik felt for the hidden pocket in the rind plate that should have concealed his own knife. The weapon was not there. Whoever had come for them in the night and thrown them in this pit must have found it and taken it away. Trust Jarissa to have somehow kept hold of hers.

He who speaks in blood had always been her first love.

'Husband!' Jarissa trod on the neck of a cannibal asp as it poised to strike, then caught the throat of a rattleneck as it flew at her face and stabbed it through the roof of its skull with her knife. 'Wake up!' A blindsnake with sapphire-blue colouration and a pattern of shifting, eye-like spots lifted its head to about a foot off the ground behind her.

Marik fumbled with his tongue.

'Jarissa!' he managed to shout.

Too late.

The blindsnake sank its fangs into the thin layer of meat that sheathed the bones of her leg.

Jarissa staggered, swayed.

'Is that all you... is that... is that... is... ssss... ss...'

The snake's lower jaw throbbed, pumping its venom into her calf.

'Ss... sss... *nnn*.'

Already dead and *changing* below the knee, Jarissa folded to the ground with a whimper. Her transformed limb oozed like a poisoned eel. Marik had never heard her utter so pitiable a sound.

'*Papayagapapayagapapayaga...*'

'No!'

Death was no stranger to the peoples of the Deepsplinter. To those scattered clans who scraped a living from blood cacti and cannibalistic rites far from the black eye of Carngrad and the Varanspire, he was taker and giver. The even-handed. The handful of rugged steadings on the Deepsplinter were without doors, that Death might come and go unhindered, and come swiftly when the moment came.

He did not come swiftly for Jarissa.

Marik dropped to all fours with a howl.

His right hand fell across a large stone.

Whoever had dug out the pit must have left it there in the ground, too much effort to pull up. Marik could see that most of it was still buried. Wrapping it with both hands and digging his fingernails into the sand around it, he pulled. Its rough planes cut into his palms. His hands, bloodied, slid on the stone, but it refused to move. Blinded by grief and pain, thoughts jumbled in his head, he reset his grip on the stone to try again.

With a murmuring *hsssss*, a great white boa reared up from the writhing mass of serpents, like a daemon conjured from a pool of ichor. It stood half again his height, thicker about the trunk than he was. Its spade-like head swayed from side to side, eyes as huge as worlds, a forked tongue flickering in-out, in-out, tasting confusion and fear.

Marik met the milk-and-oil swirl of the giant serpent's gaze.